I0551661

HALE'S STORM

Book One in the Hale's Storm Series, by

ALISSA BRIGHT

Copyright © 2013 Alissa Bright

Photo Copyright © 2013 Cindy McCauley

All rights reserved.

ISBN: 978-0615868721
ISBN-13: 061586872X

This book is dedicated to
my husband, Ben, who always
believed my words would become
a published novel; and our two little
rascals, who are so excited
that Mommy is finally done with it!
I love you guys.

ONE

August 1941

It is the dead of night. I know that I'm asleep, but I feel fully aware of both places I am right now. My real self tosses and turns, tangled up in the quilt I share with my mom and sister. I try not to rouse them from their sleep, but I'm far more present in a rich, vivid dream. I'm far, far away in a place I've locked away and shoved deep down into the craggiest depths of me. Of course, a gal can only hide her deepest desires in a state of consciousness. As I dream, this delicious vision has escaped once again.

I know this face from every angle. My fingers brush across the length of his sharp jaw, just below a set of full pink lips. The span of skin from cheekbone to cheekbone wears a smattering of faded freckles. Two curving lines form parentheses around his lips where they meet his cheeks, irresistible grooves that deepen when he grins. His emerald eyes look at me in a way that they never have looked at me outside of this vision.

Every girl longs to be looked at this way, but the way this look presses on my heart causes me a mixture of elation and pain. It hurts. Even in this illusion, it hurts. The pressure in my chest cinches down, squeezing tighter, and tighter.

Outside of this mirage, he'll never look at me this way. The stuff of these dreams can never happen in real life. I'm not allowed to love him like this. If I do, it may just choke my heart out until it goes cold.

I flip over and punch the worn-out feather pillow under my cheek. I face May, my little sister, and next to her, Mama. This bed has gotten roomier since my older brothers enlisted in the armed services, taking their best pal and the feature character of my dream with them. Since the constriction around my heart has rudely nudged me back into awareness, the vision of his strong face shuts itself back into the box I hide it in, and slinks back into its dark crevice. And suddenly, even though I'm warm from the shared heat of two other bodies in this old, sagging bed, I feel completely alone.

I'm in love, all by myself.

While everyone else on the farm still sleeps, my bare feet pad quickly over the straw leading up to the graying, dilapidated barn that is seventy paces from the rickety back door of our house. In the dim glow of pre-dawn light, I make my way through the sagging barn doors while my tattered skirt hem brushes against my calves. I pause inside to allow my eyes to adjust to the lesser light. Though temporarily blinded, my nose recognizes the sweet tang of digested grass, or as Uncle Mac calls it, cow plop, and musty straw. My best friend, Tilly, waits for me here.

Under faint beams of light that reach through the barn roof, I shuffle through the straw until I find her undulating form. I run my palm down the ridge of her reddish brown back, her stiff hairs fanning up under my fingers. Tilly requires a certain amount of romancing if you want her to hold still and surrender her milk. Too vividly, I remember learning this technique the hard way as a seven-year-old girl, stumbling after this stubborn, fleeing cow with my empty bucket clanging in my hand. My fingers find the groove above her hip bone and scratch in circles, soothing her.

When Tilly begins licking the air with her long, curious tongue, I know she's ready. I pull up the little three-legged stool that has become worn to the shape of my backside, nestling the bucket in the straw beneath her bulging udders and swiping a loose strand of hair out of my eyes.

"Here it comes, Tills," I warn, and blow warm breath into my hands. I try to rub the morning chill off of them, but when I touch her, she turns her huge head towards me and moos in surprise anyway. Her wide eyes stare at me in accusation, trying their best to induce guilt, but her hooves remain firmly planted in the straw.

Her ear flicks, telling me it's time for me to spill whatever is on my mind. I sigh and allow my thoughts to drop to my lips like candy from a penny machine.

Tilly is the best listener I know. She quietly chews on my deepest, ugliest, darkest thoughts until the last drip of her milk plops into the bucket, at which point, mid-sentence or not, she takes my secrets and hastily hoofs it out of the barn. I imagine she can handle the adolescent drama I dish at her, since the rest of her life is relatively stress-free: chewing her cud, flicking her ears to chase flies off of her head, roaming the fields for the greenest grass.

As my fingers roll in rhythmic coaxing, relief arrests her and her hooves settle into the hay.

"Today's the day, Tills," I begin sullenly, shaking my head. "Ten years. Daddy has been gone an entire decade." The rhythmic hissing of milk hitting the tin pail begins; background music for the memory of who I was ten years ago.

I haven't always been a seventeen-year-old, raggedy milkmaid finding solace in the company of a cow. Once I was Penelope Hale, budding heiress to the considerable Hale family fortune, as close to a princess as a little girl can get in the United States. Nestled so deeply in the lap of luxury, my little sister, big brothers, and I never gave a thought as to how fresh milk appeared on our table. It just was there, along with any other desire of our young hearts, but I don't take anything for granted anymore. Not milk, not food, not love or comfort.

I should've known it was too good, but how can a little girl know anything but what she has seen? How could she possibly foresee how painful an empty stomach can be until her own belly spasms with hollow, hungry aching? The tall iron gates of the Hale estate had done an excellent job of keeping the world and its cares out. The young, fresh-faced version of myself safely inside the gates had no idea what fate had in store; no idea that a hailstorm was rapidly approaching.

Devastation blew in as quickly as dark grey storm clouds in the wind. One moment I was sleepily stumbling across our ornate, glossy hardwood floor seeking a midnight drink of water from the faucet, moving toward the light of the kitchen to the low hum of Mama's conversation with the housemaid. Then the next moment, I was blown into the wall by the velocity of our stricken and panting driver, Murdock, as he barrelled through the back door.

"Madam, Madam!" he wheezed, hands supporting his weight on his trembling knees. From my vantage point in the dark hall, I could see his profile; sweat pouring down his forehead.

"I came as quickly as I could! It's... it's Mister James, Madam. He's..."

And with his message, the floor beneath my tiny feet opened up, and I began to fall. I wanted to rush back up the sweeping staircase, climb back under the blanket of my innocence and pull it over my head, to protect me from the ugly truth of the world. I still want it, I still ache for it; but once you know an ugly truth, there's just no going back.

The next morning, with the timid sun barely rousing the rest of the world, my siblings and I sat hip to hip in rumpled silk pajamas on our plush love seat. Pre-dawn light tumbled over manicured gardens and fountains, through our home's grand windows, catching in the crystal of the chandelier dangling above our heads. My older brothers and my little sister rubbed their tired eyes. They didn't know, yet.

Our pillow-pressed, tangled manes didn't quite match the room's opulence and grandeur. At eight, seven, and five years old, our short legs dangling from the love seat weren't long enough for our toes to graze the plush carpet.   All four of us were so young, too young to fully handle the message our Aunt Madge had been appointed to deliver.   Our mama was too distraught to even be in the room with us, let alone swing the wrecking ball at her four children herself.

I remember looking up at my aunt, engrossed in the creased ravines of heavy makeup around her eyes and mouth.   Her nostrils seemed large, dark, and cavernous as she spoke.   False black lashes fluttered over her cold eyes, devoid of any hint of sympathy for us.   I watched her lipstick crease, pull and fold over her lips while her words hit us in the gut: our daddy was dead.

At that moment, every floor to ceiling mirror in that room shattered into millions of glittering fragments with her words.   As it turns out, it was just my tiny heart breaking.   All the same, those shards left deep scars.

Madge neatly snipped our young branch from her family tree; a tree which money actually grows on. Her cold eyes looked away as we plunged twelve stories down through branches and branches of wealthy Hale ancestors.

Her entire face glowed with greed as she rationalized, "Family heirlooms; surely you understand," as she shooed us off of the furniture embedded with our scent and branded with our memories, and put our grand estate up for sale to the highest bidder.

We fell straight into the gnashing, hungry teeth of poverty, whose appetite was freshly whetted by the nationwide economic depression. From opulence to mud, before the sun had even risen.

You'd think the dust would have settled on Daddy's grave after all this time, and I could just be left with my fond memories of him. But every year on this anniversary, I'm reminded of just how empty all of it has left me, and this dust cloud gets kicked up. It chokes me with pain and loss. As I quietly stew inside the thick of it, Tilly turns her head and moos, lifting her hoof as a threat.

"Sorry, I forgot," I apologize. Tilly is like a child who needs a bedtime story to relax, and you don't get milk from a wound-up cow or from one who is determined to leave the barn as soon as just enough pressure has been relieved from her udders. I'm stubborn, but between me and the animal that weighs over half a ton, she'll win our battle of wills every time.

I continue simultaneously milking and explaining the world to Tilly.

"Work never ends, no matter what. Still gotta deliver your milk; still gotta go to the hospital."

She settles her hoof obligingly back into the

straw.

"Still gotta milk you!"

Her ear flicks lazily to acknowledge my comment.

"Don't worry, Tills, you're much better than Doris," I soothe and she lets down again; hiss, hiss, hiss, into the pail.

Tilly's velvety ears get a daily earful of complaints about my despicable fellow candy striper at Saint Christopher's Hospital. This Doris gets a real bang out of trampling my dignity under her sharp heels. She typifies everything I'm not: lazy, wealthy, and arrogant. One of her patients tossed his cookies yesterday, so Doris switched our room assignments on the board and I had to mop it up.

I sigh. "It would be nice if we could all be together today. This is the first year Max and Eddie won't-- hey!"

Tilly's shuffles forward nervously, mooing.

"Tilly! What gives?" I panic and lunge to steady the pail just as her back hoof kicks it. "Ah, swell, Tilly!" I bark, annoyed. My hands absorb the vibration in the tin pail.

If this milk spills, we'll have some very unhappy customers with empty milk bottles, and unhappy customers don't leave milk money. Unhappy customers find another milk service, and we don't eat until our reputation can be restored with them.

I peer anxiously into the bucket without breathing.

"Phew," I sigh, relieved. Warm, creamy liquid fills it almost to the top.

My list of daily chores is far too long for me to waste time worrying about the cause of Tilly's temper tantrum, so I just smack her rear as she lumbers away. I can hear her moos fade into the distance while I bottle her swirling white milk, setting aside some rich cream in a tin for churning into butter. I put the milk baskets into the cart and hitch it up to our horse, Nell. As usual, she moseys through our rounds like a slug, and we finally pull back home just as the August sun starts warming the air. Hungry and hurried, I trot up our back steps onto the sagging porch and through the thin door in search of breakfast. I find Mama and May bowed together in prayer. They pray for Daddy's soul every year on this day.

"Daddy doesn't need our prayers, Mama; he was a good man," I tell her after they intone amen in harmony.

"Everyone's a sinner, Pip," she drones, obviously irritated to have to be reminding me of a Sunday sermon once again. Long lashes over her large blue eyes flutter in annoyance. "Even your good daddy. We all need redemption."

The wooden floor creaks beneath my steps.

"Especially Tilly!" I grumble. "She ran out again

while I was milking her."

"What'd you do this time?" May accuses. Little Miss Mayhem, as I call her, is a champion mischief maker, hardly one to be throwing blame around.

"Nothin'. I was just talking... 'bout Daddy," I defend. "And the boys."

"Your brothers? Ha! You know those rascals were always cruel to that poor cow," Mama recalls. "They claim they used to tip her when she was sleeping."

I roll my eyes. Max and Eddie taught Mayhem everything she knows about mischief, and they are very proud of their shenanigans. If they put a notch in their belts for every wicked scheme they came up with, they'd run out of belt within a week! I can only wonder how the army likes their troublemaking.

"Aw, Mama. They always bragged about that, but nobody believes they could actually tip over a cow. Tilly doesn't sleep on her feet."
"I didn't know cows have feet," May giggles.

"Hooves," I amend, and stick my tongue out at her.

Mama continues as though we haven't spoken, "...and they'd mash spoiled fruit on her back so that flies bombarded her all day. She probably spooked at just the mention of that pair of hooligans." We all feel the emptiness those "hooligans" left in the house, and can't wait to get them back. Even if it means merciless tickle-torture for their little sisters.

"The bucket was almost full anyhow," I say to stifle any seed of worry in Mama. The woman's mind is a hotbed for troubles. Every stomach in the dim room rumbles in unison, reminding us of the last two-day stretch we went without food. Tilly has kicked the bucket over before. Turns out, spilled milk is a worthy thing to cry over.

"I wasn't worried," Mama lies, her eyebrow twitching. She points with her nose at an empty envelope on the table, ruffling her waves of light shoulder-length hair, while I rake my fingers through May's unruly mane. "Letter from Eddie came."
May offers the letter with one hand and absently butters toast with the other.

Butter. Our annual luxury on this awful anniversary.

"I'll read it when I get home. I've gotta go. Ol' Nell gets slower every day," I complain. "It's like I'm riding a hippopotamus. She'll make me late, again!" I kiss May on the crown of her head and snatch her toast from her fingers. "Thanks, Mayhem!"

TWO

I sprint along the country roads, leaving a trail of dust in my wake, to make up for lost time. At the edge of town, I hop up on the trolley precisely in the driver's blind spot so I can lean into the wind without being reprimanded. With one hand gripping a brass pole, and my feet on the wooden running board, I hang my body over the asphalt as it rushes under me. My arm dangles loosely in the wind and my rag curls blow into a more natural wave. This is a daily thrill that I like to think blows the scent of "farm hand" off of me before I get to the hospital.

By the time we reach the heart of town, I smell as fresh as sun-dried linens. The brakes whine and I hit the ground running. I climb up the front steps of Saint Christopher's Hospital, where I volunteer as a candy striper, pulling my apron over my clothes. Though its red and white stripes barely resemble a nun's habit, I always get the feeling that I'm headed into a convent when I enter under this great stone archway. Inside, the head nurse, Nurse Adler, is just as strict as a Reverend Mother. I quickly smooth my wind-styled hair to avoid her regular lecture on professional appearance.

When a candy striper doesn't become a young bride--earning her MRS degree, as we call it--she has both feet in the door to become a nurse. She has proven that she can handle blood, vomit, and bed pans alike without fainting like a lily.

Ahem. Unless, of course, she lands that MRS degree.

Well, I don't want one.

I'm barely through the gigantic front hospital doors when I hear the rapid clicking of high heels in an impatient rhythm. The shoes belong to Doris, who will never be mistaken for a nun. She greets me with a sour grimace as she shoves a full tray of urine specimen bottles into my arms. The glass jars clink together and teeter dangerously, like bowling pins. Warm amber liquid slops out and fills the tray, bleeding through my apron, and my skin crawls where the warm wetness makes contact. I can feel a hot, pulsating burn in my chest climb against my will to my cheeks, where my anger visibly radiates. I clench my teeth to contain it. I narrow all of my embarrassment and fury into a killer stare at her back as her ample bottom bounces away on heels far too high to be practical for a five-hour shift.

I am certain that this spill was purposeful; Doris, you see, is evil.

"Aw, swell," I growl under my breath, rolling my eyes. I place the dripping tray on the reception counter like a plate of hissing rattlesnakes. One of the bottles tips completely on its side, and I jump back to avoid the splash.

The head nurse blows through the main hall with an armful of charts. Under her heavy eyebrows, her razor-sharp eyes note the mess I've just made.

"Dis crumziness von't do, Hale!" she scolds in her thick German accent. Her staccato bark makes my last name sound like "Hell", which happens to suit how she treats me quite perfectly. Nurse Adler is the kind of woman who can make you feel like you're in trouble, even when you're innocent of everything except breathing.

A wayward chart slips from the top of her pile and lands on the floor, unnoticed.

"But they aren't..." I begin to shriek after her in my defense, but her wide bottom has already undulated around the corner. I suspect her ears would be deaf to an accusation anyhow. Doris's nastiness is well concealed from authority figures, even the troll-like ones like Nurse Adler.

"Ahem!" Doris clears her throat in a high, feminine tone, appearing from around the same corner with her ear cocked upward.

"These are yours, I believe," I hum warmly, pushing the tray toward my foe with one finger. Her hands fly up to block responsibility for the soggy tray, lips hissing noxious words.

I can barely stifle my grin as I eagerly scoop up Adler's fallen chart from the floor and set off to find its patient, L. Sharpe, room 13A.

"Sorry, Doris; I have work to do!"

'L', is old, tiny, and crabby. As soon as my foot touches the linoleum floor of her room, a dam bursts and a vigorous flow of complaints roll over me. She's so small and frail under the thin blanket of her hospital bed that I wonder where she could have possibly been hiding all of these words. I'm up to my throat, choking on her ramblings.

"Finally, someone has come to save me from this wretched excuse for a pillow!" she gasps and throws hers to the floor. Her spindly, liver-spotted arms flap wildly, punctuating her words, "Really, Honey, you have got to do something about this gown. It's like an itchy cotton straight-jacket! And I'm tied up in it all day while my begonias are surely wilting away at home, and I just can't trust any of my fluff-headed housemaids to remember to feed Winston while I'm imprisoned here!"

"Winston?" I whisper.

"My poodle. Maids can be so unreliable, you know."

No, I don't know, I answer silently. I can't remember having a servant to care for my whims. I step backward, briefly considering trading this patient with Doris for the urine specimens, but L continues without allowing pause for my exit.

"What does that chart say anyway, Missy? When can I be released from this prison so I can see to things at home myself?" She doesn't pause for my answer. Somehow, without inhaling, her complaints segue seamlessly into a monologue about her wretched daughter-in-law squeezing the joy out of her only son. Her rant lasts so long that I'm out of things to busy my hands with, so I just stand here awkwardly with her discarded pillow and absorb the flow of her wrath.

However, after just five minutes with the bony, hunched woman, the nasty twist in my belly is barely noticeable and my flaming cheeks have calmed to a dull burn. I can't be entirely sure, but her complaints seem to center on everyone and everything besides me; I find that I actually kind of like her. The combination of her high, feminine, finishing-school-trained voice mingled with the gravelly quality of old age is highly entertaining to listen to.

Doris can keep those urine bottles.

"May I get you some water, Missus Harp?" I interject timidly when she pauses for breath. No need to turn the knife point my direction.

"*Shhhharpe*, dear; and if I drink any more, I'll just have to tinkle! The last time that urge demanded my attention, it was such an ordeal that I'd really rather just shrivel up with dehydration and die right here on this pitiful excuse for a mattress!" she answers, pounding both tiny, furious fists into the offending bedsprings. I brace myself to have it thrown at me, too.

"Really, you'd think that Doris broad doesn't like people!" The way the name sizzles on her tongue assures me that we share a common enemy. I snigger as I realize that Doris's evil is boundless; she's even rude to a harmless, sick old lady! I'm pleased to have found an ally.

"What are you laughing at, young lady?" snaps L crabbily at the amused smile dancing on my lips.

"Missus," I pant to try and stop laughing, "Missus Sharpe, please don't take Doris's rudeness personally. Doris is reliably unpleasant that way. To everyone," I assure her while patting her veiny, withered hand. Especially to me, I think. The skin is so thin across Missus Sharpe's knuckles that I pat lightly so as not to break right through it.

"How does a nasty broad like that get into nursing?" she muses, exasperated, jabbing at the air with her small, furious hand. "Nurses are supposed to be... well, you know, nice!" I don't bother to correct her that Doris and I are only stripers, not real nurses, because the rise in station feels nice, like practice for my future career. My spine straightens up with borrowed pride.

I perch on the side of her bed and lay my hand gently on her thin, blanketed leg, looking her squarely in the eyes.

"Let me tell you about ol' Doris," I indulge.

In an instant we become old girlfriends; those thin lips curl into a mischievous grin as she senses that hot gossip is coming.

"I've only been here for three months, but word gets around this place like a bad infection. That gal's only here because her mama's using her as gold bait. Her family was real rich before the crash, you know; stocks and bonds," I begin.

"Pshaw!" L interjects, flapping her skeletal hand dismissively. "Black Tuesday annihilated that treasure chest!" Across the nation, fortunes, even vast fortunes, disappeared in a puff of smoke that day. The stock market crashed, turning working men and wealthy investors alike into desperate scavengers. When the endless streams of riches from the wealthy's "wise" investments dried up so instantaneously, the effects trickled down through the businessmen and the factory workers, restauranteurs and the hired help, grocers and gardeners who served them. I had to learn about all of this in school, as I had maintained a round belly and full cheeks inside the gates of the Hale estate.

It seems some families, like Doris's, refuse to accept that their fortunes have vanished. The economy is still healing, and they're still nursing their reputations.

L's sagging, lined eyes show no concern for the crushing effects of the Great Depression. They sparkle and squint with anticipation for more of Doris's story, so I continue.

"...and now they're just barely hanging on by a thread. Their only hope is to snag a promising fella for their daughter, and well, you know- Ivy League doctors and surgeons are the fellas who are thriving these days. Mansions come and go, but people never stop getting sick." While a hospital gown is the great leveler of pride, stripping a person of the clothes and adornments that mark their station in life, something tells me L's family thrives as well. Filthy, stinking thriving. "Well, the regular fellas, anyhow."

"Ha!" she caws in delight, slapping my hand with surprising strength. "As if any decent fella's gonna snatch up a pinched face like hers!" Her own pinched face is richly enjoying the scandal, and I'm enjoying the irony.

"You should see her put on airs around the doctors; all minxy," I laugh, rolling my shoulder with mock seduction, a cruel imitation of Doris's scandalous behavior around men. A fresh picture pops into my head of heavy-lidded Doris leaning in toward Doctor Morris to straighten his tie, or bending over slowly for an "accidentally" dropped pencil while Doctor Bodily strolls by without even noticing her overflowing bosom. She's so pathetically desperate that I almost pity her. Almost.

And then I remember the urine.

And how she saddled me with vomit duty.

And how I missed the last streetcar a week ago because I was stuck doing the extra charts she'd weaseled into my pile, and I had to trudge all the way home in the inky darkness. The healing blisters on my heels radiate with pain to remind me of that long walk, and my temporary compassion for Doris dissolves.

"And you? You looking for a PhD to give you an MRS degree?" L asks with an indulgent wag of her brow, digging for more dirt. Her wrinkle-framed eyes are so keen with curiosity that the years seem to fall away for a moment, and I catch a glimpse of who she used to be, before illness and age reduced her to the ancient slip of a woman she is now.

Inwardly, I scoff at the idea of big game husband hunting. From what I know of love, the struggle just isn't worth it, rich fella or not. In my mind, love is a vine of berries: sweet, rich fruit ripe for the picking, but one is much more likely to end up getting pricked by the sharp thorns than acquiring the sweetness. The thorns outnumber the fruit by the hundreds! If you're willing to endure the thorns and pluck off a juicy berry, the sweet sensation of the fruit is gone in a single swallow. I've seen too many gals get pricked by a briar, then go right back for more, only to bleed again. And again. Why even bother?

Anyhow, to me, only one fella is worth bleeding for, and he's hundreds of miles away over the Pacific Ocean. In my mind, he spends his military days reclining on the beach, surrounded by breathtakingly beautiful hula girls who alternate between dancing for him and sitting in his lap, feeding him fresh pineapple and fanning him with palm fronds while the tropical sun ignites his rusty gold hair. I shake my head against my jealous vision. Even if he were right here in this room, he'd still be just as far away.

"Nah, I'm actually here to learn," I say. She sighs, a bit disappointed, but clearly pleased by my ambition. Surely when she was growing up, gals were still wearing corsets and were only trained in the delicate art of holding out a pinkie properly while drinking tea. They'd never be allowed something so bold as ambition.

"Well, good!" she beams. "Because that apron's not doing you any favors, Darlin'." Her eyebrow is raised in critical appraisal.

My shoulders roll uncomfortably in startled response, though I agree with her. These boxy striper's aprons are no haute couture. Unless you're Doris, of course, who pins hers tight around her bust and waist; but I prefer "utilitarian" over "hussy".

"I'm going to train to be a nurse. Volunteering here is just the start; can't beat the experience!" I sell her in a coaxing voice suited for a radio advertisement.

My face drops as I reveal, "See, my mama works her fingers to nubs keeping us fed. I don't want that, so I gotta make something of myself. Can't rely on a man to take care of you forever!" I declare. Mama works hard, and she does it with dignity, but the memory of her carefree days when her lap and her ear were readily available to me are too vivid for me. I mourn for the mother in my memory, because that woman is as dead as my father.

Her expression looks almost sympathetic to my cynical declarations.

"Hmm," she muses. "Well, I had you pegged for a gal in heavy sugar," she cackles at her own misjudgment and flicks her wrist. "But what does this old prune know anyhow?"

"In heavy sugar? Me? Why?" Nothing about me screams "rich gal". I'm clean and I take care to keep my clothes mended, but I'm hardly the Duchess of Windsor.

"Brains, Honey. You're sharp; I can tell," she explains while tapping a bony finger to her temple. I struggle to hide the effect of the insult from showing on my face; she's just implied that you have to be wealthy to be intelligent.

"Can't a gal be be poor *and* smart?" My voice falters a little with the weak rebuttal.

"Well, of course; but, you know," she scrambles a bit, trying not to alienate her best source of entertainment. "The finest schools hone the best minds." It's a phrase from deep in the recesses of her mind, labeled "facts". "You're in school, I hope?"

"Certainly not 'the finest' school," I admit, thinking of the public school I attended with all the other working-class kids. At least, those that didn't drop out and get a job. "I graduated Saratoga this past spring. You have to be a high school graduate to get into nursing school." Otherwise, the idea of my high school education would've surely been eaten alive by the need for farm labor at home.

"Well, I'll bet you were at the top of your class," she says brightly. The repentant smile she gives looks odd on her lips, folding her well-worn frown lines into a new form. This has got to be the most fun she's had since she was admitted to Saint Christopher's; otherwise she wouldn't be bothering to strain the corners of her mouth upward. I did earn decent marks in school, but being a part-time farm hand got in the way of my studies. Anyhow, the top pupils are always fellas, regardless of who deserves the rank.

"Well," I redirect, eager to skirt the awkward subject, "can I help you to the powder room? I actually like people."

"I suppose," the old bat sighs, raising her arms so I can pull back the blanket. "And Honey, if you're going to see my backside, you may as well call me Lyla."

THREE

While Lyla takes care of her bathroom needs, I inspect myself in the mirror. My dishwater blonde hair, which Mama calls "honey blonde", bounces around my shoulders in waves. I can thank May for tying my hair in rag curls last night for the effect. *"Pay the pretty price!"* she'd said, as she always does when I groan during the nightly procedure that leaves my tender head smarting. I have the trolley to thank for softening the severity of the tight curls so I don't appear too pretentious. I've secured them out of my face with a red scarf, knotted at the nape of my neck.

My straight, small nose points like an arrow toward my rosebud mouth. My cheeks are constantly tinged with pink, and deepen with any emotion: happiness, anger, embarrassment. I see this as an utter betrayal. It's so unfair to be forced to wear your emotions like a billboard when others can ride out their emotional storms on their insides!

My large blue eyes squint at my reflection with the thought. They're my favorite feature, wide and rimmed by a forest of dark lashes.

A decade of being underfed has resulted in sharp cheekbones and a slender neck, though labor-hardened muscles hide under my blouse and striped apron. Being overworked has conditioned me to be unexpectedly strong. I'd make a great dark horse in women's boxing, if such a thing existed outside of our unofficial family bouts. May, the announcer, stands on a wobbly wooden chair with a hairbrush microphone; my brothers and I playfully hop around on the soft feathers of our bed, the ring; and I box them with all my might. Besides the time Eddie's blow knocked out my loose tooth when I was eight, I win more often than not. That is, until they took their fight to the army.

I barely have Lyla settled back into bed, mumbling about the new crummy hospital pillow I've supplied her, when Nurse Adler enters like a single-minded hunting dog. She stops, pointing at me with her porous nose. The way she pants, cheeks aflame with anger, strikes a bolt of nervous fear in my heart. It vibrates out to my limbs; my hands are shaking. I know I'm in trouble.

"Dere you ah!" she accuses. "I hev bin looking every-vere for you! Lolly-gakking, I see!" she grunts, tapping a pudgy foot impatiently on the linoleum. "Der is a pa-chent screamink at de top of his lunks that he is stranded on de toilet wis no toilet tissue! Git him some tissue so he vil stop yellink! Now!" She attempts an authoritative nod but her double chin quickly bounces off of her thick neck. I can't help but think that it would have been far more efficient to just get him the tissue out of the supply closet herself, but stripers are too far down on the hospital food chain to point out such absurdities. I scurry down the sterile hall to the supply closet with the speed of a frightened rabbit, so when I turn the handle and the door doesn't swing open, my face bumps into it.

"Ow!" I moan, and rub my sore nose. I hold my hand up, expecting blood, but it's clean. I try the handle again; stuck. I drop my hand from it and sigh, resting my defeated forehead on the door. Through the steadily throbbing pain of my nose, I remember Adler's orders to report back to her when this job is complete. But how can I complete the task with a locked door between the toilet tissue and me?

If I were Adler, what would I do? I imagine her ramming the door like a linebacker. I step back and charge the door with my spindly frame, throwing my shoulder at it.

The door wins the match. I barely notice the pain of my nose because of how badly my shoulder throbs. Tears well up in my eyes and I start to sway dizzily. My legs threaten to crumple beneath me. I stamp my foot to snap me back into focus. A gal faints in the hospital, and she can kiss a nursing career goodbye! I manage to stay upright, but I can't squelch the stinging tears pooling in my lids. They spill over and splash onto the linoleum at my feet.

I hear the jammed door crack as it opens from inside. Quickly, I swipe away my tears and stand up straight.

"Mind over matter, mind over matter," I swiftly mumble. "Mind over matter."

A figure steps out from inside the closet.

"D-doctor Sweeney!" I chirp to mask any sign of my near-fainting.

He scans my waifish form skeptically. "You're the one making all the racket out here?"

I laugh nervously; this man gives me the willies. He's older than my father would be now, and he always finds a way to touch me with very un-fatherly intentions.

"Yes, sir, I... Nurse Adler sent me to..."

"No further explanation needed, Sugar;" he replies, stroking my cheek with the back of his short fingers. "We're all a little afraid of that beastly woman."

When I instinctively squirm away from his

touch, he coughs into his fist and starts down the hall. My skin crawls where he had made contact. I wish I had a moment to wash my face. I walk into the closet, shaking off the creepy feeling. As I scan the tall shelves for a roll of toilet tissue, a soft crackling noise pulls my attention to the floor behind the linen rack. Nervously, I peer around the back, expecting to see a rat. What I see instead shakes me considerably.

"D-Doris?" I stammer, unbelieving. The crumpled girl huddling in the corner barely resembles her usual haughty demeanor. She sniffs, wiping at the wet black tracks on her cheeks; mascara dissolved into liquid by her salty tears.

"What do you want?" she snaps like a wounded tiger.

"I- I'm looking for toilet tissue. Adler sent me... wha..." I stutter, dumbfounded. She offers up a roll in annoyance. From the big pile of used tissue next to her, I can see that she has been blowing her nose repeatedly with it.

"Here. Now get lost!" she barks like a snarling Doberman, but her body language tells me she does not actually want to be alone.

"Listen, um, Doris," I begin with softness. It feels unnatural to let down my guard and address her this way. "I have to deliver this tissue to 16B or Adler's going to skin me alive!" As a fellow striper, I know she understands the threat. "But I'll be right back," I promise.

"Don't bother," she squeaks, her snappish tone warring with the hope in her voice. I scurry down to 16B, knock loudly, and enter the bathroom with one hand shielding my eyes and one hand blindly offering the roll.

"Sir? Sir?" I call out. I cough instantly when without thinking, I draw a breath. The smell is thick and terrible in the small washroom.

"Over here," croaks the man. His voice sounds hoarse.

I shuffle toward the sound until I feel the roll snatched from my fingers.

"Finally!" he sighs. "Bless you, Doll." I turn and retreat quickly to find fresh air. When I remember Doris's messy mascara, I hold my breath and shuffle backwards into the washroom to wet a towel.

"Excuse me, sir. I'll be out of your way in just a moment," I say out of the corner of my lips. With the damp cloth in hand, I trot back to the supply closet, slip in, and close the door.

"Doris?" I whisper.

"What?" she snaps back weakly. A hushed sob follows. I kneel at her side with motherly compassion; I have a weakness for tears. My disdain for the girl evaporates, seeing her this helpless.

"Here," I soothe, dabbing softly at her cheek. "Your mascara has, um, exploded."

She turns her face up to me. Her features look almost soft and innocent without her usual scowl marring them. She winces when I start wiping at her other cheek.

I pull my hand back. "Too hard?"

"No, it's... that's..." she pauses.

"What?"

"He smacked that one," she sighs.

"Doctor Sweeney? *Hit* you? Why?" I can't recall him ever disciplining a nurse or striper with physical force, but here she sits in a heap on the floor of the supply closet, sobbing in pain. I'm baffled.

"He's mad at me," she offers. I'm baited and curious about what she means.

"Sweeney is mad at you," I repeat to clarify. "What'd you do?"

"What did *I* do? *I'm* the victim!" she pants defensively, clearly trying not to start sobbing again.

"Whoa, whoa, calm down," I coax her like I'd coax Nell. "Just... explain it to me."

"Why? Why should I tell you anything? You hate me," she accuses, sniffling.

"Well, yes, sort of. Until now," I admit. She scoffs. "You hated me first," I remind her.

"Ha! You noticed." She rolls her brown eyes.

"Why is he mad at you?" I ask again, hoping persistence will prove that I'm a captive audience. "And what in the name of Heaven were you doing alone in the supply closet with Sweeney?" I wrinkle my freckled nose.

"I gave him some news he didn't want to hear. And he called me a liar," she mumbles.

"What? Like you lost all his charts or something?"

"Are you thick?" she asks, annoyed, snatching the damp towel from my fingers. "I'm... I'm expecting," she admits in a harsh whisper. Angrily, she presses the cloth to her bad cheek.

My mind is literally blown at these words. Thoughts fly wildly through my brain. "With... his...?" I go over the facts: Doris is desperate to land a wealthy doctor for a husband. They were locked in this closet together. This is probably not be the first time they've locked themselves in this closet together. Sweeney preys on young gals... ew. Ew! I start to gag.

"Don't start that or you'll make me vomit!" she cries, and I can see her choking on a gag of her own.

"Sor-sorry," I say and gain control of the reflex. "I'm just surprised that he would slap a gal who's on the nest!"

"You think a fella like that abides by some code of decorum? Pshaw!" Her face pinches with bitterness. It seems she has learned this about him a little too late. At least she's stopped gagging.

"So, I'm guessing you didn't get a marriage proposal or anything," I joke lightly. Maybe that's overstepping; she probably had been hoping he would hear the news and drop down on one knee. If the rumors about Doris are true, this could have ended her hunt for a husband. She would have been able to bring home her kill on her shoulders and proudly hang his head over her family's fireplace. Only, it seems Sweeney's animal instincts have told him to run away in fear, and Doris has spent all of her bullets.

She snivels and looks at the towel in her hands. "No... no," she whispers. New tears well up in her eyes and her body convulses with restricted sobs.

Now I've done it.

"There, there," I coo, and timidly wrap my arms around her. She cries heavily into my shoulder. While her chest heaves, I stare at the ceiling and marvel at what's happening in this supply closet. For three months I have endured unchecked hazing by this girl. By anyone's standard, she has been downright nasty to me. If I'd been interviewed just this morning, and someone had asked me, "*Who is your greatest enemy?*" I wouldn't stutter before "*Doris Abernathy*" tumbled out of my mouth. Yet here we are, embracing as I stroke her hair.

"It's going to be alright."

She sits up and glares at me. "Alright? Alright? How can it be alright?" She hiccups. "I have to land a husband; a good, rich guy!"

There you have it; the rumors are true. Doris is here to snag a wealthy Joe.

"And now I'm a cast-aside hussy who's... on stork watch! Of course it'd all be alright if he had as much interest in me as he did when we made the thing," she rambles hysterically.

I feel another gag coming on. I don't want those pictures in my head. Ick! The creepy feeling I'd felt a few moments before rushes over me like a sneaker wave, and my hand rises up to the place where he'd touched my face. I shudder.

"But, nooooo. *'How do I know it's mine?'* he says. *'You never know with a loose gal like you.'*" Her brow furrows as she mocks his serious expression. "He called *me* loose!"

I don't say it aloud, but I think the whole hospital thinks Doris is loose. Even the mail room gals chatter about her fame for it. In fact, they're the informants who I learned about Doris' family from in the first place.

"What decent man will take me now? My mother is going to fillet me. I'm a dead gal walking!" she cries.

"Doris, there is always a way. Your head is just

foggy right now," I say sensibly. I know all too well how emotions can cloud your world.

"My head has been foggy for three months!" she snaps. "There's just so much *pressure*! And then, with the nausea, I can't think straight. I'm always on the verge of tossing my cookies!"

I interrupt her when a revelation dawns on me, "Is that why you handed off those nasty urine samples this morning?" Another gag threatens my throat at the memory.

She smiles weakly as she admits, "Yeah."

"And the vomit?"

"Mmm hmm."

"Well, how do you justify sticking me with all those charts?" I challenge, scrunching one eye shut.

"That's just because I don't like you, remember?" She manages a weak smile. "You're just too pretty not to be competition." I roll my eyes at her. *She thinks I'm "too pretty"? Can't she see my home-made, mended clothes? My rough, cracking hands?*

"Trust me; I'm not in any kind of race to the altar," I assure her with my palms up defensively. "And especially not for a creep like Sweeney. You know, we should really get out of here before Adler gets her nose out of joint," I suggest and stand up.

"You go. I'm all puffy," she replies and sniffs, waving a hand around her face. Same old Doris, dodging work where work can be dodged.

"Are you going to be okay in here all alone?"

She looks up at me with her large, sad eyes and squints appraisingly. "You sure are nice to people you hate," she muses, sniffing. "I hate that."

"I don't hate you, Doris," I reply sincerely. "I just don't understand you." Perhaps after learning some of her sad secrets, I'm starting to; but by nurture and nature, we are two different people. I could never feel right signing a time card after spending my shift in a supply closet with one of the doctors.

My head swirls, jumping from pity for her predicament, to revulsion at the mental picture of that creep's hands moving over her, to a deep, deep sadness because of the pressure she must be under to keep the wolf from the door. That fear I can understand. The memory of hunger and desperation are too fresh in my mind; and although I chose another way to help my own family, I can see how Doris landed herself in such trouble. I can't imagine her mucking out Nell's stall in those sky-high heels.

I slip back into the hall before Doris can morph back into her usual self.

FOUR

I don't see either version of Doris for hours, so I'm saddled with both of our duties. Without her drama or the welcome distraction of Lyla's complaints, today's gloom settles over me again in a thick veil. It rots within me just as ripe and consuming as when I woke up; my stomach feels ill. As I straighten a pile of crooked charts on Adler's desk, I gasp at the wall clock that insists that I'm already twenty minutes past the end of my shift. The ol' reliable trolley will arrive in ten minutes, and I'm still wearing this urine-stained apron!

I jog to the trolley stop dodging rain puddles, pulling the soiled apron over my head and stuffing it into my bag. Clearly, it has sprinkled this afternoon, and the sun busies itself burning up the puddled dregs. The vapor this makes is thick in the air, magnifying the unbearable heat. Wet heat.

I blow out a sigh as I hit the trolley bench with only a minute to spare. I blow a stray strand of hair out of my eyes, legs reveling in relief. Finally, I'm off of my feet! The soles of my shoes carry remnants of dust, hay, urine, and a thin layer of hospital germs. I fan the steamy summer heat away with my pocketbook and close my eyes, drinking in a deep breath. I want to grab my skirt hem with both hands and fan it wildly to cool my thighs, but I know Mama would never bail me out of jail if I were arrested for indecent exposure. As I sit in a slump that would send her through the roof; *"Sit up straight, Penny! You'll be an old hag in no time with that posture!"*, my mind swims with thoughts of Doris.

Both of her parents come from high society bloodlines. Her job is to uphold her family's good name by marrying high. They may be near broke, but they're still Abernathys; around here, that means something. Even though our ancestors helped fund the American Revolution to declare our independence from England, all wealthy east coast families still seem to cling tightly to aristocratic castes. It's a wonder she doesn't require us to call her "Lady Doris of Saratoga". As a Hale, I could claim a similar title: "Lady Penelope", but I don't want it.

I don't doubt that the life she seeks will lead to swanky parties, an overblown, grandiose wedding and an easy existence with her wealthy husband and plenty of privilege, despite her unappealing personality. Her family tree qualifies her immediately, though getting knocked up will certainly yank her down out of those lofty branches. No gentleman willingly accepts used goods, and no one, rich or poor, wants to raise another man's child. Sweeney may have just ruined her life.

Until I lost my daddy, I was headed down the same smooth track as Doris, ending with a place in society and nose pulled permanently upward by some invisible string. I wonder if I'd be as stuck up as she is if things hadn't changed so drastically. Would I be gliding atop a self-important carriage that rolls on the gilded wheels of arrogance? Since we were derailed, my mother has made it her personal mission to wash our heads of that superior mindset. In Mama's mind, the arrogant rich are our enemy, and she and her house will have no part of it.

The day Daddy died, my new destiny was set: to help my family scrape by until I can find a man of a similar station who appreciates my strong work ethic and cooking abilities; have a modest union at city hall, then scratch for every nickel and dime that comes into our home. We'll have a herd of children who'll grow up to do the same, and dogpaddle to stay afloat until we die. Unless, of course, that husband leaves me or dies early, whereupon I'll be left to my own devices to feed our brood. This possibility is why I sacrifice my only free time to volunteering at the hospital; so I can write my own fate. With the fresh memory of Doris's pickle on the brain, I think I've made a lucky trade! Doris went for a berry, and now she's completely tangled up in the thorns. Gals just need to stand on their own two feet, and that's exactly what I intend to do!

Splash! A car careens by, sending the remnants of an oily black puddle splashing over my benchmate and me.

I gasp, momentarily frozen while my hair drips. As I wipe dirty, gritty drops from my face, my luck doesn't feel quite so keen anymore.

The sun beats down on my scalp, baking the crust of that puddle into my hair in seconds. In my head, Mama's sermon about never leaving the house without a hat plays at the forefront. Despite her constant fatigue, she reserves special store of energy for doling out lectures. Quietly, though, I agree that she is right this time. I'll have a red, itchy flaky scalp for a week. The other lady on the bench gets up and shuffles away, grousing and dripping.

My options are limited: either continue hopefully waiting for the elusive streetcar, hail down a yellow cab that I don't have a nickel to pay for, or walk on my newly-healed blisters the twenty-eight blocks home and try not to melt into a street grate from the choking heat on the way. I peer through the traffic again, hoping for some sign of the trolley. Nothing. I must have missed it after all.

I'll have to hoof it. I stand up sighing, glaring warily at the empty trolley tracks, where no shiny green troller appears to rescue me. My feet ache in protest before I even lift them to step, and I resolve to lose my shoes once I'm out of the center of town. As I lean over to reach for my handbag, the tinny whine of brakes perks up my ears. I look up hopefully for the trolley, but instead I see a sleek black car slowing as it hugs the curb. The buildings and sky, even me, reflect back like a mirror image in the glossy paint of the car.

"Pardon me, Miss, but can I offer you a lift?" A young driver, stretched across his wide bench seat, calls out his passenger window.

I've been taught all my life never to accept rides from strangers, but my fatigued feet cry out against the daunting thought of twenty-eight blocks on weary feet. The lure of relief from the heat and the hike is currently much louder than Mama's warning words shouting in my head. I examine the would-be rescuer: a young, clean-shaven, respectable-looking fella in a plaid cap and suspenders. He looks nothing like the wild-haired, hump-backed maniac I envision when Mama doles out her "stranger" warning; not a hairy wart on him, and he looks a whole lot less threatening to me than creepy Doctor Sweeney.

I stand up and gesture to my damp hair and clothes, two feet from the car. Between the two of us, I'm the maniac; the car reflects the odd shape my hair has been flattened into.

"S'okay," he nods, accepting my wetness. He seems totally unfazed by the impatient honking, cursing and shaking of angry fists of the delayed drivers behind him as he puts the car into park on the busy street, effectively bottlenecking the afternoon traffic. He opens the passenger door from inside.

I gratefully swoop down onto the pale cloth seat and try to touch it with the damp parts of my body as little as possible. "Thank you," I say politely from my perch at the seat's edge.

"It's nothing," he answers with a lopsided grin. "Where to?"

In the pause during which I consider if answering "the cemetery" will make me look like a lunatic, my stomach lets loose a low, rumbling growl. It's so loud that there is no chance that his ears missed it. My cheeks flush with embarrassment, betraying me once again.

"Well, this damsel *is* in distress. I know just the cure for that sort of thing. You like Ovaltine?" The car's engine growls happily as it lunges forward, and

I'm forced to stabilize myself on the seat and door with my grimy hands.

"Oh, um, ha, eh," I stammer, positively humiliated that my stomach and cheeks have betrayed me. I'm always ravenous after my shift, but the streetcar usually gets me near the house within twenty minutes. This time of year, I can cut through the orchard on my walk home from the stop. The trees droop with peaches large and juicy enough to serve as my dinner and my dessert. I cross my forearms tightly over my rebellious stomach, hoping to stifle any possible future uproar from it, and concentrate on the bottles of urine to spoil my appetite.

I blush and find words, "Oh, thank you, really, but my trolley never showed and I'm supposed to be home in ten minutes. If you could just..."

His brow furrows under the brim of his cap as he interrupts, "Surely there's a solution for something as simple as that. You can ring home; I've got a nickel here somewhere." He mans the wheel with his left hand as if there aren't seventeen yellow cabs surrounding us, weaving alarmingly through the downtown city traffic while his right arm searches for the coin. Clearly, my *"no, thanks"* is deaf on the ears that peek out from beneath his cap.

I don't bother explaining that only business owners and rich folks have home phones. If he drives a car this fine, he's probably oblivious to that fact. Mostly I abandon my protest because I am famished to the point of being lightheaded, and besides a peach, the only thing waiting for me at home is a shovel and a small hill of horse apples crawling with flies. It seems the very thought of malted chocolate milk has allowed my stomach to realize its full scope of hunger, and it spasms in anticipation.

"What makes you take such pity on me?" I ask him.

He chuckles; I think he can sense the surrender. "I passed you a few times, and well, I couldn't call myself a gentleman if I didn't rescue a damsel, could I?"

We've only gone a few blocks when he slows to the curb outside a bustling diner without signaling. He is a terrible driver! I wonder how long he's had his license. Or maybe...

"Do you have a driver's license?" I blurt out in panic. My traitorous cheeks flare red again.

"Yes Ma'am." he replies proudly, snapping a suspender with his thumb. "Shall we?" He offers his arm to me after tossing his cap on the dash and helping me from the low seat. His clean shirt sharply contrasts with my damp, dirty blouse; but his pomaded hair is tousled enough to smooth the disparity. As we walk, I feel like I'm only playing the part of a well dressed, poised socialite. I'm three years old again, shuffling around in my mother's heels.

"Table for two, would'ja please?" he asks a minxy waitress. As he turns to do this, I notice that his hair has an unruly lock in the back, at the end of his part. I become warm with the memory of Eddie dodging Mama and her comb, insisting he's well old enough to comb his own hair. My brother usually has a similar unruly lock of hair arching off of his crown, frozen in place with Dapper Dan's. The resemblance endears the fella to me.

I shrink down into my shoulders as I become aware that we're gathering stares from the other patrons. I'm severely aware of what I look like next to him; we're surely rather mismatched pair, even if I weren't spattered with dirty street water. This fella treats me as though I am a perfectly well-dressed socialite anyhow as he leads me to a small booth, gallantly gesturing for me to take a seat.

"Hey, uh, I just realized that I don't even know your name," I laugh.

FIVE

"Jackson. But friends just call me Jack," he answers and holds out a hand to shake. I take it as daintily as I think a lady should and hope he doesn't feel how calloused my hands are against his smooth palm.   As our skin meets, I feel a sting shoot through my hand and up my arm, where it rains down over my chest.

What was that? I wonder, sparks still fizzling inside of me.

"Penelope," I smile calmly, trying to conceal my surprise. "Everyone calls me just 'Pip'."

"That's a nice dimple in your cheek, Just Pip," he comments, smiling back. I can thank Grandpa Hale for drilling his finger into it every time I smiled at him, ensuring the little indent would be there the next time.

He smiles back and holds eye contact wordlessly. I look down, flushed. A moment of silence passes at our table while the jangle of silverware plays throughout the rest of the diner. Seated across from this stranger, I have a head-on view of his face when I look back up at him under my lashes. Creamy skin, almost translucent, holds the light from the diner windows. His cheeks burn pink, like he's been running. A distinctive round freckle decorates his left cheek, just on the apple. The irises that caused mine to look away are rimmed with dark blue; stark, silky light blue inside with a sunburst of yellow at the center, gold flecks dotting the pale blue. The yellow glows, giving the impression that they're lit from within. They're almost difficult to see through his hedge of lashes; straight, light brown lengths that could fan a gal on a hot day like today.

His shoulders have a sturdy look, though the muscles aren't hard with labor like Eddie's or Max's. One juts farther up than the other, mirroring his lopsided grin: dark pink lips, one side pulled up in a smirk. The smooth lips aren't really extraordinary until they move, curling into a grin or feigning a grimace as he talks. I go ahead and admit to myself that he's handsome.

Two tall glasses of foaming malted chocolate milk clink together as they're set before us. They drip with condensation, which makes my hot, dry mouth pucker. Ovaltine.

I take a sip. I nearly shudder with the heavenly sensation of the cool, sweet, creamy stuff swirling over my tongue.   My eyes sweep up to my benefactor.

"So, you really have me curious.   You stopped because...why? I'm not that pathetic. What gives?" I pry.

"Well, ah..." he swallows and ducks his head, looking uncomfortable.   My curiosity is piqued, as he's looked completely cool and collected- relaxed, even- up to this point. "I was driving by and sort of, uh, flew past your bench.   I saw the aftermath I caused," he continues, and a mental replay of the wall of dirty water shows in my head, "so I came back to... um..."

Through his stammering, the realization rolls over me that my hand rests inches away from the hand of the *"careless idiot!"* driver that swerved into that puddle, so I snatch it back to my ribs. Come to think of it, I did remember the distinguishing high rear windows of his car as it drove away from the scene of the splash. A brand new Mercury, distinct in style with a huge curving humpback in the rear; the shiny black paint acting as a mirror for my stunned expression. My reflection had shrunk away in moments as the car sped away.

"Yooooou..." I draw out, beginning at a high pitch and plunging into a growl.   I'm freshly reminded of the disgusting street water that had flown into my eyes, nose, and ears.   Every movement I've made since has reminded me of the lingering street grit in my clothes and hair.

"Aaaand I see that I, uh, sort of soaked you there on that bench..."

I groan and listen to the rest of his explanation with smoke rising from my head, eyes narrowed and arms crossed. However, his boyish pink cheeks repel annoyance, melting it away before it settles too deeply.

The corners of his mouth twitch. "May I call this... an apology?" He raises his hand to flag the waitress, but keeps his dancing eyes on me. He's waiting for my response, hoping for exoneration.

She shimmies over. "Miss," he tells her with mock seriousness, "I am in quite a pickle. I'm gonna need you to give this lil' doll anything her heart desires, or my keister is toast!" She grins at him like she'd love to toast his keister.

"Hmmm," I growl, sitting tall, and watch him squirm. "I suppose you could consider it a start." I turn to the waitress. "Um, perhaps a... sandwich?" My eyes flicker to Jack. I don't want to overdo it; I don't know how much it will cost.

He doesn't seem fazed by my request. The waitress juts her hip out, and her pencil bounces against her pad of paper impatiently.

She smacks her gum three times before asking flatly, "Which one?", far less enchanted with me than with him.

"Uh…" I haven't been to a restaurant since I was seven and Daddy would take me out for a malt. I haven't the first clue what sort they offer. Clearly annoyed with my slowness, she looks across the table to Jack.

"Chicken club, crispy bacon," he tells her, watching my eyes for approval of this choice. I must be drooling, because he amends, "Two, please."

She nods and leaves, scribbling.

"You won't be disappointed," he assures me. He couldn't know that I haven't had a shred of chicken or bacon or any kind of meat since Reverend Bell brought us a thick slice of honey ham last Christmas Eve. I salivate at the very thought.

A vindictive thought passes through my head. "I wasn't the only one you soaked on that bench, y' know. There was a rather *fragrant*-smelling lady grumbling about cats sitting next to me when you sent up that wave of street grime." I gesture to the matted state of my tresses to punctuate my words. "Should we order her a sandwich as well? Plenty of room in our booth," I bluff. I feel smug remembering the stares we caused as we walked in. The woman's potent smell and those filthy wads of wiry hair would have caused a more sizeable ruckus.

He looks amused. His lopsided smile creeps back up; its magic not lost on me. He clears his throat.

"Actually, I really hate cats, so, redemption will just have to start with you. For now."

"The state of your eternal soul rests on me, then," I tease. "Though Saint Peter might just be a cat lover. Better work on that." We both smile. Teasing feels right at home to me; I relax a little.

"Will do," he grins crookedly.

"You're just lucky my big brothers aren't around," I threaten. "They could do more damage to ya than ol' Saint Peter." I knock a fist into my palm to demonstrate.

A cock of his head to the side asks where they've gone.

I feel myself light up as I tell him about Eddie and Max. I guess I'm proud of them for getting out and seeing some of the world. While I don't necessarily miss regularly finding a frog in each of my shoes, they're my big brothers, and I miss them.

He smiles as I tell him about the secret swimming hole in the river that they and our pal Phin snuck off to in the summers, and how I'd follow them until we were far enough from home that they'd have no choice but to let me come along. I tell him about my unbeatable cannonball, and brag how I'd always out-splashed the boys, to their everlasting disgust.

As I talk, Jack rests his chin on his fist. This

position causes his fringe of eyelashes to nearly cover his eyes completely. It lends him a cool, casual air.

Phin and my brothers have remained close partners in crime despite our move over the railroad tracks. His wealthy parents, multiple ranch owners, were hit hard by the drought. They'd been able to keep their house, but were humbled considerably by their brush with poverty. Phin's bicycle saw a lot of miles between our houses as he pedaled over the tracks to our new home. The trio has remained so inseparable that they'd enlisted together just after Christmas last year. After many letters home describing the agony of basic training, *"They're not training us, they're killing us!"* and *"It's freezing here! I can't get a wink of sleep when I'm too busy shivering all alone in this bunk!"*, all three were rewarded for surviving the cold by being stationed in Oahu on an army base that defends the Naval outfit there. Hawaii! Warmth at last!

Jack lazily raises one eyebrow. "Phin... a cousin of yours?"

Hearing his name aloud is like a jolt.

"Naw, just a family friend," I answer as calmly as I can, but my heart skips a beat. A picture of my ginger-haired Phin riding his bike, the unbuttoned top of his henley flapping as he rolls into our orchard, plays at the forefront of my mind. I scold myself internally for allowing the thought.

"He your fella?" Jack asks.

My stomach drops deep into my lap and I flush pink. "No way! He's like a big brother!" Truthfully, while Phin sees me as a little sister, a pest, I don't view him in a brotherly manner. Lately, I just view him in my dreams.

"Methinks thou dost protest too much," he answers, grinning.

"Shakespeare," I note appreciatively, very willing to change the focus elsewhere. Anywhere else besides my one-sided romance! I try to stuff the vision of Phin and his impish grin back into the deep recesses of my thoughts, where they belong. These aren't thoughts I allow out in the daylight.

"Yup," he answers and takes a sip.

"My daddy was a big Shakespeare fan," I tell him and clear my throat. "And it's '*the lady doth protest too much, methinks*'".

He raises his brow. "Thanks; I'll keep that in the bank." He taps his forehead. "Was?"

Here we go. "Yeah, he, uh, passed away ten years ago. Today," I explain hastily and gulp from my own glass to give me something to do. My eyes flutter, searching for something to rest on. I settle for the thumb of his left hand. The nail is smooth, pink and clean. I fold my hands in my lap under the table; they look downright shabby in comparison to his.

His brows furrow while he runs a whole hand of those clean fingernails over the side of his head.

"I'm sorry to hear that. That's a shame."

"Thanks," I whisper. "The boys aren't even here to, uh, *celebrate* with us. Kind of a long trip, you know?"

"Hawaii. Lucky dogs!" He sounds truly envious.

"Yep."

"You know, your boys are the clever ones," Jack starts, poking the table with his index finger. "Nazis keep on this rampage and there's no way the we can keep our hands clean! Sooner or later all us fellas are gonna be snatched up by Uncle Sam, willing or not, and those early birds will be pulling rank on all the new peons. Gives a fella something to think about." He drains his glass so thoroughly that his empty straw rattles loudly against the bottom.

I don't let the idea of my brothers within a hundred miles of Hitler settle in my head. "Let's hope that doesn't happen. England will smash him first with all those fly boys they're training."

A light illuminates his eyes from within. "Wouldn't I love to be one of them."

I raise my brows. "You want to *fight*?" It makes me wonder if Eddie and Max signed on for more than the paychecks. Do they want to fight, too? I sure hope not.

"Well, nobody likes a bully," he says, grinning.

I roll my eyes. *Boys.* Always looking for a fight.

"Hitler is the worst kind of bully. 'Sides, I don't want to fight; I want to *fly.*" His eyes sparkle as I consider his words.

Isn't flying the exact same thing as fighting when you're alone in a cockpit, flying a plane and manning a gun? When hordes of enemy planes are trying their best to shoot you down?

He settles back against the seat and sighs. "My mother would flip her lid if she heard me talking like this."

"My lip is buttoned," I assure him, pulling my bottom lip over the top one. Then I mumble out of the corner of my mouth, "What's your mama want you to do?"

"Follow in my father's footsteps. First stop: Columbia. Then wear a tie every day of my life." He pulls his collar and feigns choking.

"You sound bored," I note.

"I am." Golly, he reminds me of Eddie.

I tap my chin and squint my eyes. "I think those fly boys actually *are* wearing ties under their scarves."

"It's not really about the tie," he explains. "Even if there is a draft, my mother wouldn't let my brother or me off of American soil. She'd break our legs herself to render us disabled before we could be shipped overseas." His smile goes tight. I try to imagine the kind of woman who'd disable her child to keep him safe. One who would do anything to have things her way.

"Well, you'd better brush up on your Shakespeare then, college boy."

The waitress sways her hips as she walks over and sets down our sandwiches. My stomach gurgles at the sight of the food. I wait politely for him to take the first bite, then lift mine to my lips. It smells savory, heavenly. It takes all my effort not to shove it down my gub; I feel like a hungry dog at her bowl. I count through my chews to keep from swallowing each bite whole...*one alligator, two alligator*; the emptiness in my stomach reaching eagerly up my throat.

As the weight of the sandwich calms the hungry spasms of my stomach, I steal glances at Jack. His cheeks are as pink as a little boy's, though he's plainly on the upward slope toward manhood: clean shaven, but with a subtle darkness to his chin that hints that a beard is hiding just under the surface.

"Nineteen," he tells me.

I wonder aloud why I didn't know him when I was young. Our parents certainly would have been in the same circles.

"My brother and I were raised down in Georgia," he answers. A southern boy; that explains his fine manners. "As soon as Prohibition was lifted, Pop moved us up here to revive the Ferring plantation," he explains, then salutes. "Serving his country by providing fine red wine to the masses. Plus, my gran was living here all alone, and he figured we better keep an eye on the ol' lady."

Breathing life back into a winery seems like a funny reason to uproot your family.

His father must be a drunk, I hear in my thoughts.

"I can't believe that a slight thing like you can polish off an entire plate," he muses as he slips a crisp bill under his plate.

It's not the reference to my figure that flushes my cheeks. What he doesn't know is that while he was fooling with his billfold, I'd slipped the remainder of my meal into a napkin and stuffed it into my handbag. I can certainly live with this 'ravenous' façade for the benefit of May and Mama. Chicken- any real meat, really- is practically a delicacy in our home, and I can't bear to just leave it on the table to be thrown out. May probably won't even recognize it.

I'm a lousy liar, so I just smile in response.

SIX

We stroll lazily back to the car. I doubt he's really repairing his eternal soul, though mine has certainly been soothed, whatever his actual intentions. I haven't felt the bitter hollow of loss even once since the irritation of being splashed chased it away. His huge black car roars to life when he turns the key.

"So, where exactly is this mysterious swimming hole?" he shouts over the engine noise. The very idea of sharing its top secret location makes me gasp.

I stare at him sideways, considering the possibility of betraying my brothers. The Spot's location is a spit-sworn family secret. Best fishing, deepest water, best trees to climb in and a huge willow tree to nap under. My brothers had put me, their own flesh and blood, through a stiff round of hazing just to be worthy enough to have this knowledge. The only other person who knows about it is Phin.

"But I hardly know you," tumbles out before I can control the high, screeching pitch of it. The fear Max and Eddie have struck in me is deeply ingrained. Sense reminds me that they are way across the country with the Pacific Ocean between us. They won't know if I reveal the location of The Spot. Still, I'm hesitant.

"Aw, c'mon, gal-with-the-famous-cannonball. Spill!" he coaxes. "Don't you want to rinse that muck out of your hair?" He wrinkles his nose as he holds out a stiff strand of my hair. His grin is wide. I can't deny that even though it feels as though my brothers are already sitting on my chest, subjecting me to merciless spit torture, Jack has proved himself to be a great distraction on this awful anniversary. Max can hold my mouth open while Eddie suspends a string of spit just over it, as I kick like a mule in futile protest. Perhaps, when they come home, they'll trap me in the quilt and pollute the air inside with their gas. But since it's as hot as the fiery depths of Hell today, I decide that I'll welcome their torment in exchange.

"Then I'm drivin'," I compromise, against my better judgment. "Move on over. You just keep your eyes shut, and I suppose I'll take you there."

"You know a three on the tree?" he asks skeptically with an arched brow, referring to the high shift knobs stemming from the wheel.

"Been driving tractor since I was seven," I assure him, feigning confidence. Even though the shifting configuration is higher in this car than the rusty old tractor, it can't be too difficult to adapt to. My heart thrums at the idea of driving. I don't even have a real license! I keep to myself that the tractor is the only motor I've ever been in control of. Hopefully it won't show while I maneuver through the streets of town. Remembering his own terrible driving, I reason that he probably won't even notice my inexperience.

Instead of opening his door to trade places, he lifts me easily over him and slides over so that we've exchanged seats. I study his face for a moment, stunned. My sides tingle where his hands have been; I felt that same zing at his touch this time, too. It has run down my legs to the sensitive nerve endings of my toes, where they continue to tingle inside my shoes.

I perch myself on the very edge of the seat to reach the pedals and coax the car into drive. My body tingles, and I can't seem to stifle the little floating sparks of electricity that center where he's touched me.

"Just keep your eyes shut."

He covers his eyes to prove his feigned in-observance, abruptly peeking through his fingers. The car lunges forward and I stomp on the brake to counter it. We rock from the force of it.

"Vee eight," he purrs. "Your tractor have that kind of horsepower?" I shoot him a look. 'Ollie', our old Oliver tractor, moves about as fast as an aged cow. He takes a lot more coaxing to get moving than this machine.

"Close those peepers!" I command, channeling Nurse Adler's authoritative bark as best I can. "Do you know how much trouble I'll be in if they come home to a crowd at the river?" I nearly hyperventilate at the thought, rethinking the wisdom in taking him there. He recoils from the blow of my outburst.

"Gee whiz, you have so little trust in me! I can keep a secret," he defends.

"Squeeze 'em, or this becomes a blindfold," I command severely, one hand on the tail of my scarf.

"How will you drive with a blindfold?" he teases. I give him a stern look. He sighs and obeys, resting his lashes atop his cheeks. After checking twice, I sigh and begin making my way toward the hills. The game of 'red light, green light' has given me some sort of idea of how to read the stoplights that have just debuted in downtown Saratoga, but I find that no corn field has prepared me to drive amongst other cars. Once over the bridge and on a straight dirt road, the cars are sparse and my teeth relax their clench. Blood flows back into my whitened knuckles.

The speedometer tempts me, ranging all the way up to one hundred and ten. Even down at twenty miles per hour, the wind blows my hair wildly around my face and cools my body. My mouth hangs open in a grin reminiscent of a kid at the circus, and my heart pumps just as excitedly. As I pull away a strand of hair that's stuck to my tongue, the thrill of being at the wheel almost overshadows my nerves.

Max and Eddie are going to kill me!

When the clean whitewall tires bounce along the slim dirt path toward the river I spend my summers in, sense is shaken back into me and I slow the car. I guess I had lost my better judgement in the excitement of driving.

"Wait, Jackson..."

"Jack," he corrects me. "I insist. We're on a road trip together; we're chums now."

"Okay, *Jack*," I repeat, rolling my eyes, "I don't have my swimming suit."

"Me neither, Doll. But, I am a gentleman. I won't look," he smiles, but the way his eyebrow dances makes him look contrarily devilish. I roll my eyes again, trying not to let my amusement show. His teasing reminds me of my brothers, but there's a definite un-brotherliness to his jabs.

I stick my head out the window as soon as the brakes whine and the car slows, breathing in the clean air of solitude. The passage ahead will soon become too slim for the wide car, so I park in the middle of the path. I kill the engine and hop out the window, knowing his shiny car, now coated in a thin layer of dust, won't be disturbed all the way out here. He follows behind me as I maneuver through the thicket.

My toes wriggle instinctively out of my shoes while I survey the familiar L-shaped bend of the sparkling river that's nearly enclosed with a jumble of boulders and trees. I duck under the tendrils of the great willow tree and they drag across my back, as they always do. A feeling of being right at home floods me, and I stifle the nagging feeling that I'm betraying my brothers' sacred trust. At the water's edge, my toes grasp the stony sand and dig, burying themselves in the cool feel of it. I pluck a stone from the bank and throw it into the glassy water. It plops in, sending rings expanding toward both banks. My skin shivers with anticipation. I know this calm surface conceals a deceptively swift current rushing below.

Just standing here triggers movie reels of memories in my head, all playing at once: my brothers with homemade fishing rods. Phin, our family friend, lashing driftwood logs together with river grass to construct a raft. The Hale family jump offs: an ongoing rock jumping contest where the only prize is pride. My young heart pounding while I attempt a terrifying feat to prove myself to them.

The young, green foliage just across the bank glows bright green against the rest of the ancient trees. I crack a smile, remembering the day we set that little grove aflame while trying to cook a two-inch minnow Max proudly caught.

"Didn't your brothers teach you how to skip a rock?" Jack asks as he skims a stone expertly across the water. It skips six times before it disappears beneath the surface.

"I can skip a rock," I defend. "It's just an off day for me, all around." A pang of the rotten, churning stomach shoots through me; but it leaves just as quickly as it came. He scoops up another rock and walks closer to the water's lapping edge. This time it bounces seven times across the surface. Seven! Not to be outdone, I pick up a rock of my own and skip it properly. Seven rings ripple on the water, and a cat-like grin sits on my lips. Tied for first, and I'm a mere gal. *Ha!* Maybe it's this place, but I've spent a lifetime proving myself as able as the fellas.

"Huh," he muses, looking appreciative. He saunters to a low boulder, throws his hat on the top of it and drops his suspenders off his shoulders. He pulls his shirt over his head and my heart picks up pace again. He's well built, though his muscles are soft. He throws his shirt over the hat and bends to remove his shoes. I realize as I watch the proceedings in a dumb stare that he is stripping down.

"I am a lady, you know!" I say in a barely suppressed shriek of near panic. "I know you bought my sandwich, but I hope you're not expecting...I, I'm not..."

Am I really a lady? I wonder. A lady might not stare as blatantly.

"Turn around, then, *Lady*," he mocks, grinning. I flip my body around and watch the willow's drooping leaves dance in the light wind, in time with my pulse.

"What're you doin'?" I call to him over my shoulder, eyes defiantly straining in my peripheral view to see how much further stripped he is. I'm really hoping that God isn't paying attention to me right now. Jack is down to his skivvies and stepping his way to the taller boulders. I yank my gaze back to the dancing leaves, but my dancing mind replays the sight of them over and over again. I've observed my mother sewing pair after pair of undershorts for my brothers. I've scrubbed them over the washboard countless times, hung them on the line and seen Eddie and Max shuffle to the breakfast table in the things, so they are a familiar sight; but the sensation I'm experiencing now bears absolutely no resemblance to those memories. I pluck one of the leaves and busy myself by shredding it in my fingers. I sigh at my sinfulness. I'll be the one needing reparation with God by day's end. I try to stifle this feisty imp in me.

He answers, calling, "Jus' putting an experience with your description. So, where's the best spot to jump?" I can hear him scrambling up the rocks.

"Curiosity killed the cat, you know," I warn, but I hear him grunt over the largest stone near the top. "If you jump straight out from where it juts out, there, you won't hit the bottom," I point over my shoulder, peeking just a little. "But don't step on the green patch. It's slippery." I turn to watch so I can guide him away from that danger zone. For safety's sake only, of course.

"Okay," he says and lunges up the last few feet to the landing. He steps carefully across the flat surface, then launches from the rock. As he jumps, he tucks his long legs up to his chest and breaks the smooth surface with a cannonball that leaves every cannonball I've ever seen in the dust. Boom! The impact of his landing upsets the water with a great splash. River water rains down on me where I stand on the shore. My hands are still protectively held in front of my face, dripping, when the current pushes him to the shore and he starts out of the water at me. Virtue keeps my eyes squeezed tight; I know well from the washboard that cotton becomes totally translucent when wet.

"Your turn, Lady Penelope. Here, lemme take your scarf." There's a smile is in his voice as I blindly surrender the dripping fabric. It's silly to spare it from plunging into the river with me when it's already soaking wet.

"That's the second time you've soaked me today, Mister!" I accuse with my eyes closed.

"You needed it," he teases.

"Will you, uh, wring that out for me? Over there, in the trees? I don't want you watching when I jump," I tell him.

"Sure. But ya know," Jack begins. I can hear his feet ambling away over the river rock. "...a guy can see right through a wet blouse."

I frantically shuffle my arms across my chest to conceal the lines of my brassiere, but the sound of his steps have already retreated into the trees.

"My daddy is most likely looking down upon this event, and I'm pretty sure he is not smilin'!" I call to him while I hesitantly unbutton my skirt behind a boulder. In just my shirt and underwear, I'm bare legged, but hopefully covered enough to please my daddy if he really is watching. I scamper up the rock as quickly as I can. My bare legs are no more exposed than they'd be in my swimming suit, but they tingle with exposure anyway while I climb.

From my vantage point, I can see that he's respectfully keeping his back turned. I'm hoping to get him back with a tsunami of river water, so I curl into a loose cannonball and will my body to hit the surface with heavy force.

I plunge deep. Bubbles rise frantically all around me, but my soul sighs with the relief of plunging into my cool sanctuary and I allow myself to sink toward the rocky bottom. A younger Pip would swim across the river bottom with her ankles crossed, imagining her legs and feet to be a mermaid's tail until her human lungs burned for the need of air. Today, I can't linger. I want the satisfaction I've earned by soaking him with that ferocious, long reaching cannon ball. When I kick to the surface and shake the hair from my eyes, I expect to see my freshly soaked victim on the shore. But as my head turns back and forth, scanning the bank, I don't see... anyone.

"Uh, Jack? Where are you?" I'm answered by a great splash. Water flies into my eyes and mouth, and rocks me around while the culprit surfaces.

"Hey, my mouth was open!" I complain and blow my waterlogged nose. He looks like a dog with just his head visible, riding the river's current over to me. His hair is wild and a mischievous grin lies triumphant on his lips. I'm treading water, but when he makes it to me, his feet reach the bottom. He easily picks me up and I'm plunged into the deeper water again. My heart pumps with adrenaline and exertion. Its feels so very opposite of the feeling I was expecting today, and I'm finding myself slightly addicted to this new sensation.

I come up coughing and set off after the predator. My spindly muscles strain to dunk his head, but he flips me over his shoulder and I'm under again. I furiously scramble for the surface, and wrap my arm around his neck to take him down. I throw my weight back and my arms wrench at his neck, but he pulls forward so that we're both immersed.

When all of my muscles burn, I concede that as tough as I've tried to be, I'm not the stronger of the two of us.

Treading in surrender, I fling a lock of hair from my eyes and muse, "I suppose this is what a gal gets when she wrestles with a bear." It's a white flag. Without adrenaline, my muscles feel fatigued and I'm sucking heavy breaths. I pant and lie back so I'm floating on my back, looking into the canopy of trees above us.

Jack laughs his deep, throaty laugh. "A bear? What does that make you, a fish?" He feigns a roar and kicks toward me with claws bared. A jolt of self-preservation electrifies my muscles back into action.

I swim quickly to the shore and scramble up the rocks.

"Cover your eyes!" I screech to him when I see his playful grin. My blouse isn't doing the job it's meant to; it's as good as wet tissue paper; so I hug to the rock for modesty as I climb.

"Too late." A big boyish grin spreads across his wet, dripping face as he looks up at me from the water.

"I thought you were supposed to be apologizing," I scold as sharply as I can muster, though my voice warbles. I'm humiliated that he's seen the lines of my bra. "You're going to be begging forgiveness from the good Lord if you don't wipe this sight from your memory!"

I flail awkwardly on the landing, attempting to cover my more delicate parts while I scramble behind a rock.

"Close your eyes, or get out a bedroll, because I'm not coming down until you're not looking!"

He answers by turning toward the opposite bank. I gingerly tiptoe toward the launch point, still hunched, but he doesn't turn back. When I push off of the rocky bottom and break through the surface, he turns around to look at me.

"Well, ain't you just waterproof?"

I blush. It's nice to hear; a gal always wonders how she looks when water spoils her careful hairdo.

Charmed, I scramble back up the rock and jump in, splashing into the warm water. He's only a moment behind me. I get lost in the amusement, so it's nearly dark when reality regains its footing in my head. When the sun sets in Saratoga, it takes the day's heat with it.

"Jack. Ahem, Jackson..."

"Aw, c'mon now, Doll; anyone who spends time in their skivvies with me is considered a friend. *Jack*," he corrects, wiping water from his mouth.

I blush deeply, ashamed. I've allowed myself to get lost in the sparks.

"We should probably go soon". I squint toward the sun, which is tucked just behind the rocks. "There's no way I'll be home before Mama begins to worry, but if we leave now I can stem the flow before the dam bursts and the Saratoga police comb every ditch in town for my dead, maimed body."

He nods in mock solemnity and swims toward me.

When he's close, I watch tiny beads of water rolling down his straight nose and the way his lips look particularly pink, all wet. He picks me up effortlessly and throws me over his shoulder while he walks out of the water. As it becomes shallow, I wonder if he realizes that the thin cotton of his shorts betrays the shade of his skin underneath. I squeeze my eyes against the desire to gawk; one less repentant prayer to beg tonight. I feel the tendrils of the willow sweep over us and I jostle in his arms while he ducks and swerves through the thicket. He sets me down next to the car.

"Cold?" he asks as I slide onto the seat. All the warmth and energy in me has set with the sun. I'm tired.

"A little," I say with closed eyes. I hear him shuffle around in the trunk. I feel a blanket being laid over me carefully, and murmur my gratitude. I'm too exhausted for my lips to form a real word.

"Home?" he asks as he swoops into the driver's seat. He has to tuck his long legs under the wheel to fit. A yawn stretches my mouth open wide and won't let me answer until it's through. I cover my mouth.

"Mm-hmm," I mumble through my fingers. "Sorry, I get up really early to milk Tilly." Under sleepy lids, I watch the familiar trees and boulders whizz by much faster than when I'm walking this path. The silence we ride in allows my thoughts to drift back to my dad. Oh, I miss him. My skin longs to be tickled by his large, strong hands. I ache to be lifted and twirled around with my legs flying behind me, watching the familiar happy crinkles form around his sparkling grey eyes. If there were ever such a thing as unconditional love, my daddy possessed it for me.

He called me "Princess", even when I wore long strips of scabs from forehead to chin from falling out of the tree in our orchard. It looked like a giant tiger had taken a swipe at me, but he still looked at me like I was the world's most prized, flawless gem. He was always so calm and relaxed; top collar unbuttoned, sleeves rolled up his forearms. I loved to lie on his chest and absorb the tranquility he radiated. I have half a mind to direct Jack to Green Valley Cemetery so I can lie face down on Daddy's grave and soak up any wisps of lingering peace, but the other, sensible half of my head directs him to my house. When we're near Radcliffe, my directions are sandwiched between guilty rants that I know I'll regret tomorrow, but I can't make them stop.

"I am not the dame I've put on at the river, Jack...oh, turn up here... I mean, I don't go around whipping my skirt off with any ol' Joe! And, oh, I'm for sure gonna be strung up in the orchard and beaten for showing you the Spot. It's the green one, up there, at the end all by itself," I point out my little hovel. "No, no; that's the outhouse. Keep going. I appreciate the ride and the meal and the company, but I must declare that the devil overcame me today in a moment of weakness, what with it being ten years since..." I trail off when my lungs are completely depleted of breath.

We pull up to the house.

As I suck in a refill, he interjects, "Miss Hale, you are bleeding purity.   I've met a share-cropper or two, and you sure aren't one of them. Our waitress, maybe; but not you." His hand slides into mine. My entire body stiffens like a plank of wood.

I examine his compliment while my hand radiates with heat. So, he can tell I'm not a hussy. *How can he see a halo shining over the head of a girl in wet skivvies?*   I wonder nervously if he's thick enough to dare try to kiss me goodnight. Any gentleman should know he shouldn't attempt that on the first date, if they've ever even heard of Emily Post, famous etiquette columnist.

Is he a gentleman? I wonder. *Is this even a date?*

Truthfully, I've never kissed anyone. Or, you know, dated anyone. It's somewhat limiting for a gal to carry a torch for one fella her whole life, especially when you're like his pesky little sister. Of course, no one else has weaseled so much as a toe through the rusty gate around my heart before, and here is Jack with all five toes stepping on in without my permission.

I pull my hand back to my lap. My eyes tell him, *Don't waste your time on me. I'm no good.* He just smiles and comes around the car to open my door. Maybe he has heard of Miss Post.

"See ya around, Pip," he says, leaning into the

door.

"G'night," I sigh and saunter up the steps, still wrapped in the quilt, still wrapped in the jumble of feelings that the day had brought. He waits until I open the creaking, paint-peeled door to pull his car away. I sigh into the doorframe and bite the smile on my lips. I watch his tail lights fade away until they disappear from my sight.

The sensible gal in my head scolds, *Don't get mixed up with him.*

The more mischievous one produces a vivid replay of his transparent skivvies.

I shake my head to rattle them both into radio silence. I'm sure if Jack knew I regularly hear voices in my head: a devilish Imp on one shoulder competing with angelic Sense on the other, he would never have invited me into his car, let alone tried to hold my hand. When I light the lamp on the table, low so as not to wake Mama and May behind the sheet that creates a "bedroom" in our little one-room home, the letter from Eddie sits lonely on the table in its light. I scoop it up eagerly, consuming the words with my eyes while my damp bottom blindly finds the chair.

"Hello... how are you... don't worry, Ma... we're fine... wish I could be there with you on the awful anniversary of losing Dad..."

I scan through his boxy penmanship. Then my eyes hone in on a phrase that leaps from the page at me. It's somehow darker, larger, and clearer than every other sentence.

"...a decade later and we still can't prove a thing".

Prove what? What does he mean? When Daddy died, he was hunting with his club buddies and his horse got spooked. His foot was caught in the stirrup, so the frightened, fleeing horse dragged his struggling body through the woods. When the horse jumped over a fallen log, Daddy's head was smashed right into it, crushing his skull on impact.

I close my eyes and shake the dark vision away. *What does Eddie know that I don't? Was there more to my daddy's death then simple tragedy? What does he want to prove? Have I been fed a consoling story about an accidental death when there was really foul play involved?* I was only seven... My chest starts tightening in spasms while my eyes blur. If so, someone's lied to me. The thought makes my stomach churn with renewed vigor.

How many people know this? Am I the only one kept in innocence? If so, how infuriating! *Oh, don't tell poor little Penny, she's far too weak and fragile to handle such sensitive information.* My cheeks flare with a scarlet burn; hot, angry flames lick over my vision. I knew it! I *know* it. I really can't trust anyone.

The Sense in me peeks out from the curtain I've shoved her behind. *Don't get ahead of yourself. Get the facts first. Breathe.* I accept her coaching and fight the constriction of my lungs to draw a deep breath.

There, she soothes as I release in a breath the fiery sparks of my hissy fit. My body relaxes into the chair; my eyes flutter sleepily. I'd better get to bed.

However, a toiling imagination does not make for a good night's sleep.

SEVEN

I'm ascending at the end of a night of vivid dreams circling around Eddie's letter, mingled with water droplets on Jack's pink lips and his throaty laugh. My dreams have plucked insignificant bits from the text and sprinted off in their own distorted paths, but still they keep bending back around to the same thought: murder.

Moving further toward consciousness, I'm becoming aware of the pressure of a heel in the small of my back. I can feel the stem of a chicken feather in my pillow poking my cheek, but I struggle against waking to cling to this limbo a little longer, because my subconscious mind is so much more liberal with information. Ed's not one to hold a grudge against a horse, and I seriously doubt he was referring to a mossy log. So... *who planned my father's violent death?* I search my vivid dreams for a clue, any clue.

Awareness wins, and my dream evaporates into

wisps that I can't cling to. *Groan.* The chance to glean any more insight into this new shock floats away with them.

I roll onto my back and sigh. I peek out from under sleepy lids and watch flecks of dust dance through the dim light that streams in through the crack in the curtains. The only sound is May's soft breathing next to me as she dreams. Her hair is swirled around her face like she's been tossing throughout the night, yet she's curled up in the quilt without a toe uncovered.

It's Thursday... I need to milk Tilly, scratch up some breakfast. I'll just grab a peach from the orchard. Then I'll drag Nell through deliveries, ride downtown to check on the crate boys and the produce they sell for us, put in some hours at Saint Christopher's, get started on those mountainous piles I've let build up in Nell's stall... I sit up quickly before the weight of the day's load crushes me.

My feet hit the gnarled wooden floor softly and I hum a quiet little tune as I walk to the closet. Inside hangs the usual worn display of shabby, hand-me-down garments that I must treat with care so they're fit for May to inherit. I sigh and settle for the grey blouse and white skirt with faded red polka dots. I just love a skirt in summer. When it's hot out, all it takes is a swish of the fabric to provide a rush of cool relief to my legs. Not a perfect match; the dots will clash with the stripes of my apron; but who am I, Doris? I don't need to get gussied up to change bedpans. Tilly seems unimpressed with my retelling of yesterday. She chews her cud lazily while I fill her ears to the brim with the details.

"Can you believe Doris got herself into this mess? Just goes to show you, fellas are creeps." Based on her reaction to the mention of my brothers yesterday, I'd say she agrees. "Of course, I met a sorta un-creepy fella. A nice one, really."

She doesn't ask his name.

"Jackson," I offer.

She switches her tail.

"He bought me Ovaltine at a *diner*. I can't even remember the last time I sat in a diner!"

Silence.

"Nothing like your milk, Tills," I assure her, "but, *wow!* Chocolate is just divine!" I shiver, temporarily drunk with the memory of the malted milk. Once the sugary cocoa hit my veins, the ache in my muscles had faded. It was as though I'd ingested a magic potion and they were instantly vigorous. And then the sandwich! Oh, golly! Words cannot express the sensation of a full belly. And not even just being full... I mean, you can fill yourself to bursting with onion soup, but the sandwich left me... *satisfied.*

Tilly lifts a hoof to threaten my silent daydream.

"Sorry, Tilly. Anyhow, the fella was a fair distraction on a crummy day."

She turns her head to me, which is saying something for the world's laziest cow.

"Aw, don't get your hopes up, girl. I can't go pecking around with some rooster and fly the coop. I've got plans!"

She turns her head forward again, ignoring my declaration of independence.

As I replay yesterday for Tilly's entertainment, I run into the last event of the night. My stomach sinks with the fresh renewal of the sordid possibility. "Eddie said something really curious in his letter. He said *we still can't prove a thing*. As in, he was *murdered?* So, that would mean he didn't just die in a fluke; someone killed him." I whisper the word 'killed'. It sounds new and strange to say it aloud. "I don't know what to believe; if that's true, then I've been lied to for ten years." My words hang still in the cold morning air while I examine them. In the long quiet, I have to snatch up the pail quickly as she begins lumbering her way out of the barn.

When I come back in from the barn, Mama is sitting at the table with a bandanna tied up around her head, chewing toast with her homemade peach jam. I hold the rattly door so it won't snap shut and wake May, and I nestle it softly into the frame.

This little farmhouse sees seasonal meals: the same scanty supper night after night until the leaves change, redundant rations of leftover food that the crate boys can't sell from our farm. Onion soup all winter. Thin potato soup in the early spring months, and then the sweet respite in spring and summer's crops. *Variety.* Anything that's going bad or the crate boys can't sell is divided between our table and Uncle Mac's. Peaches and peas, apples and carrots. Melons! Beets, tomatoes, berries! My body revels in the relief of fresh roughage in these warm months.

"Mornin'," I whisper. For some reason, my heart is pounding and I feel almost guilty as I approach the table.

Mama stares at me; sizing me up. I should have recognized the dampening of my palms which only that intent look of hers can trigger. Her children have been trained to react to it like Pavlov's dogs. *The Stare.* She watches me with squinting eyes as I sit and spread jam on my toast. The hairs on my neck stand warily at attention.

"What?" I ask her with a nervous, breathless laugh. I'd almost forgotten the winded feeling that accompanies the sweating palms. And, right on schedule, the slow wringing of my stomach.

"You don't look particularly well-rested this morning," she states in a leading tone. It sounds dangerously close to an accusation.

"Oh?" I respond before I stuff the toast into my mouth.

She raises a sharp eyebrow, but doesn't break her gaze. "You were mumbling in your sleep."

I flush. "Me?" I hate that I talk while I'm unconscious and dreaming. I wonder nervously what I'd said in my sleep last night. I sure hope I didn't mention swimming in skivvies with a fella.

"And you came in rather late."

I nod guiltily.

"Anything you want to share?" She chews slowly, carefully inspecting my face for any clues. Yesterday's scene replays in my head, again. It seems impossible that Mama could know all that transpired yesterday: that I had been caught in a hailstorm of street muck; that Jack had picked me up, then taken me to the diner; that I betrayed the secret location of the Spot, and swam in just my skivvies and blouse; but if I've learned anything in my seventeen years, it's that mothers have eyes in the back of their heads. And intuition, to boot.

We're in a staring standoff as I squint my eyes at her, trying to deduce what she could know. I applaud myself for stuffing Jack's wet quilt far under the bed to keep her from discovering it. She squints back, trying to climb inside my pupils and read my mind. The hairs on the back of my neck stand at attention.

"I didn't have a chance to muck Nell's stall, but I will today right after I get home," I promise her.

"Oh?" she asks. It's only one word, but you don't know interrogation until you've been raised by Edith Hale and subjected to her penetrating stare. Words that I don't want to share press on the inside of my tightened lips as her eyebrow raises higher toward her hairline.

Blood throbs loudly behind my ears.

When I can't take it any longer, the bull bursts through the gate: "Well, my trolley didn't come and I got sprayed with a disgusting puddle when this idiot- well, not an idiot- but anyway," I bumble on rapidly. "I'm wet and dirty and this fella offered me a ride." I suck in a breath while Mama's other eyebrow rises to meet its twin, "but then my stomach gave this loud, humiliating 'roar!' and he heard it, so he insisted on feeding me as penance for soaking me with muck, he said. He took me to a real restaurant, a sit-down joint, ya know, even though I was all wet and dirty, and I brought some home. It's real white chicken, Mama! But I told him about how the boys and I used to swim in the river and he wanted to see it..." This all escapes in one breath. I can't tell her the finer details; her eyebrows have already reached her hairline.

The Stare finally breaks when her brows fall

back into place, and I can breathe. "You accepted a ride from a stranger?" she asks with a cheekful of peach. Her long lashes bat in disbelief. I sigh. Didn't she hear "chicken"?

"Yes, Mama, but don't get all in a lather. He wasn't a creep or anything."

"How could you have known that? Many killers who prey on young girls are normal looking fellows," she lectures in the cautioning voice I know so well. The way she sips her tea makes her seem somehow more disapproving and prim.

"Am I chained to a pipe in his basement?" I challenge, palms up. I learned sarcasm from Mama herself. It doesn't faze her.

"No, Penny, but that's just dumb luck. You never know! Anyhow, go on," she prods, rolling her finger in the air. Why she thinks I will share things with her when I just get harangued in return, I will never understand. I just shrug.

"Nothing more to tell," I answer curtly and button my lip.

"Hmmm, I'm not sure I believe that," she answers and stands up. "Is he a normal looking fellow?" she asks with an eyebrow arched, Mama-style. I think of the sparks of electricity at his touch and my cheeks flush; it's all the answer she needs.

"Better than normal, hmmm? Well, if there's a fella who'd like to spend time with you, he should meet your mother first." I roll my eyes when she walks into the kitchen. Mama may not have attended finishing school, but she's well trained in the delicate art of lecturing.

"What's his name?" she calls over her shoulder while she rinses her dish. The lecture is over, and I sense girlish curiosity in her voice.

My buttoned lip comes undone. "Jack. Well, Jackson," I tell her.

"Jackson...?" She leads, fishing for his last name.

"Actually, I didn't catch his last name," I admit.

"Well, how will I know whose pipe to check when you go missing? Bring him by the house. I'll be in the orchard all day," she says as she dries her hands on a ragged dish towel.

"No need. I won't be seeing him again." Mama ignores my comment. She kisses my forehead and heads for the door. I respect her. So many years of pouring from a nearly empty pitcher. Busy as a beaver, she can still keep an eagle eye on her children. But after Ed's letter, I have to wonder: is she hiding something under her protective wings?

"Mama."

She pauses mid stride.

"What did Eddie mean when he said 'we still can't prove a thing'?"

She waits a beat too long before she turns back to face me, her features carefully arranged in innocence.

"What do you mean, Penny?"

I narrow my eyes at her, hyper vigilant of her every move. I watch her right eyebrow, which will twitch when she's really uncomfortable. "His letter."

The telltale brow is still, but she sighs heavily.

"He just wants someone to blame, I guess. They both do. It's tough for a boy to lose his father." Her tired, beautiful eyes look sad. Sad for the thick layer of crust on their young hearts. Sad for the tragic reason for those hard shells. But no twitching brow.

"Who?"

"Hmm?" she asks, as though she hadn't heard my questions at all. I know a good stall job when I see one.

"Who do they think killed Daddy?" Thick tears are threatening just below my eyes. It stings, and not at all in the nice way I'd been stung yesterday.

Her shoulders sag. "Oh, I don't know. Your brothers have a long list, Penny. Why don't you ask them?" I tighten my lips with frustration. With the tortoise speed of the postal service, it will take weeks to get an answer.

I decide to voice my impatience with that plan. "But..."

"Argh! I don't have room in my head for all that weighty business!" Mama repels any further discussion of it by shaking her hands and head.

How can you not care who killed your husband? Imp wonders.

"Oh, and Penny..." she turns to me with one foot already out the door, "please remember that this is Mac's house. Take care of the stall. We do our part to have the privilege of living here."

"Yes, Mama," I sigh and the screen door rattles against the frame. My shoulders fall dejectedly. I'll have to wait for an answer. I can't decipher Mama's thoughts, and I guess there's just no escaping horse poop.

When May rises, I spread her toast with jam for her. I'll forever be her 'other mother', I guess, even though she's fourteen this month.

"Hiya, P," she says sleepily, rubbing her eyes. Her long lashes crunch under her fists like wheat stalks. Her pillow has styled the curly brown hair on her crown into a bird's nest. "You were talking in your sleep." She yawns, but her eyebrows dance excitedly. I know girlish interrogation is coming; we're a regular sorority around here. Nothing gets by these two.

"So I hear," I answer sarcastically.

"Why-y?" She sings. She's much more direct than Mama, and I'm much more liberal with the details with her than I am with Mama.

I give her the same story, with added notes about Jack's blue eyes and handsome smile. I decide it's safest to withhold the underpants part. I never know how The Stare will affect May, and I don't need that incriminating tidbit leaking out to Mama. I expect her to revel in the details with me, but instead, she looks slightly scandalized. It looks comical with the fluff on her head.

"What?" I ask her, somewhat put out. A girl should be able to count on her little sister to enjoy good gossip with, especially when it involves a handsome stranger with a swell black car.

"Well, what about Phin?" she asks.

The sound of his name aloud cuts through the air, and catches me off guard. I blush and stammer instead of displaying the cool mask I've practiced in regards to his name. "Wha-what about *Phin?*" I ask, my reply coming out much more flustered than the casual tone I wanted. I try to regain control of myself by retrieving the chicken from yesterday's sandwich in the icebox and chopping it into bits with furious hands. I stuff a huge bite of bread into my cheek. May just smiles the impish grin that's earned her her nickname, 'Mayhem'. It's enough of a response to indicate that I'm not fooling anyone.

A memory of Phin pulls me off of the grey wood planks of the farmhouse floor into the past. I met him when I was six. The summer before I turned fifteen, we'd been rigging up a zip line over the secret spot for three days. As usual, the guinea pig was the runt of the group: me, and I slipped my legs into the circle of rope, grasping the top of the loop with a death grip. Max shoved me off the launch point and all at once, I was flying. I shrieked in delight, but then the "expert" knot dissolved and I was plunged into the shallow far side of the bank. My feet slammed into the rocks. The fall jarred me and I fought back tears. It was humiliating. I knew that being with them was a privilege, and crying was not acceptable. Max and Eddie were doubled over in laughter, but Phin had shown real concern. He dove in and surfaced near me. He'd scooped me up and carried me all the way home. I fought desperately to hide my wiggling chin, and he had graciously looked away to give me privacy to blubber in pain. My eyes watched his neck, collarbone and chin for two miles that day. The memory of his handsome face fades to darkness.

When my awareness comes back to our tiny kitchen, I spar, "Mayhem, he's miles and miles away." The wad of bread in my cheek muddles my argument and weakens its intended strength.

"What's he ever done that says, *'I'm sweet on you, Pip'*? Nothing!" I insist while the knife moves furiously.

A dot of wet bread flies from my mouth onto

May's forearm. She scrunches her nose and wipes it away, but she won't stop watching my eyes for a chink in my armor.

"He's like another big brother, like a triplet or somethin'," I dispute, gesturing with the knife hand. A chunk of white chicken flies off of it onto the floor. "Besides, Eddie and Max would never have it. They'd murder us both for even thinking about that!"

"Five second rule!" we yell in unison and scramble for the scrap. May blows on it to rid it of germs and pops it into her mouth. Her eyes close appreciatively. I know the new feeling she's experiencing, like instant vigor to one's limbs. I swallow the bread. It's a thick lump in my throat.

"Anyway, to him, I'll always be Little Pip Squeak, following him around like a pathetic stray dog."

"I'm sure Phin likes dogs," she says, smiling. "I do."

"Oh, you would," I grumble. I'm envious of how she can say his name without blushing. "Point is, nothing will ever happen between him and me."

"But you want it to," she teases in a sing-song voice, poking my shoulder.

I growl, frustrated. "Not happening, May. Not with Jack, either. Yesterday was fun, but it'll have to hold me over for awhile. I've got plans, and nobody's blue-eyed, handsome face is gonna drag me down. I don't want my kids rescuing scraps from between the floorboards."

We're momentarily hushed by our humble circumstances.

I lead her by the shoulders and sit her down. My fingers begin untangling the nest on her head.

"So, you're going to have babies all by yourself? I'm pretty sure that's physically impossible, Sis. Maybe you oughtta ask Mama again about all that 'birds and bees' business," she suggests with her sassy head bobbling. Sarcasm is deeply ingrained in all Hale siblings.

"Nooooo, no thank you," I protest uncomfortably, trying to hold her head steady while I work through the knots. One torturous fifteen-minute discussion with Mama, a period of sweaty palms, a tied tongue and blushed cheeks, was wildly uncomfortable enough to last me a lifetime. It felt like a bucket of embarrassment had been dumped on my young head. My cheeks flush just thinking about it. *Darn it, May; now I'm not going to be able to look Mama in the eye for at least another month!*

"I'm getting my nurse's certificate, May. Then, when I'm a working gal, maybe I can consider a... a guy."

"Gee, sounds romantic," she says and rolls her eyes up at me. Her cavalier attitude has been inherited from our parents, the ones we had when we were young, and bears the hallmark of carelessness. She is far too casual about her future. It causes my anxiety to multiply spilling out of me in an attempt to fill her gaping hole. *Is she blind to our surroundings? Hadn't we both just skinned our knees for a pea-sized hunk of chicken?*

"Romantic, May? What, you wanna end up like Mama?" I snap, fingers working furiously to tame her mane and her attitude. "You can't rely on some fella to take care of you! You've got to make something of yourself!" I'm trembling as I holler the words.

"Ow! Gee whiz!" she complains, craning her head away from my angry fingers. "You're ripping my hair out!"

"I am not." I pick up the brush and comb extra softly to prove it.

"I never knew Mama's bitterness got you so bad," she says quietly.

"I'm not bitter! Just... realistic."

Her large green eyes start to swim in her tears, and she says shakily, "Daddy didn't leave us on purpose, you know." The cleft in her chin dimples over and over as her chin wiggles, melting the heat from my heart. "That doesn't always happen."

I swoop down on her and enfold her in my arms, just the way our maid, Honey, used to soothe me.

"I know, May. I know," I coo and stroke her chestnut hair. My fingers begin their daily routine of smoothing her curls into two braids, then pinning them across her crown. "It's just... well, sometimes, husbands die. And sometimes they just have no ambition. Or they get injured and can't work, or they just plain can't provide. Or they stop loving you and leave." I secure her braids with one pin for each grim possibility. "Or they go and get murdered." The last pin goes in severely.

"Ow!" she complains, recoiling with her delicate hands protecting her scalp. "Murdered?" She's staring at me like no one ever gets bumped off, and scoffs. "Yeah, if you marry some fella in the mafia."

I sigh. I can tell she'd glossed right over that part of Eddie's letter. Innocence is bliss.

"Just sayin', May, if you put all your eggs in some fella's basket, he will very likely let you down. *Crack*." I throw my hands out in a dramatic gesture. "It's a big gooey mess."

"So you think you can't live a good life without money?" Her tone tells me she doesn't think so.

"No. Well, yeah. Remember Mama before, you know, before we came here? She was so, you know, mild?" I revel in the memory of a younger, smoother mother basking in the backyard sun while we played around her; not a care to wrinkle her forehead.

"Sort of," she answers thoughtfully. She was

only four when we came here. "But wouldn't you be bored if you were one of those rich ladies? Nothing to do all day but clean your jewelry and lie in the sun, and gossip about your friends?" she laughs.

I smile back, knowing I will probably never experience such a thing as boredom. "Well, we're in no danger of that." With that, we stand up to get on with our laundry lists. May grabs the egg basket and I reach for my hospital apron. As we walk down the steps, she pauses and scrunches her nose.

"So, I don't get it. Do you like this Jack fella, or you don't?" she asks with a scrunched nose.

"It was fun. But its not going anywhere," I reply. "A guy like that wants a nice, quiet gal who's seen and not heard, ya know?" I try to envision my dirt-embedded nails cradling a delicate teacup, pinkie daintily up.

"Even though you're bent on being a man-hater," she begins, and I roll my eyes, "Don't count out Phin, 'kay? I'd like it if he really was my big brother," she smiles and jumps the last step.

"*You* marry him, then!" I jab. I push away a threatening pang of envy as a vision forms in my head: a band of dazzling white gold encrusted with tiny jewels that symbolize the undying devotion of one Phineas Emerson O'Shea; on the finger of my little sister. I shudder in disgust.

She ignores me and bobs toward the henhouse, basket swinging.

EIGHT

The hospital halls are rather quiet today, so Nurse Adler has me catching up on charting for her. It's tedious work that makes my eyes water and cross without my permission, and it makes me seriously reconsider this career path. If I wanted to sit on my rear all day, I'd have become a secretary. However, if I've learned anything here, it's that you don't argue with a lady with a beard! The forest of coarse white hairs that dot Nurse Adler's chin reach out at me like fingers when she comes close; they can make me agree to anything to avoid their graze.

The only break in the brain-bending monotony is a momentary visit from Doris.

"Listen, Miss Goody Two Shoes," she hisses threateningly through her teeth with thin arms crossed over her chest, "if you so much as breathe a word of what you know to anyone around here, I'll wring your skinny neck. Do you understand me?" She's bent so far into my face that I'm reclining in midair. Without mascara streaks and a dripping nose, she is back to her brassy self.

I push my neck toward her nose. "Ease up, Doris. I won't rat you out."

She squints her eyes at me, sizing me up. She wrinkles her nose. "Well, don't think this makes us girlfriends or anything."

I pull my face away from hers and nod. I suppose she's satisfied, because she turns and bounces away on her heels. If she ever saddles me with vomit duty again, I know just what to hold over her head.

Hours later, my hand is cramped and my rear end is aching in the wooden chair. I rise to stretch my legs. Just then, around a cheerful green fern with a stem card that reads, "Get well soon" in handsome cursive, a tall figure curled over the handles of a wheelchair catches my eye. He's smiling down at the twiggy, shriveled occupant of the chair as her tiny arms gesture wildly. I gasp and shrink behind the fern. What is he doing here?

In twenty paces, I'll be exposed in his view. I really don't want to have a conversation about my loose behavior yesterday, and I sure don't want him to expect it again today! As I'd told May, I can't get all mixed up with a fella, so my plan is to just avoid him. I drop to the floor and press my back up against the files. With the brass handles digging into my back, I close my eyes like a toddler playing hide-and-seek. I can't see you, so you can't see me.

I can hear his steps and the squeak of the wheelchair approaching. My heart thumps so loudly against my ribs that I worry its drumming will expose my hiding place. I hear the half-door of the information desk swing open and I squeak in terror.

"Hale! Vat are you do-ink down zere?" Adler barks.

I open my eyes to her hairy, sausage legs straining the threads of her stockings, and I sigh in surrender. I scramble for the pencil by my toe and hold it up.

"Here it is," I say feebly with a forced smile. Her look remains suspicious. I'm forced to rise, or offer another explanation that my brain is refusing to fabricate for me. I stand slowly and turn back to the charts. "I'm nearly..."

But the breath required to finish my sentence is gone, because I'm staring right into the collarbone of the person I've been hiding from. My eyes rise to meet his and my face burns pink. He smiles, which looks fetching under his cap, sitting stylishly cockeyed on his head. The gold flecks in his eyes brighten. My sides tingle reminiscently, remembering his hands on them yesterday. I brush at my apron, trying to wipe away the feeling.

"So, *this* is where you volunteer?" he asks, too innocently, while he leans one elbow on the counter. His sharp jaw rests on his fist.

"Yeah, here; the *only* hospital in the county," I reply sarcastically, pulling a file from under his elbow.

"Oh, well, I was just visiting Granny," he explains, gesturing toward the stooped occupant of the wheelchair, "and they said I can take her home today." His smile holds a hint of mischief.

"Thank goodness, because I'm bored to tears in this place!" the occupant croaks. "If I had to spend one more night here, they'd be shipping me upstairs to the loony bin!" Lyla Sharpe's liver-spotted hands slice the air with punctuating gestures. "My neck is aching just thinking about that wretched excuse for a pillow. Perhaps with one of those tranquilizers they have upstairs for the nutjobs, I might've had some decent rest!"

"Lyla? This is your grandson?" I ask. Her going-home outfit matches her haughtiness quite well: velvet, silk, pearls, a stylish feathered cap.

"Yes, Dear. The only one left in that family with a sense of humor. His mother's squeezed the life out of my boy and his big brother, but I'm still hangin' on to this one!" She shakes a handful of his shirt in her fist while she talks, making him sway like a tall stalk of wheat. I smirk because she's been able to work in a jab at her daughter-in-law in the forty five seconds we've been talking. Jack glows down at her like she's his favorite person in the world.

"You've met my gran, huh?" he asks me. The vision of her wrinkled, sagging rear peeking out from her hospital gown has been seared irrevocably into my memory. Oh, I've met her alright.

"Oh, we're old friends, Jack-Jack! Aren't we, dear?" she coos at me in her gravelly voice.

"Yeah, Lyla kept me company on my shift yesterday." She's not the sort of woman you disagree with. "I'm sorry you'll be leaving," I tell her sincerely.

"Oh, nonsense!" she snaps and swipes the air at me. "I just talked her ear off, and she was patient enough to listen." Behind the wheelchair, Jack's eyebrows are high in a comically understanding expression. I sense that he's been on the listening end of her rants before.

"However, we do share a common foe," she says darkly. Doris's pinched expression flashes in my head. I don't know how to soften Lyla's feelings about Doris without revealing her secrets, so I just nod. "You know my Jack?" she asks me.

"Well, sort of," I say hesitantly.

Jack snorts. "Alright, Gran, let's get you home," he tells her and starts to push her chair.

"Wait! When are you through, Dear?" Before I can answer, she's scolding Jack, "Aren't you going to offer this young lady a ride home?" She turns back to me. "You don't want to take the smelly old streetcar, do you?"

I look up at the clock. Five minutes to go. If I accept the ride, then I'll be tangling myself further into a web I don't want to be in. If I lie and say I have to stay here, surely they'll see me walking to the trolley stop. If I hide out and miss the trolley, I'll have to hoof it home. I chew my lip while I consider my options.

Adler kicks a foot back through the swinging half door. "Hale, are you qvite feenished? You may go; your sheeft ees nearly up anyhow." My mouth tightens against my tongue to keep it from poking out at her. She hasn't released me one minute early ever before. It's as though she has a delicate sense of my wants, then cruelly sends them through her meat grinder with a wicked, stubborn grin.

"Wonderful!" Lyla claps her thin hands together. "Shall we?" Apparently she has made up my mind for me.

"Well, only if I get to push," I concede. I come out the swinging door and take the handles from Jack.

I can give my trolley pennies to May for her "indoor toilet fund". She'll like that; that jar is filling up pretty slowly. I'll do this for May. It'll be over in ten minutes, and she can clink the coins in with the rest of her meager collection. No sweat, I tell myself. But my palms are slick on the handles as we roll through the exit doors.

We all pause at the top of the stone steps.

"Uhhhh," I mutter, envisioning a very bumpy ride for Lyla down this staircase. We should have exited the west doors, where there's a smooth ramp and a roundabout for patient pick-up.

"I'll just carry you down, Gran," Jack offers.

"Nonsense!" she waves him away and positions her feet to stand. I lunge forward to support her by the arm. "I can walk. Just a little stiff from that bony excuse for a mattress," she grumbles and looks pointedly at me, as though I designed, manufactured and installed the uncomfortable hospital beds myself. "Just need to stretch my stems." She grunts, but seems nimble enough with us at her sides.

In the car, we haven't gone two blocks when Lyla gasps. "Oh, Jack, pull over! My hair is a rat's nest!" It seems the city air has reminded her of the need to be presentable, in case the Queen of England comes sauntering down the main avenue. He pulls over immediately, cutting off a yellow jitney, and we roll to a stop in front of a posh beauty parlor.

"Best not to argue with her," he whispers to me

behind her head.

He hops out of the car and leads her to the salon. As he swings open the door, I faintly hear Lyla crying out, "It's an emergency!" to the staff inside.

I smirk.

Jack is grinning as well as he jogs back to the car. "Well, I don't have to pick up Granny for at least two hours. She's a real yakker," he explains, but I'm already keenly aware of her gift of gab. "Where to?" His eyes sparkle with mischief.

"I hate to spoil the fun, but I've got a big pile of horse apples waiting for me at home."

"Sounds tasty," he laughs. "And speaking of tasty, I know you're hungry."

My face goes red from the memory of my rumbling stomach. *Will I ever live that down?*

"Wanna grab a bite to eat before you go shovel some fudge?"

"Hmm. Emily Post says it'd be my turn to pay. They don't pay me at the hospital, ya know. I volunteer, so you could stand in a bread line with me..." The idea of clean, polished Jack standing in line for a soup kitchen is comical, but I'm bluffing. Mama is far too proud to have ever taken us to a bread line. I'm being somewhat standoffish toward him, sure; but Mama was right. I can't get tangled up in the thorns right now.

"Tempting," he bluffs in return, tapping his

finger on his chin. "Or, we could save time and I can just buy you a burger," he offers. "Emily Post can eat her hat!"

My resolve to avoid him wanes. My mouth salivates at the mere thought of a warm, juicy hamburger dripping with ketchup. Still, somehow I drag up the strength to resist.

"I'm fine; the peach trees are so ripe, they're dropping fruit. I'll just grab one at home."

Now *his* mouth salivates. He licks his lips. "Fresh peaches. Mmm."

Emily Post would agree it would be rude to accept the ride without offering him some fruit, Sense reminds me, drawing up an image of one of her articles on proper manners.

Oh, *fine.*

I show him the way to Mac's side of the farm so we're closer to the orchard. He opens my door over my lap and I'm left in a cloud of his scent. It's nice; woody and clean. I'm briefly intoxicated as I get out of the car. I shake my head to clear it.

We walk toward the trees, where I know Mama will be filling baskets for this year's batch of prize-winning jam. Jack doesn't bat an eyelash at the effect the chunky dirt clods beneath our feet are having on his shiny wingtips. They're coated with dust by the time we round the corner. I can pick out the forms of May and Mama from a hundred yards away, but they're not working; they're playing.

I watch Mama stalk May around the peach tree. Her shoulders, which usually sag with the visible weight of responsibility, are loose and light as she moves. She springs forward to catch May around the waist. May shrieks, and Mama's face softens in a laugh, peeling back her usually dark under-eyes and wrinkles to reveal a relaxed, youthful version of herself.

This is where she finds her respite, I realize as I watch her. Her children are the well from which she draws her strength in small bucketfuls. I know the hands that tickle May are rough, red and cracking, but you can't tell now as they're suspended in the air, curved into bear claws, ready to strike with another round of tickling. I guess you'd need something to keep you afloat after losing everything. I respect her. She has never allowed herself to be a victim.

"Hiya, Mama," I call from fifty yards, and their flushed faces snap up from their wrestling poses. Mama stands straight and brushes her hands on her apron when she sees my companion. Her neck straightens regally, hinting at the poised woman I once knew. She gazes at Jack curiously as we move toward them.

I fold my hands properly as I say, "Mama, May; I want you to meet my friend..."

"Jack," he interrupts, striding forward and shaking Mama's hand animatedly. His cheeks look especially pink in this light.

"Edith, Penny's mother," she introduces herself, panting slightly with either exertion or embarrassment. She pushes her blonde hair out of her eyes with her free forearm. "Pleased to meet you. I hear you got Penny out of a bit of a pickle yesterday." That's polite, seeing as how he's the one who threw me in the pickle jar in the first place.

While the two greet each other, Mayhem catches my eye and mouths, "hubba hubba" with wide eyes and a rolling neck. I stick my tongue out at her. She's not supposed to be rooting for this fella.

"I hope Penny has learned your last name by now, Jack," Mama smiles and looks at me for proof. "Sharpe, ma'am, Jackson Sharpe. Though most folks just call me Jack," he replies. With the afternoon light washing over him, he looks somewhat angelic. Mama must be lamenting yesterday's assumption that he was some creepy, stalking killer. Before I turn back to her, I can see her thin face in my mind's eye. Admiring Jack with adoring eyes, imagining his features on her grandchildren, begging me to relinquish my nursing dreams so she can secure him as her son-in-law.

However, when I look at her, the image I expect is twisted into a cold sneer.

"Sharpe," she parrots flatly. "Hugh and Ruby's boy, hmmm? The winemakers on the Ferring Plantation?" The name rings in my head. I've heard it before, but I can't place it.

"Yeah," he says with a confused smile; her tone is downright rude. Where had her welcoming smile gone?

"Well then, what're you doing over on this side of the tracks? Little rougher over here, ya know. Excuse me, but I've got work to do." She brushes her once delicate hands on her skirt and turns her back to us. She kneels under the tree she'd been chasing May around, and goes back to collecting the fallen, bruised fruit for jam. Nothing is wasted around here.

My jaw drops. Is this not the woman who put soap in my mouth for forgetting to say 'thank you'? I didn't realize she was capable of such rudeness.

"Mama!" I scold. "Apologize to him!" Blood thumps in my veins, flooding my cheeks with color. Some compelling instinct drives me to want to protect him against her.

She is silent under the tree except for the plunk of fruit into the basket.

"I'm sorry, Jack. I don't know what's come over her," I apologize loudly in her direction, so she can hear me.

"Show him out, then get back here and pick up a

basket. We *work* in this family," comes Mama's stony voice over her shoulder.

I'm humiliated by Mama right now. I loop my elbow into Jack's arm, pinning it to my ribs and marching him toward the field to the street. Five steps away, I turn on my heel and pluck two ripe peaches from a low branch. The branch snaps back up and bounces in the air. Hopefully it whaps Mama in the leg, like she'd whap ours when we were little and would forget our manners. I trot back to him.

"That went well," he grins. While he seems amused, I'm horror struck. I grab his arm in mine and hold it with all the rebellion against Mama I can muster.

"I know; I'm sorry," I apologize again, even though it seems Mama's tongue lashing was entertaining to him. "I oughtta wash her mouth out with soap," I grumble as we stomp through the dirt.

He laughs. "You've had your mouth washed out with soap?"

"Yeah," I answer.

"Lately?" he teases.

I poke him in the ribs as we maneuver over clods of dirt. "Naw, when I was little! Octagon soap; all the time. Tastes awful." *How can he be laughing?* "Pleh!"

"Ha! The brown, nasty stuff for laundry? I

thought that was my nanny's special brand of torture." My arm, pressed against the side of his ribcage, absorbs the vibrato of his laughter.

"Jack, I'm really, really sor-" I begin, but he cuts me off.

"'Sorry'. I heard you. Don't worry about it."

I button my lip, but apologies are still chanting in my head.

"Well, it was very nice meeting your mother," he offers when we reach his car. I snort and slap my free hand over my mouth to cover the offending sound; too late. At least someone in that encounter had manners. Clearly both Mama and I fall short in that area.

"No, no, this isn't goodbye," I tell him, pinching his arm even more tightly in mine. I can't stand the thought of this nice fella driving home with the bad taste of Mama in his mouth, thinking her reaction is somehow his fault. His eyebrow rises. "You need to know some things."

NINE

Jack's face seems mostly unaffected as we drive, though his occasional squint tells me that my mother is still on his mind. He mechanically eats his peach with his thumb nail resting against his lower lip. He pulls up to the bluff overlooking the bridge in the heart of town. We step out of the car, and I eye the wet grass.

He follows my gaze. "Sorry; I used to have a quilt in the car, but this loose dame stole it," he teases. I plop down defiantly. The grass makes a perfectly soft blanket beneath our backs as we lie on the knoll, watching clouds move slowly but surely in the slow, steady breeze. I ignore the moisture seeping onto my back as fluffy white cumulus pillows form shapes and lines over our heads on a canvas of grey blue sky. He stares away from me, at the river, while he chews.

"Mama is..." I'm struggling to find the words to explain while I watch the hollow in his cheek move with his jaw. "Mama finds it very hard to trust, uh," I pause, scrunching my mouth into a side-winded heart shape, "to trust a trust fund, basically."

I watch his reaction carefully. He just watches the river.

"You see, we used to run with your pack. My daddy came from money, you know, 'Hale Oil'," I say with an eye roll.

His eyes shift in surprise. Hale is a household name.

"We were spoiled rotten back then. No idea at all there were so many hungry bellies in Saratoga... well, in the whole country." I shake my head at my ignorance. "Mama was never a raving fan of the aristocratic game, you know? When she married my daddy, she was sure marrying up. She was no debutant," I continue, and scoff. She certainly hadn't acted like one just now.

"She and my Uncle Mac were orphans. That's Mac's farm we live on; he earned it out of dirt. Their daddy died in the war and she says her mama just died of grief soon after. When my dad courted her, she had a lot to learn about kid gloves and luncheons and proper speech; pinkies up and all that. Grandma Hale liked her a lot, though, so she took her under her wing and polished her up. Until, that is, she passed away; before I was born." I think of the beautiful portraits of Grandma Hale. As a little girl, I used to sit with her framed photo by the mirror, wearing strings of her pearls, and try to hold my face as glamorously as she did. She was a real looker; her photo oozes dignity and class.

Jack's brow furrows as he listens, chewing the peach slowly.

"Well, once Grandpa died, my Uncle Harry and my dad and all their club chums went on a hunt in Grandpa's honor, which, you know, is really just a thin excuse for a drinking binge." He laughs at my cynicism. "They were all schlepping along on their horses, teetering through the trees; just a bunch of drunk Joes with guns. Then there was this big snap that spooked Daddy's horse. He bucked Daddy off, stepped right on his chest and dragged him through the woods." I'm momentarily stunned at the vivid scene in my head. The pictures were originally composed by the understanding of a seven-year-old girl as she was told the story, and therefore the details are exaggerated to fit a scene of horror: giant, gnarled trees; a dark swirling mist; a horse with the build and defiance of a bull, his hooves as heavy and forceful as a wrecking ball. This isn't a tale I like to drag up to the surface often.

"The doctor told Mama that since Daddy was so drunk and loose, the fall didn't really harm him; just some light bruising on his back, but the horse's hoof broke three ribs and punctured a lung. Supposedly he survived that, but he was dragged three hundred yards before the horse jumped over a big tree stump, and Daddy's head smashed right into it. His face was so mangled, they couldn't repair it enough for viewing." My imagination supplies more of the scene: the drumming of frightened hooves fading away, the rough bark on the ominous log, a pool of scarlet blood growing steadily under Daddy's still head. "So I never saw him again."

When my voice fades, Jack rolls onto his side, facing me. Tears pool in my ear. His eyes move, resting on each of my features.

"Without Daddy, our family was entitled to nothing of Grandpa Hale's inheritance. Mama never had to work, so Madge claimed nothing we owned was Mama's; and Daddy never made a will. Of course, civilized family members wouldn't ever entertain the idea of stranding a young family for a minute, regardless of paper, but that's not Aunt Madge." Her name shoots from my lips with the heat and force of a bullet. Angry tears spill down my face in rivulets.

"It was more like a pack of scared puppies being chased away with a broom. We didn't put up much of a fight." I lost it all that night, not just Daddy or the comfort of my bed. I lost my sense of security. I lost my innocence. And with every day of hard labor, my light-hearted mother became more and more encased in a thick, crusty shell of stifled hate and bitterness.

We were swiftly moved from our comfortable, sprawling estate to the cramped 'guest quarters' at the back of Mama's brother, Mac's, ranch. The tiny, rickety house, more suited to horses than guests, was built as a bunkhouse for traveling farmhands; maybe two or three. Our family of five strained its seams.

Though it was a long fall from cushioned upper class, Uncle Mac's calloused hands caught us just before we tumbled over the the edge to be dashed to bits on the jagged points of rock bottom. As uncomfortable as it was to wake up in a dog pile with snoring Eddie's arm smothering my nose and mouth or May's frozen feet pressed against my calf, sleeping on our farmhouse feather bed was considered the Ritz Carlton compared to the sleeping conditions of some of our ragamuffin schoolmates. They woke up each day on the hard ground, beneath a cardboard roof in a cluster of ramshackle huts that surely didn't provide much shelter from winter's bite. Even over ten years later, I'm still waiting to wake up sprawled out in my own warm bed, pad down the curved staircase and crawl into Daddy's lap, blocking his view of the New York Times.

His forehead creases. "So... she hates people

with money because she was left without any?" he asks.

"No," I defend, though I'm not sure Mama deserves defending right now. "Because of what greed for the stuff can do to someone. If it can make someone throw four innocent children and a fresh widow to the wolves..." Hot tears spill down the same avenue on my cheek over and over. I swipe at them swiftly, and a new wave of emotion comes over me. "I don't even know if that's all true anymore. My brother thinks someone planned for him to have that accident."

You think so, too, Imp insists.

Maybe I do.

"I'm sorry," I say and hiccup. The scarlet of my cheeks, burning with anger, deepens with embarrassment. Heat emanates from them, and I shrink into the grass, trying to cool them against its green blades. "This is a lot to dump on a fella all at once." I laugh through my wet smile.

He smiles back and takes my face in his hand, thumb swiping at my thick teardrops that won't cease. He scoots closer.

"You're warm," he says, and puts his cheek against mine. The light stubble on his cheek sweeps across mine, aggravating the fully inflamed capillaries. It's a pleasurable pain. His mouth slides over the bridge of my nose, and his lips catch a tear perched on my cheekbone. He presses his mouth into my cheek long enough to exhale warm breath onto my face.

Don't, my eyes silently warn him. *I'm not your kind of gal.*

The Imp inside of me wants to kiss him, fighting forward in my chest, straining hard.

What would Emily Post say to this? I recoil. He pulls back, and we roll to our sides, facing each other.

"I'm sorry to hear your mother has lumped me into the same category as your aunt."

"That's not *your* fault! You didn't do anything to make her think that; she's just... she's as stubborn as a mule," I grumble into the grass as I pick at it idly. "She's so busy building walls around herself, she can't appreciate a nice fella who comes around to say hello." I look up at him to assess how the compliment is received, and see that he's biting back a smile.

"What?" I ask. "What?"

"Nothing. Guess I see where you get it," he laughs.

My jaw opens when I realize his implication. Me, *stubborn?* Well, yeah; I guess I can be sort of tenacious sometimes. In desperate situations, when it's called for...

Ahem, Sense and Imp clear their throats

suggestively.

Okay, *I'm as pigheaded as she is!* But not in the same way. *How had he picked that up about me so quickly?* I've only known him for one day!

He's grinning as he watches the cogs turn in my head.

"What's your aunt up to now?" he asks, and my mind is distracted with forming the answer. That was probably his intention when he asked.

"They moved near the big city, I think; but we haven't seen her since that day. Good riddance." I wave her memory away. "She's a vulture! Daddy wasn't anything like her. There wasn't a mean bone in his body," I say. I wouldn't have to defend his character to anyone who had known him. He really was a good man.

"You don't seem to have a mean bone, either," he grins.

I laugh, which feels exhilarating after tears, and ask, "So I'm a mule, but a nice mule?"

"Sure," he answers.

He's empathetic, I decide. Understanding. And kind.

Sense groans internally.

I'm not doing a very good job of keeping him out of my gate.

TEN

Later, when trying to explain his good merits to Mama, while she leans against the stall wall and watches me shovel a few days' worth of horse poop, she argues that it's easy to be empathetic, understanding and kind when you're lusting after someone.

"Lust is a driving power so strong that it can compel you to do stupid things, like eat escargot, like I did on my second date with your father. Snails, Penny. Slimy, rubbery shelled slugs!" She shivers in disgust. "There is a reason why lust is the deadliest of the seven deadly sins." Since my face is pointed at the ground, I take the opportunity to roll my eyes. She eats up every word of Reverend Bell's sermons with a spoon.

Lust, indeed.

"Henry the Eighth started beheading his wives when he lusted after the next one."

"Mama, I'm not *lusting*," I defend with hot

crimson cheeks.

"Potiphar's wife lusted after Joseph and it landed poor Joseph in prison, even though he..."

"*No one's* lusting!"

Oh, really. Could've fooled me, Imp jeers, bringing up a fresh memory of the feel of his lips on my cheek. I slap away the thought with both hands.

"Maybe not you, Dear. Not *yet*, anyway."

But love, she explains, compels even stronger moves, such as bearing a child. Or caring for someone when they're sweaty and covered in vomit. Even loving them when they've made a huge mistake.

"You can't build a relationship in just a few days. You mean nothing to this fella, except you're some pretty doll with nice gams."

I consider her comment. *Do I want to mean anything to him?* Of course not.

Liar, Imp accuses lightly.

I just don't want Mama to be so rude to my friends.

Or pig-headed.

Or bitter.

"Yes, I was ill-mannered," she admits lightly, and I roll my eyes at her gross understatement. "But I did it for your own good, Penny! You don't need some sugar daddy roping you in and taking you off that smart track you're on! You don't have time to entertain a fella, do you?"

It must be a rhetorical question, because she continues with her arms crossed. "Didn't even have time to muck out the stall, because you were so busy goofin' on him." Her head shakes back and forth.

"I'm mucking it out now!" I cry in defense, holding out my shovel as evidence. I'm standing in horse poop; that should be good for something.

"Yes, *now* you are. But you stormed off with that boy and left the peach picking to May and me," she scolds.

"I didn't come back because I was *mad* at you!" My voice rises. "If you just hadn't been so rude..."

"Penny, don't take that tone with me! I'm sorry for being rude to him; I shouldn't have acted that way. I admit, it was quite un-Christian-like of me." If only Reverend Bell could have seen her. "It's just... when that handsome face walked into the orchard, I saw you dropping your training and having his babies and giving up on your dreams. I just don't want you to get hurt." Her face droops sadly to punctuate her last words.

Though I can see right through that baloney- I know she doesn't like him because of his pedigree- I am weary of this argument. If I'd brought home some ragamuffin guy from the next farm over, she'd have treated him decently no matter what he drove me to give up.

Or Phin, Imp teases. Phin's family skated through the depression and survived the drought; they still have plenty of old family money and social standing. But even with their elevated status, I know deep down that Mama wouldn't be as bothered by a courtship with him. Somehow, since we knew him before we moved over the tracks, he's exempt from our crusty outer shells. Mama has always treated him like another son. And even though I've vowed not to allow some fella to distract me from making something of myself, it seems he was already in my heart before I closed it off.

However, Mama was genuinely interested in Jack and his sparkling smile until he revealed who his parents are.

"I'll get my chores done," I promise with a rigid jaw. "And I'm no fool for that guy! I still plan on training, Mama. I'll stand on my own two feet before I let my head get in the clouds." She smiles serenely at my surrender.

"Come here, Penny," Mama coos and I tangle myself into her. My chin finds the hollow of her shoulder, exactly like it did when I was a three-year-old, and she pats my back.

"I churned it already," Jack argues and wipes his brow with a handkerchief before he stuffs it into his back pocket. He's shown up at the hospital again, conveniently near quitting time. It's a boiling August day, the kind where all you want to do is plunge into cool, deep water. Apparently we both feel the river luring us, only I had hoped to go alone like I always do on these days. At least since the boys left. Last summer, we would have shared it together.

I've told him that I have chores to do, so I don't have time to swim. He trots along next to my hurried strides while I march toward the trolley stop, explaining that he went back to my house to "have a chat" with Mama. May had intercepted him, and told him not to disturb Mama when she's making jam, because that's just a recipe for ugly trouble. I agree with May that he's lucky he didn't knock on that door. Her claws really come out when she's interrupted during a task so methodical.

But, she'd told him if he wanted to hang around and wait... Isn't it just like little Miss Mayhem to rope a willing pair of arms into helping her with her work? To hear him tell it, she'd reclined on the hay bales across from him in the barn, grilling him while his arms turned to noodles churning the butter himself. After that, she'd persuaded him to fertilize the carrot patch. I snicker at the thought of Jack shoveling dried cow pies under the scorching afternoon sun while May fanned herself in the shade of the trees. Tentatively, I lean in and sniff him.

The faint tangy scent of digested grass lingers on his shirt. His wingtip shoes bear the remnants of dirt clods scraped from their soles.

"She didn't even let me drive the tractor," he sighs, crestfallen. I shake my head at May's impishness. I shouldn't worry about her. Poverty won't eat her alive; she's cream! She rises to the top. And she'll butter any man's toast who tries to tie her down.

Though I find the thought of escaping under the shady willow and cooling off in the river alluring, I refuse his offer. Why does he even bother with me? The Spot's location is secret, but there are plenty of other swimming holes closer to town. I examine the lines of disappointment in his downcast face. Is he hoping for another peek at my brassiere? I cross my arms over my chest, even though the lashes resting on his pink cheeks seem so innocent that I suppose I can't assume he's a pervert hoping for a look-see. There are easier ways to get a peek at lingerie than farm labor, and I'm sure this fella can afford one, if that were his intention.

He can't be thinking long-term. I can only imagine him bringing me home to his parents, flies buzzing around my head. *"She's real sweet once you get past the smell of horse fudge, Ma."* I wipe a stream of sweat from my forehead.

"Well, that's just lousy. I'm gonna waste all that

watermelon in my cooler," he sighs. My ears perk up. The crate boys hardly ever have unsold melons, and they're my favorite.

"I can't possibly drink two ice cold Dr. Peppers all by myself," he whispers dejectedly. A chill runs down my spine. He has my attention, though his shoulders sag so dramatically that I can tell he's putting me on. Apparently, I'm transparent as a ghost; *"Feed her, and she will come like a horse to a carrot".*

"Gee, and all that fried chicken, going right into the waste bin," he laments. The very idea of wasting perfectly good food disarms me. On a moral level, one cannot let fried chicken go to waste!

"Fine! I'll come!" I shout, exasperated, and we both turn on our heels. I still have one reservation, and I plant my feet into the sidewalk to assert it.

"I need a swimming suit. And you do, too," I tell him sternly, poking his tee shirt. The well-worn suit that's sitting in a basket in the cupboard is no ritzy Rose Marie Reid, just Mama's old green Jantzen that fits me too loosely to let down the straps, like it's designed to do for sunbathing. I'm not much the sit-around-sunbathing type, anyhow.

"I'm way ahead of you, Miss Hale," he tells me, grinning. "I brought my trunks."

"We can't both fit in your trunks." My hands sit firmly on my hips.

"Fine. We'll swing by the farm."

In under ten minutes, I'm dashing up the spongy, rotted wood of my front step. The pungent smell of cooking peaches accosts my nose from the street. No doubt Mama will be inside, beaded with sweat, in a jam-making trance. When I open the door, hot, peachy air blasts me. It's not unpleasant, just strong. Mama hears me cough when its perfume tickles my throat.

"Letter from Max!" she calls over her shoulder from the stove.

"Hiya, Mama. Did you read it yet?" I call back to her.

"Yep. It's all yours," she sighs, wiping her slick forehead with her forearm. "I sure could use a tropical Hawaiian breeze right about now." It's stifling in the house; I don't blame her. I grab my swimming suit and tuck it under my arm. On the way back to the door, I pick up the opened letter and a photo from next to a plate with a peach pit on it. The photo shows three fellas with surfing boards: Max, Phin, and Eddie, flexing their biceps on the sand, facing the camera, smiling because they're flanked by girls wearing leis. I toss the photograph back on the table and dash to the door with the letter in my fist.

"Bye, Mama! Come up for air sometime!" I call to her. I pass May on the steps outside.

"Hiya, P," she says, smiling innocently.

"Hiya, Sis," I mumble. I'm too lost in Max's letter to get after her for putting Jack's nose to the grindstone. When I hop in the Merc, a basket of peaches sits between Jack and me. The smell of ripe peaches warmed in the sunshine fills the car, and Jack is sucking the juice from one in his hand while it drips down his arm. May must have paid him a visit while he waited here, though I think the deep upper arm ache from churning butter deserves much more of a reward than a few peaches. We sit there for a full minute while I absorb the letter.

Jack clears his throat.

"Ahem. I don't know how to get there, remember?" he prods.

"Really? You drove me home last time."
"Backwards, at dusk. I could never guess which of these turnoffs I should take."

I direct him there, leaving out the loop around the Bayard's farm that I had taken last time to confuse him; or maybe to prolong the joy of driving, but who's counting? I eat up the little details in the letter and enjoying the pleasant twenty-mile-per-hour breeze on my face and neck. The letter flaps in the wind and I have to smooth it on my lap to read.

"Hiya Ma, Squeak and Mayhem,
I'll bet my three best gals are melting away in

Saratoga's August. Of course, me and Ed are living it up on the island. Each of us was issued a lei and a native gal right off the boat, ya know? They serve us rum punch and fan us on hot days..."

I knew it!

"...and you know we deserve it something ugly after that murderous training. I'm just joshin' ya! The best they gave us was a few sets of army-issue undershorts and a hope chest full of cigarettes. Lucky me, neither Ed or Phin took to smokes, so I get all the ciggies I can handle. Don't worry Ma, the army doc says that all that cancer talk is just a bunch of baloney.

It's warm on the island, so I'd welcome some of that rum punch anytime. Pearl Harbor is a really large inlet with just one little channel coming in, like a big boiling flask from science class. Sorry gals, no real pearls here to send home. The spot was named for them hundreds of years ago, but they're long gone now. Otherwise you'd find a string of them for each of you in this envelope.

Most of the harbor is Navy land that us Army boys are here to protect. There's a Naval station on the island in the center of the harbor, and Battleship Row. You wouldn't believe the size of the things! There's a native legend about the shark goddess,

Kaahupahau, who protects the harbor from man-eating sharks and evil spirits alike. So don't worry Ma, we're safe as kittens over here, what with a real goddess keeping watch.

Life can get a little dull on base, but if we can get into Honolulu- and trust me, we're there as often as we can be- there's a heap of joints where we can shake a leg and meet some local dames. Who knows? I may just handcuff one of 'em and bring her home to meet you, Ma! That's if I can get a dance in around Phin. He's the real ladies' man out here. Even the native girls go gaga over his red hair. They all want to touch it and pet it and smooch him. "

I shift on the seat to stifle the pang of jealousy rising in my chest. "Um, turn right up here," I direct.

"Lucky dog! He barely even combs that mop. Why couldn't I have been born a ginger, Ma? Of course, it's always swell to be the wingman of a gent with that much attention. Me and Eddie catch the scraps every now and again."

Do I feel actual smoke rising from my ears?

"How's the farm? I'll just bet you're all sick of

peaches and kale by now. We're living on cafeteria grub, so some of your homemade jam sounds just lip-smackin', Ma. Would you send some my way? I've enclosed a george for the postage and the jar. Don't send it back, or stuff it in the college jar, because I know you need it more than I do. Maybe you can use the clams we send home to hire a farmhand or two so you won't break your back. Heaven knows you're getting old, Ma.   Just kidding! You're much younger looking and far prettier than Ginger Rogers.

Oh, Ed says please send some jam for him, too, because he knows I won't share.

How's the hospital, Squeak? That nurse with the hairy chin sounds darb. I'll bet if you sent her over, the boys would just eat her up! Gals can be sparse around here, what with four thousand uniforms to each one. But you can tell that Doris that with an attitude like hers, she'd be hard pressed to catch a fella in all of Pearl Harbor, regardless of the slim pickins'.

You stay out of trouble, Miss Mayhem. I've got Squeak keeping an eye on you. Stay in school! If you get hot at night, I guess you have my permission to sleep up in the old tree house. You can sweep it, just don't go making curtains for it or having tea parties up there. It has a reputation to uphold."

"Turn into the trees up here. Yea, right here," I tell him.

"Well, with protection from the shark goddess, your boys will be home someday safe and sound. I'm off to iron my shoelaces.
   All my love to my three best gals, Max "

At his valediction, I let my eyes unfocus and imagine the big harbor. Huge ships, aircraft... and Phin, making the native gals go wild. It doesn't make sense, but I'm mad enough at him for it that my nostrils are flaring repeatedly over a tight mouth.
Well! So much for the fuzzy, distant dream of becoming Missus Phineas O'Shea! Goodbye, little flame-haired O'Shea boys and little strawberry blonde O'Shea girls. No one will be whitewashing that picket fence or tending to those flower beds. I wave away the wisps of those fantasies. They catch in the wind and fly out the window, but my heart still burns with pain.
   Ouch.

ELEVEN

Jack parks in the undisturbed tire marks we'd left two days ago. We change into bathing suits on opposite sides of the car. His navy trunks nearly cover his navel, with a smart belt trimming the band that tells me his mother didn't sew these trunks for him. I feel like a country bumpkin in my old, ragamuffin bathing suit. More than that, I just feel mad at Phin for being a ladies man on a tropical island while I pine for him back here; so I crash through the thicket without concern for my bare legs. Jack follows with a woven basket. When we settle against the willow's shady trunk, I notice that my leg is bleeding.

"It's just a little scratch," I tell him with mild annoyance to wipe away the concerned look on his face. I have to remind myself that this poor fella isn't the traitorous Phin that I'm peeved at. I manage a small smile for Jack. He nods at me and dives into the basket, handing me a thick wedge of watermelon without looking. It's cold and crisp; a real luxury! The tempting scent of fried chicken wafts directly for my nose as if it knows where it will be best appreciated. It intoxicates me so that when I'm handed a crispy breast, I press it to my face and dive in. I look up at Jack, my eyes wide with delight as I chew. I'm a child tasting chocolate cake for the first time, such is the euphoric sensation that biting into the crispy meat brings. Jack can't possibly understand how amazing this feast is for me. My jaw bounces and rolls over the stuff while its savory juice runs over my eager taste buds. I no longer feel annoyed, but I am feeling that I really like chicken. It settles into my stomach with the contented flutter of a falling feather.

Like a doting parent, Jack nods his approval. However, Emily Post would never approve of the way I'm devouring the thing, hastily chewing and licking my fingers. After just three heavenly bites, the walls of my stomach groan at this excess of food and I set it on my napkin. I'm so pleasantly full that I think I may fall asleep.

The head of the bottle fizzes as he cracks open a Dr. Pepper for me, and I wash down the salty chicken taste with its bubbly sweetness. The liquid finds its way into the crevices left in my stomach.

And then, the caffeine hits my veins. I'm instantly perked up. I want to run for the water, but the strides I can manage around the unaccustomed sensation of a full belly resemble a penguin's rather than a gazelle's. Jack is still eating, at a civilized pace, so I wade in on my own.

My skin sizzles when it hits the water. *Ahhh.* I dip under, reveling in the feel of the silky coolness. Along with relief to my overheated skin, the river water tempers my overheated feelings toward Phin, and I begin to relax.

It only takes a moment for the miserable effects of the letter to wash down the river, and I'm completely content. A full belly; floating in cool, silky water; the company of a fella fine enough to put that tropical womanizer to shame; a day's work behind me. I wade upstream and float down to the bend of the "L" in the river, where it eddies, again and again.

The little boy in Jack peeks out through his voice when he suddenly calls out, "You've got a rope swing?"

My eyes open and I follow his gaze to a knotted rope in the trees above. He's just discovered the old frayed thing hanging there.

"Yeah. I'm not sure how sturdy that contraption is anymore, though," I warn. "You've got to come at it at an angle so you hit the deep spot..."

"Hey, if you're an expert, I want a demonstration!" Jack retorts, grinning. I don't have to be goaded twice. I scramble up the boulder and find the rope, tugging to check its hold on the branch above. It still seems sound enough, so I decide to give it a go.

"Start here, just right of this little bush," I tell him. I tuck my legs up and pinch the rope between my legs. The adrenaline that courses through me while I whoosh through the air feels brand new. I let go and drop over the darkest spot; the deepest part of the river.

He tries the swing out after me, whooping and hollering like a little kid. I can't help throwing my head back and laughing at his antics. When he surfaces, he says, "You know, Pip, I can't imagine any of the debs I know doing this. You are just one of a kind." I'm warm in the cool water with his compliment. I feel my cheeks revealing my appreciation, against my will, so I punch him in the arm to deflect the compliment.

"Ow," he complains, cradling his arm. "Right in the sore spot! These boys aren't used to churning butter." He gestures to his biceps as he tries to hang on to some of his pride.

I can't help laughing; *Oh, Mayhem, you little stinker!* Butter churning can turn anyone's arms into sore, limp noodles after a while, especially someone who's probably never even scrubbed his own laundry. My little sister is a heathen.

He lets me drive back to the farm, even though my swimsuit makes a wet spot on the cloth seat. Since he sat in the passenger's seat in his wet trunks, it seems that he doesn't pay too much mind to taking care of the things he owns. I suppose I'd assumed that rich folks were careful with their nice things, but Jackson keeps proving that since he can easily replace what he has, he treats his things like tissues. Disposable.

Would he treat a gal like that? Will he treat me *like that?*

When I kill the engine, he sighs.

"Sure could go for some peach jam right about now," he hints. How can he be thinking about eating? My stomach has barely been able to handle what I've stuffed into it. A more daunting thought occurs to me: Mama will be inside. After yesterday's matinee of her dark side, I don't think Jack walking into our kitchen bare-chested and snatching a jar of the jam she's been slaving over is a wise idea. *What if we get a replay of yesterday's rudeness?* Nervously, I catch my bottom lip in my teeth.

He reads the warning in my expression carefully. "I'll bring in the chicken," is his solution. He even pulls on his tee shirt.

As it turns out, Mama is obliging. She even invites him to sit at the battered table while she and May attack their chicken. Whether the Christian in her has resurfaced or the smell of fried chicken has overcome her, I'll never know; but my God-fearing Mama is trying her best to pace herself as she gnaws on a chicken leg within a minute of our arrival. I slip into the chair across from Mama, hoping a severe look or two will remind her to mind her manners. Slightly stiff in my seat, I'm ready to be the referee if needed.

"I owe you an apology," Mama says to Jack with smacking lips. May's head jerks up from her own piece of chicken, surprised.

"Pip has explained, uh, well, things to me. I understand," he replies and smiles. The way he watches her devour her piece of chicken is really sweet. I think he must enjoy bringing people pleasure; he'd watched me the same way with mine, with the same quiet satisfaction.

"Penny has responsibilities here, you know," she says in attempted authority. It's not as imposing as intended with a cheek full of chicken thigh. May and I both sense a lecture coming and we roll our eyes.

"I understand, Ma'am," he nods, sounding like the proper southern boy he was raised as.

Mama must sense a ripe opportunity to scold someone, because she continues, "And she has plans to fulfill. She'll be starting nurse's training here soon..."

Mama seems oblivious to the severe look my eyes burn her with.

"Yes, Ma'am," says Jack.

"...so it would really dampen her plans if she got married and..."

"*Mama!*" I shriek, breaking the sound barrier. I bury my face in my hands with humiliation. I can feel heat rushing to my cheeks.

"Yes, Ma'am," he replies in attempted stoicism, but the vibrato in his voice sounds a lot like chuckling.

"I'm just sayin'," Mama says, "in case you had a mind to... Penelope! Why on *earth* are you kicking me under the table?"

"*MAMA!*" I shout, effectively shutting her mouth and deafening everyone in the room all at once. My eyes are strained and teary, and I am deep scarlet from my forehead down. Oh, I want to die! I want to melt into a puddle and slip through the floorboards. I want to be anywhere but here, being humiliated by Mama playing the intimidating father figure.

"He just wants some *jam!*"

TWELVE

September 1st, 1941

If Jack knows that the way to my heart is through my stomach, then he must be keen to Mama's weakness as well. The day after the jam incident, I'd walked home through the orchard with a peach in hand. When I opened the kitchen door, laughter rang through the room, both soprano and tenor finding my ears at the entryway. Curious, I walked in and blinked my eyes at the scene before me. Mama and Jack stood hip to hip at the sink, smiling at each other. Both wore frilly aprons, though the bow tied at Jackson's hip looked far more unnatural than the one at Mama's.

"Hello, Dear," Mama had greeted me breathlessly, wiping a stray hair out of her face with her forearm. Her wet fist was curled around a wrinkled rutabaga. Jack grinned over his shoulder like a cat who just got the canary. He didn't seem the least bit uncomfortable to be standing in our ramshackle house, washing wilted old vegetables with her.

However, I was extremely uncomfortable. I'd immediately bolted out the back door and snatched three sets of my unmentionables from the clothesline before the rickety door slammed shut behind me. With every ounce of blood in my body concentrated in my flaming cheeks, I bunched them into a ball to mask their identity. I tossed the wad hastily up into the treehouse and hurried back toward the house just as Jack walked out with his ear cocked upward.

"Hey, can I go up and see the treehouse?" he teased. "I've heard the view is real special up there."

Of course, I groan inwardly. Something about him disarms me in every way. It's as though the parts of me I'm most ashamed of, he discovers and accepts without a blink. I don't know if I like that or not, because, well; I don't know if I want to like him or not.

For a week since I'd found Jack and Mama in aprons at the sink, he'd shown up every day except for the Sabbath and assisted with laborious tasks. May tells me that Mama says she's just seeing what his lust for me will compel him to do.

When his company coincides with my home hours, Mama's hawk-like stare watches us as though a moment's turn of her back will earn her an early grandchild. She barely allows herself to blink when he's around.

Little does she know, the tools he uses around the farm have seen a lot more action from him than I have. The most thrilling moment has been a twilight stroll through the peach orchard, now just leafy trees picked clean of fruit, when the back of his hand brushed mine. I'd stiffened like a con on the run. Now I lament the thought I had the first night he drove me home when I thought he might try to kiss me.

He's got to be keen on me, otherwise he wouldn't be breaking his back doing heavy chores on our farm. The way he looks at me, and the way the yellow of his eyes brighten, that says a fella's sweet on a gal, right? There is no way he's just hanging around for the peaches.

Not that I want him to be or anything. A gal just likes to understand a fella's motivations. He can work all he wants!

Mayhem is in a vicarious tizzy, high on the tension between us and the fulfillment of having a brotherly figure hanging around. When Mama's soft snores float through the dark bedroom, May attacks me with hushed questions.

"Sooo..." she squeals as quietly as she can muster.

I groan.

"Did he kiss you yet?" The question is an excitement bubble about to explode.

"No." My answer tumbles out as more of a complaint than I'd intended.

"But he's going to. I know it!" she whispers through the inky darkness. Her excitement is barely contained; I think she'd be squealing if hushed tones allowed the sound.

"I don't want him to *kiss* me," I whisper back harshly. Half of me believes that. The other half knows it's a lie, and brings to memory the heavy, sweet smell of his skin.

"I mean, he does *want* to kiss you, right?"

"I don't know, May," I whisper in frustration, but she is certainly not the cause of it.

"You want him to, don't you?"

That's an understatement, Imp jeers.

"Go to sleep, May," I tell her sternly, but there's no way that either of us can drift off quickly with the combined fourteen-year-old exhilaration and seventeen-year-old confusion wafting around the room.

My head is full of Jack. It sure is hard to watch someone pull his shirt over his head and wipe his forehead with it when he's sweaty with August heat and the exertion of farm labor. That is, of course, only when you're watching beads of sweat roll down his neck, resting in the hollow of his collarbone, wishing mightily to be that salty bead so you can caress that neck.

Aw, crackers, I think. My head cannot find a comfortable spot on the pillow. *I'm the frog, the frog in the pot!* Throw a frog in a pot of boiling water, and it'll jump out immediately, acting on survival instinct. But if you put a frog in tepid water in the same pot, then heat it slowly, the dumb thing can't sense impending danger, and just sits there until pretty soon its dead carcass is rolling around in boiling bubbles. Cooked.

Well, things are heating up, and I'm jumping out of this pot. I flip my pillow over and grouchily punch all of my frustration into its feathers. I'm calling things off with Jack before I'm completely boiled!

September 7th, 1941

Mama has been cool to me since I told Jackson not to bother coming around anymore. If I call her on the near-silent treatment she's giving me, she'll surely proclaim that she really needed that extra set of hands. However, I know she likes him for more than his help around the farm. Her long dark eyelashes haven't batted for anyone else other than the Reverend in years.

May has been awfully mopey as well. Tilly is bored to tears with me; *I'm* bored to tears with me.

Can't go to the Spot since it'll be a public pool; Jack surely must have shared its location by now. So when I'm not working, I've taken up reading in my brothers' tree house with my skirt up to my waist to stay cool.

I've been putting my best foot forward at Saint Christopher's. Besides finding a great distraction there, I really need glowing remarks from Nurse Adler to get into that nursing program, but based on the immovable grim set of her mouth, earning her approval is looking like a feat of epic proportions. Still, I'm trying to soften her up: I'm staying much later than the other stripers, performing the eye-watering charting at record speed and bravely balancing several bed pans at a time. Tilly almost trampled me when I fell asleep against her belly while milking her yesterday. If I keep up this grueling schedule, I may just need to learn to strip her udders and keep a running commentary for her in my sleep.

Doris, on the other hand, has become a bit of a recluse. Missing shifts; disappearing in the middle of the shifts she actually shows up for; leaving early. I can't blame her. Her stomach muscles have given up holding back her pooch, and no fella's gonna be drawn to the smell of vomit on her breath. With a baby on the way, moving into a nursing career isn't feasible for her. I'm not sure why she shows up at all. I saw her earlier, taking a bite of a biscuit from her sleeping patient's tray, but it has been hours since then. I'd assumed she'd gone home, until Adler sent me to the supply closet to get fresh sheets for her patient who'd soiled the bed. Again. I throw open the closet door in irritation.

"Unnngh." A moan of anguish startles me. I wasn't expecting anyone to be inside the supply closet. I look around for the source of the sound, knowing something isn't right in here. "Unnnngh."

My eyes snap to the same corner I'd found Doris in last time, only the pathetic, sobbing heap she'd been back then was a picture from a facial soap advertisement in comparison to the horror I'm witnessing. Doris is on the floor, barely conscious and moaning in pain. A pool of rich red liquid widens across several squares of linoleum before my eyes. Her bare calves and feet are splayed awkwardly, covered in her blood.

"Doris!" I shriek, stiff with shock. Her head lolls around, and she looks up at me as best she can with half-closed lids. The skin of her face is ghostly pale, a greyish green that looks like death. Combined with the beads of sweat on her brow and her shallow panting, I'm terrified she *will* be dead in minutes.

"I'm going to get somebody!" I assure her, though I'm not sure she's conscious enough to hear me, or even realize I'm here. Shakily, I draw a deep breath, preparing to scream at the top of my lungs for help.

"Mmmngh, no," she moans, and the lump of air catches in my throat.

"Help!" I trumpet over my shoulder.

"No one. Mngh. They'll know."

"HELP!" I shriek, right in her face, my eyes wide. I scramble to my feet, slipping in the pool of blood, and run to the doorway, arching outward with my hands on the frame. I barely notice the bloody handprints I leave there.

"Help me! Someone! It's an emergency!" I stumble back to her side. My knees and shins complain as they smack against the hard ground, but I ignore the shooting pain as my mind quickly fans through pages of memories of life-saving measures I've watched the doctors and nurses here perform.

"You're going to be alright, Doris. You're going to be fine," I babble in panic. I'm not sure who I'm trying to reassure: Doris, or me.

"No, no," she moans weakly.

"What *happened* to you?"

"Dd. Duh. Doc," she stutters feebly, and her eyelids flutter closed, only to fly open again in pain. She needn't say more. Doctor Sweeney, the spineless creature, is responsible for this. I just know it. My hands flutter over her while my eyes hunt for her wound.

Stop the bleeding. Find the source. Pressure; steady pressure.

"Where is it? Where are you hurt?" I ask her, and scream over my shoulder again, "HELP ME! PLEASE!" I turn back to her, scanning her body for the wound that spills so much blood.

Arms: intact.

Belly: undamaged.

Legs: lying in blood, but whole.

"Dori- oh," I whisper, sickened as I realize the source of the flow.

"Baby," she murmurs shakily, eyes closed. Her entire body trembles, and now, so is mine.

"Somebody help me, please!" I scream, now truly terrified. I'm shaking while a shock of horror bounces around inside me. Doris's stockings and shoes are missing, and her skirt is raggedly torn up her thigh. I can't even begin to imagine what sort of damage has occurred here.

"PLEASE! HELP!" My voice is growing hoarse with the desperation of my screams.

The night janitor stumbles in, looking angry to have his buzz interrupted, until he sees the blood and his bushy white eyebrows fly up.

"Oh!" he exclaims raspily, and runs rather steadily out the door for a man whose body trails a thick cloud of liquor fumes behind him. His hoarse cry of, "help!" fades down the hallway.

If only I had already begun my nurse's training already! I've never felt so completely helpless, where a dire outcome teeters on my back. All I know is that if I leave her here all alone, she might just slip away for good.

Doris flutters her frail fingers until they close over a bloody object. The shine of metal glints through a coating of her blood. Bile leaks into my mouth when I realize that this is the weapon she's been assaulted with, and I clap my hand over my lips to hold it in. I squeeze her hand, silently willing her to hold on.

The janitor returns with a sweating doctor whose tie has flown over his shoulder in his haste. He assesses her in less than the tick of the second hand, then sweeps her into his arms and barrels out of the closet. I squeeze my eyes shut, grab the bloody instrument by its scissor-like handles, and stumble after them. I slide on my blood-slickened shoes over the linoleum as I try to keep up.

The doctor rushes into an operating room, and places Doris's now-still form on the table, shouting orders. Nurses flood the scene.

"Get the girl out of here!" one of them calls after I accidentally bump her shoulder. I hold up the bloody instrument. Another nurse takes it from my hands and it clinks into a dish.

"She's in the family way," I croak hoarsely. I can't tell if anyone has heard me. "She. Is. With. *CHILD!*" I shriek. The attending doctor looks up with annoyance. Two nurses shove me out of the double doors, ignoring my cries. "S-Sweeney... Doctor Sweeney is the father! He attacked her with that thing!" My chest heaves with fresh anger over the barbaric creep's crimes.

I hold up my palms for inspection. They glisten with Doris's blood. My stockings are stained from the knee down with dark, rusty marks. Doris's blood. I stumble to the reception desk and grab the phone.

"Operator. What number, please?" a disembodied voice asks disinterestedly.

"A girl, she's hurt!" I begin breathlessly, ribs hanging over the counter.

"What's your location?" the nasal voice asks lazily. I can only imagine the operator on the other end of this line filing her nails or fixing her lipstick while she half-listens with the phone cradled on her shoulder. I'm so frustrated by her indifference in this emergency that I want to somehow reach two arms through the line and strangle the neck at the other end.

"Saint Christopher's Hospital, Saratoga!" Pant, pant.

"You're at a hospital already?"

"It *happened* at the hospital!" I shout. Condescension is thick in her tone as she asks, "*Oh-kay, is there a doctor or a nurse present?*"

"Yes, she's in surgery now-"

"Miss, if she is in surgery, then she is in good hands."

"No! I know, I mean, Sweeney hurt her, they took a metal object and..." I start to hyperventilate, and squeeze my lids tightly so that I can hang on. *No fainting. Don't faint.*

"Miss?"

Pant. Pant. "He needs to be arrested!" I sputter.

"Miss, I'll notify the police. What number are you calling from?" I rattle off the prefix and numbers for this line.

"*Thank you,*" I sigh into the receiver. When I hang up the blood-smeared phone, I slump completely over the desk. My limp arm falls from the side and hangs in the air. Finally, she'd *heard* me, so I don't have to carry this load all by myself! Moments later, the phone jangles. It's metallic ring causes another rush of adrenaline to course through my veins. I snatch it up with fumbling hands.

"H-hello?"

"Is this the party who reported an injury?" the same nasal-voiced operator asks.

"Yes. Yes!"

"Two policemen are on their way, Miss."

When the officers arrive, we follow three sets of bloody footprints backward to the smeared scarlet puddle in the supply closet. I explain about the illegitimate child and Doctor Sweeney's creepiness and his clear motivation to attack her with the long, thin, pointed metal instrument with the scissor handles.

"Where is the weapon now?" the younger cop asks. His light hair is so slickly pomaded and shiny against his head that the rain outside hasn't misplaced a strand. Beads of water remain on his shiny nameplate: "Officer Dalton".

"I gave it to the nurse. In the operating room," I explain, trembling. I haven't heard a word about how Doris is faring in there.

Why do you even care? Imp jeers. *She's an ornery crumb.*

No one deserves this, Sense laments from her quiet corner.

When I return to my vigilant perch outside the operating room, Doris's condition is still a mystery. No one has come out or in, which I take to be a good sign. If she is... *dead,* then they wouldn't be bothering to hang around. I gulp the lump in my throat down. It sits sickly in my wringing belly.

Fellas are scum.

Not all *fellas,* Sense and Imp protest together.

I examine the two familiar faces floating in my

head; the ones that my mind's main argumenters have supplied to prove their point; the ones that don't fit into the "scum" category. One face is littered with freckles from his copper hairline to his sharp jaw. His hair is tousled. The skin next to his eyes is crinkled by his easy smile, pink lips stretched wide over his teeth, framed in delicate curving lines from his nose to his chin. His playful eyebrows take turns lifting and falling- a move I've never been able to replicate.

The other face is creamy pale, tinged with pink at the apples of his cheeks. Raven hair is smoothed and slick, with the exception of one short rogue lock at his crown. Low brows, impossibly long lashes, pale blue eyes glinting with mischief. His smooth chin reveals the shadow of dark hairs waiting to emerge. The crease that appears along with his lopsided grin is a small, backward 'c' that is so entrancing that it may as well be a spinning hypnotic spiral.

"Lust is a driving force so strong..." Mama's voice in my head blows the images away in a puff of smoke.

Phin, well, Phin is busy smooching his way through the nurse's roster on Pearl Harbor; and Jack's just a playboy looking for a challenge. *Lusters. Lusting, lustery lusters!* You can't rely on them. If you do, you end up lying in a pool of your own blood in a supply closet. And then the image of Doctor Sweeney appears in my mind unbidden. *Some doctor he is!*

The louse! How could he do that to her? She's a spring chicken in the prime of her life. He must've known she'd lay bleeding out in the supply closet, too weak to crawl for help. He is a doctor after all, he knows the risk. I scoff. *He won't be a doctor for long.*

Nurse Adler lumbers out of the operating room and I scramble to my feet.

"Hale," she acknowledges me in her scraping, throaty German accent. "I net a cigarette." Her thick ankles shuffle toward the back door to the alley. Her shoulders slump with exhaustion, but I trot behind her eagerly. I need to know what's been going on in the operating room.

"Wait! How is she?" My fingers tremble at my quivering lips. I can't breathe.

"Phee-sick-ly, she vill recover," she reports. A rush of relieved breath escapes my lips.

"Oh," I squeak, relieved. My lungs finally fill fully with air, and I realize I've been short of breath since I found Doris on the floor. "Swell."

Nurse Adler shakes her head in disapproval and her loose jowls jiggle. "But zet girl hes gotten herselv in qvite a mess."

Tell me about it.

Adler's mind seems to snap back to the tasks at hand, and she snaps at me, "Hev you jest been sitting here? Git to verk! Empty ze vaste bens!" Two hours have passed since my shift ended, so I have no responsibility to 'verk'. However, my other option is to begin my walk home in the moonless dark, among inky shadows filled with lusting creeps waiting with those long, pointed instruments in their eager hands. I shudder. I'll take out the trash.

"End clean up your hends. You vill scare ze pachents!" she barks with a critical once over.

No more than you do on a regular basis, Imp snickers.

I decide to clean up after I've made contact with the grimy lid of the dumpster in the alley. In five minutes, I've collected the trash quietly. I make my way toward the back door and shove the heavy metal door to the alley open with my hip. My eyes, expecting to behold the dimly lit alley with its usual scabby alley cat pawing through the dumpster, strain at the scene before me. Just to the right of the bin, someone is pressed to the wall, curled like an armadillo, encircled by a mob of drunken men.

"Dirty Hun!"

"Nazi!" a man sneers, throwing a bottle at his prey. My neck swings back and forth rapidly, trying to make sense of what I'm seeing. The terrified victim is Nurse Adler!

"Filthy Jerry!"

My fingers absently release the waste bag when I take in the face of their victim. *Of course,* a voice in my head reasons. *They're picking on her because she's German.* Adler tucks her face away to dodge an oncoming shoe.

"Get the dirty Hitler lover!"

She's outnumbered seven to one by a horde of barflies. The motley crew of men, obviously intoxicated, must have stumbled over from the bar with liquid courage fueling them. Alcohol has fanned their sparks of hatred into wildfire. One large, brutish man holds the thick leg of a broken chair like a club. A slim Joe with a thin mustache wields a busted bottle. When my wide eyes take in its menacing broken points, I imagine this mob at the bar, working themselves into a frenzy until this little man smashes his bottle on the counter, demanding action. Adler must have been the first victim they'd come upon. I'm frozen in horror.

This is not helping my outlook on fellas.

THIRTEEN

A man in a suit looks like he left his office job at five and has been deteriorating ever since.   His bloodshot eyes and teetering posture make me wonder if he will fall over at any moment. The fella to his left is holding a torch. An actual *torch*.

"Hey, what is this, a witch hunt?" I shout with my filthy, blood-encrusted hands raised upward.

The slim man jerks his gaze my way.

"Hale!" Nurse Adler cries hoarsely. "Help me!" I've never heard her low voice reach this pitch. Her tired body visibly trembles with fear. My heart is stung by her desperation and the terror in her bulging eyes. "I hev no luff for *Heetla!*"

The brute slaps her cheek. Hard. "Pipe down, Heinie!"

"Leave her alone!" I shriek as I rush down the steps at the crowd. Adrenaline courses through me; my muscles feel swollen with the stuff. My heart pounds against my chest wall, trying to beat its way free, while my darting eyes widen in alert. I'm suddenly a wild animal defending her young. I back up and crouch over Adler's short, squat body.

The slim man ignores my presence. He reprimands the brute who slapped her with a bump of his shoulder and says, "No, Felder, let's hear what the dirty Kraut has to say." He settles back, arms folded, and awaits her reply while licking his lips hungrily. The tip of his tongue fans the short bristles of his mustache as it moves across his lip. The torch blazes on ominously in the near-quiet night.

"You eed-juts," she spits at them over my shoulder. "Jes, I am from Germany, but not all are Nazis! Ven you say dis, you ah as bed as Heetla himself!"

The mob grumbles.

"Can it!" the thin man directs them, his glinting eyes trained on Adler.

She continues her defense. "Ven he took ovah, mekking people hate Jews and Poles, efun people who were dees-abled or seeck, menny people agreet out of fear. But my hesbent vas kvippled, his leks, and his muzza vas Polish. Ven ve hert he vas exterminating dees people, ve hed to flee our home in da dark of da night to escape. Ve took nothink vith us." Incredibly, the crowd listens quietly to her solemn words.

"But, Nazis ah vigilant. They ver vatchink for runnas. Mein Christoph was kilt, right in front off me, shot t'rough his eye und left to bleet to death in de street. I ren alone, all de vay to dis country."

My anger at Adler, all my resentment, washes down the walls of my chest in the acid of guilt. I have always loathed this unbending woman, but now I'm lost in softness for her tragedy. I'm ashamed of my cruel thoughts.

Tears stream from the outer corners of her eyes and push their way over the round apples of her large cheeks. "I could neffah feel loyalty to de man who kilt my hesbent!" she trills.

The sobered group watches her; the silence thick after her words. My muscles begin to relax their tight hold, my protective posture. I think these men, too, must be remorseful for how they've treated this poor woman. They all seem to be absorbing the heartache that Hitler has personally caused her.

Then the thin man clears his throat. The mob's eyes collectively turn to him.

"Did 'Heetla' teach you to lie like this, spy?" he hisses and flicks his tongue. He clearly hasn't bought her heartfelt protest. Fueled by adrenaline, liquor and hate, he must've missed the genuine pain screaming through her words, twisting her features in agony.

Clearly, Nurse Adler is not a spy. If Hitler's agenda is to weary young candy stripers, and frighten grown men in a country that he's not even at war with, then perhaps Adler could be considered an operative. But the only dictator *I* know is Adler herself, who cracks the whip for *"verk"*, *"verk"*, *"verk"*. She's an army of one, but it is obvious that she isn't a Nazi. I'm convinced, but the creepy, slim man's thin mustache bends into an angry sneer on his lips; it tells me that he doesn't want to be convinced, he wants to feel hatred coursing through his veins. I wear a sneer of my own for his twisted desire.

As the mob leader, his unbelief rouses his crowd to action again. After all, a witch hunt can only end with burning a witch, whether she's evil or not. I'm tossed aside to the concrete by the brute, banging my hip and my elbow as I land in a heap. I'm lost in the sudden agony that explodes from the affected bones, the torn skin.

The mob roars like warriors. Through spinning eyesight and a haze of pain, I watch them close in on Nurse Adler. My body stiffens, muscles absorbing the adrenaline that again rushes through me, and I shove aside the dizzy pain to try to stand up. I can't let this happen! I have to help her!

"Hold it right there!" A deep, authoritative voice bounces down the brick alleyway. The mob freezes in place, and reminding of a schoolyard game of freeze tag. Some of the thugs teeter on one foot, arms outstretched, but all of our faces turn toward the two figures who stride swiftly toward us in the darkness. As they draw closer and closer to the torchlight, their faces come into view. I recognize one of them is Dalton, the slicked blonde policeman who interviewed me about Doris's attack, his gun drawn. The other one is... Jackson.

"Hands up!" the narrow-eyed officer booms as Jack relieves the torch-wielder of his load. The mob turn their faces to the light the torch casts, palms up in surrender at shoulder level. I rise to my feet and raise my hands as well, though I can't claim any guilt here. The officer's eyes scan the mob of miscreants. When his eyes settle on the thin man, they stretch wide open with excited recognition.

"Stark," he growls, and immediately trains his gun at the creep's heart. I can hear Nurse Adler sobbing noisily behind me. "Captain's gonna reward me big time for capturing you! You're wanted in every state down the east coast, fella!"

Stark's eyes dart around the scene warily, his spindly frame stiff. Suddenly, he grabs me by the throat and pulls me up against his chest, shielding his body from the path of the gun with mine. His bony ribs press into my back, and I feel the jagged point of his broken bottle resting lightly against my throat. I shudder and then go still, standing as stiff as a dead cat in his grip.

"Don't move, or the dame gets it!" he threatens. His rapid, ragged breath sounds excited as his words hiss right into my ear. It's as though he would really get a bang out of slitting my throat in right front of this audience. I hear the sick wet sound of his tongue tracing his lips.

"Drop your gun!" Jack screams at Dalton. The policeman holds his rigid pose.

"Nothin' personal, Sugar," Stark hisses into my ear, stepping backward slowly with my body still in his clutches. His breath is wet and his words stick in my lobe. I cringe against them.

"See, I'm a wanted man. The fuzz wants me in the slammer and the mob wants me dead. If I get thrown in the joint, I'm as good as sleepin' with the fishes." I imagine his thin frame at the bottom of the harbor, swaying with the tide. At the moment, my wishes line up perfectly with the mob's.

"Let her go!" Jack threatens.

"Or what? You'll come get me?" Stark mocks, shouting. "You've got ten steps to take before you reach me, and sure enough this lil' gal will be lyin' in a pool of her own blood by the time you've made five." My eardrums throb. Images of Doris collapsed in that crimson puddle flash like a shuffling deck of cards. My lungs are compressed with fear; I'm fighting a full-blown attack of panic.

Jack takes a slow step toward us.

"Ah!" Stark presses the bottle tighter to my neck. It slices through a layer of skin, stinging, but not bleeding. Jack halts and puts his hands up.

Stark warns, "Don't wanna do that, Mister," and licks the lobe of my ear slowly. I squirm with disgust. The cold air bites the moisture on my skin, intensifying its unwelcome presence.

Jack stands still, his burning eyes trained on Stark's, but he bellows to the officer beside him, "Shoot him!"

"Lower your weapon or this gal is gone." Dalton's eyes dart around.

"Lower it!" Stark's tongue flicks.

"Shoot him!" I scream. "Do it! If he cuts me, we're already at a hospital!" Suddenly, a vision of my limp body on a gurney flashes through my head, intermixed with Doris's greyish green face on the operating table. We're both limp and unconscious.

In my mind's eye, I'm being rolled down the hall with a deathly pallor that matches the image of Doris. Nurses and doctors wave their bloody hands over my still form, trying to staunch the blood pouring from the jagged gash at my neck. One nurse swabs my lobe clean of Stark's poison saliva with alcohol. I long for this part of the vision to be real. In fact, I'll take a cut throat just to have someone cleanse me of Stark's touch.

Stark's snakelike voice is low in my ear again, but loud enough for the officer to hear. "Aw, Sugar, you've got a big, thick, juicy artery right here," he begins, running the tip of his tongue across the strained diagonal muscle that runs from my clavicle to my ear. I cringe, willing the vomit in my throat to stay put. He presses the bottle in tighter. It cuts my skin, and I gasp as thick drops of warm blood spill down my neck.

"If I go any deeper, you'll bleed out in minutes," he hisses, drawing out the 's' like a snake. The vomit rises to the back of my tongue. I wonder how many times he has committed this very act to warrant being hunted by good men and bad alike.

Jack's eyes look frantic. He is frozen in a forward stride. I can almost see his heart beating its way free of his ribs. *This is not the face of a fella driven by lust.*

My mind races. My heart thumps. The survival instinct in me takes over, and my body knows it must fight. I start to sway gently, rocking from heel to heel, positioning my feet where I want them.

"What are you doing, Sugar? Dancin'? This ain't no Sadie Hawkins, trust me," Stark jeers.

The smile drops from his lips when my right heel arcs upward, slamming into his groin. His limbs go limp; he groans and doubles over in pain. He loses his grip on the bottle and it hits the ground, shattering into hundreds of shards on the pavement, glittering in the warm torchlight.

Jack barrels forward and grabs me around the waist, lifting me off the ground. His wingtip shoe lands heavily on the back of the man's neck, forcing his face down into the broken shards beneath him. Stark arches his neck back and turns his face just before his nose makes contact, but Jack increases the pressure until the creep's cheek grinds into the ground. Stark wails as the glass beneath him slices his face.

"How do you like it?" Jack growls through his clenched jaw. He teeters with the weight of both of us on Stark's face and back. I am as still and rigid in his hold as I was in Stark's.

Officer Dalton cups a hand on Jack's forearm. "Alright, Tiger, I'll take it from here. Get her out of here." Jack hops from Stark's body, and Stark wails in pain as my feet touch the pavement. I hear a boot land heavily on Stark's back while we stumble out of the alley at the rate of Jack's galloping heartbeat, and know that Dalton has the beaten, writhing creep under control.

When I fail to keep pace, Jack lifts me so that I'm cradled in his arms. Near tears, I tuck my head under his chin while he runs. My breaths can't be any deeper than shallow pants against the tension of my chest and body. The adrenaline that had fueled me evaporates into a mist, trailing down the alley behind us. The fight shakes out of me as I jostle in his arms.

I am so... *so* worn out. Truly, I know weariness, but the way I feel now sinks much lower than any amount of tired I've ever felt. I whimper against the dip between his clavicles, where his pulse pounds rapidly. The side of my lower lip rests against the skin above that restless vein. It registers every throb. I think our pounding heartbeats race in time with each other's.

"It's okay, Pip," he soothes, voice vibrating with his steps. "You're safe now."

I do not feel safe. *Nothing* about me feels secure, except for the places where he holds me. I am crumbling like a cookie in a toddler's grip. My resolves, my stubbornness, my thick outer shell. Crumbs. Dust. I don't want to fight anymore. I can't fight anymore. I just can't.

The feelings I've stuffed deep down bleed through these new cracks. Every throb of my pulse pumps more, more, more of them up. The liquid emotion runs over me, smoothing the cracks, the bumpiest crumbs. It soothes me, and for the first time in a decade, I let it flow.

FOURTEEN

Out of the alley, Jack lays me on a bench just in front of Saint Christopher's front steps. I mourn the break between my skin and his. He takes in the blood covering my throat, hands and shins; he looks horror stricken.

"Let's get you inside," he says nervously. I grin weakly, trying to calm him.

"It's not all my blood. Just here," I say as my fingers graze across the crusted wound on my neck. "And it's only a little surface scratch from that bottle."

He doesn't look convinced as he gently fingers the wound.

"We need to get you to a doctor."

"No, no," I insist as I sit up slowly. "I'm fine. I just... I just want..."

His eyes watch me, terrified, but eager to fulfill my need.

"...you to..."

The yellow in his eyes illuminates.

"...hold me."

Jack looks troubled, with his brows furrowed. It is not the reaction I'd expected.

"You really have my head spinning, P."

"C'mon, if I were on death's door, I wouldn't be able to be talking to you right now," I insist. "It's probably all just old blood. Is it even bleeding anymore?" I try futilely to look down at my own neck.

He inspects it for me in the light of the street lamp. "No, I guess not. But we can't just sit here, out in the open. Those goons will be making their way out of that alley soon enough, and I don't think I can keep myself from pounding that creep." I wobble to my feet.

"Okay. Let's go."

He helps me to a standing position, supporting me at the elbow. The hottest of my emotions burns brightly at his touch. Molten lava moving through the liquid, a slow boil. I cannot stuff down my feelings for Jack any longer. The exhausted shell of my body feels weak, and broken, and I simply don't have it in me to keep fighting him away. *Why did I ever want to push him away, anyway?* As we walk slowly away from the hospital, I lean into his support. *Can he know that I'm leaning on him in every way?*

"Where to?" he asks.

"Anywhere," I breathe. I'm exactly where I want to be.

We turn down the next alley. Jack scans for predators, but it's hard to see straight through with several steaming grates dotting the ground. I falter just past the first one, and we are shrouded in the cover of its mist.

We pause. It seems both of us know this is as good a destination as any. He encircles my waist and pulls me to him, moving tentatively as if to ask if this is allowed to be more than just the supportive hold I'd permitted when he saved me. My tense body shudders, trying to relax into the curve of his arms. I rest my head on his shoulder.

He burrows his face deep into my hair. His breath warms my chilled ear, making it tingle. I have the odd vision of sun-warmed honey pouring thickly into a bowl as the heat of his breath moves from my ear down to my toes.

Suddenly, he moves forward with force, pushing me toward the building. Soon, I'm as stiff as a board with my back pressed all the way up against its bricks. I've run out of space between his chest and arms and the brick wall behind me.

"Jack," I breathe, way beyond feeling overwhelmed.

"Penelope," he says, sending the name through

his hot breath into my ear, across my cheek and into my hair. It hits my lobe with a sensation completely different from the sound of Stark's hiss. Jack's head dances back and forth, tracing his nose along my cheekbone, then rests his forehead on mine. The ridges of our noses are magnetized together. My heart pounds so hard that it feels like I need to bind it down with my arm, but my arms are trapped in his encapsulating hold on me. My breathing rates dangerously close to hyperventilation. I hardly hear the noise of the street over the rush of blood in my head, and the light sound of his breath on my skin.

"I... I have..." he starts to speak through husky breaths. I turn my face a little more toward him to give his words my attention. In the delicious nanosecond after I realize that his mouth is going to meet mine, but it hasn't yet, my lips vibrate with nerves, my mind racing with worry that I've somehow misread his signals and he'll pull away at the last second. Blood courses through my veins, pounding like a drum with each accelerated beat of my flurried heart.

He doesn't disappoint me. His mouth touches mine with unexpected softness. Our lips hold there, unmoving, but fireworks explode behind them just the same. My rigid body melts toward his. Warmth bleeds through me, searing the broken bits of myself back together, welding the shards in place. Quite unexpectedly, it feels like relief.

He pulls me in closer and kisses me more firmly. A tremble starts at my feet and races up my legs, causing my heel to bounce off the ground. I am positively burning inside; I can only inhale to take in all that's happening. My chest fills with swirling, burning emotion and whimsy. The arm that I had balanced on his shoulder, which was weak and limp at his advance, comes to life and coils around the back of his neck. He moves so slowly, so firmly, and so tenderly. He pulls back and places his cheek against mine. Mine is one hundred and twenty degrees, scorching and, no doubt, deep scarlet.

"I have never known a girl like you before," he finishes in my ear. His eyes bore into mine in the relative darkness. My head falls to the side, melting away with the rest of me. He wraps his free arm around my shoulders and hugs me to him tightly. I wrap my other arm around his neck, repeatedly lifting my hands and grasping him tighter and tighter. I just can't get close enough, perhaps even if I could climb inside of him. He lifts me off the ground and whirls me in a circle. My blood-stained, rag doll legs fly out behind me and I let my head fall back as we spin. Upon return to the ground, I rest my head against his overcoat. Finally, I exhale. The vapor it causes in the cold floats upward and away. It feels exactly like I'm floating, just like the vapor.

His hands find mine. They're not soft, but not calloused either.

"Let's get out of here," he suggests.

Why would we ever want to leave this place? I wonder. The steam rising and slowly swirling out of the street vents match how I feel. Steamy. And wobbly. My knees are still weak from that kiss as Jack leads me to his car. I follow alongside him in a zig-zagging trail while the scent of elation wafts from me. When we arrive at the vehicle, I fall onto the seat, sighing. He shuts the door behind me, and I'm abruptly alone in the cold car. A giddy grin spreads over my lips.

A moment later, he joins me from the driver's side door. We stare at each other. The tiny creases materialize slowly as his mouth twitches upward, and the temperature in the car begins to warm. My eyes fall to the wide, horrific blood smear on his sweater.

"Oh no," I whisper, one set of fingertips touching my lips.

"What, this?" he answers casually, brushing lightly at the deep red stain. "It's just a little surface stain." I smile at his coy replay of my own words.

He hesitates, squinting, then crawls slowly across the seat toward me. His fingertips replace mine at my lips, each charged with its own buzzing electric current. My eyes close as he brushes them up my jaw, carrying the static up to my earlobe. This completely new sensation feels so nice that it twists my stomach into a tight coil. His breath fills my ear; I shudder. He shakes my hair from his face, blowing it off of his lips as he pulls back, and slips his fingers around both my ears. He tilts my head back as his pinkies slide simultaneously over the pounding veins below my ears.

"Pip. Are you nervous?"

My laugh is shaky and embarrassingly high pitched. "Very."

"Why?" he asks.

"Because you scare me."

He drops his head and shakes it. His hair tickles my chin and his fingers brush down my neck, lifting carefully over the gash. His lips fit against my jawbone and he holds them there for just a moment before pulling back. My touch sensors can't seem to decide if it feels nice or nerve-wracking. He growls playfully, holding his hands up like claws in the air, and then lets them fall. He scoots back under the steering wheel, wearing a delicious half-grin. My heart rate refuses to mellow down.

As Jack drives me home, I float a few inches above the seat, buzzing with all-over warmth. He scoops up my blood-crusted hand, and our tangle of fingers rests on the tweed houndstooth of his thigh. A ridiculous grin dances from side to side on my lips; I can't stifle it, though I'm really not trying very hard.

What did I ever fight him for?

"Here we are," he murmurs as he slows in front of my house. I enjoy his profile as he cranes his head down and forward to confirm that we're in front of the correct ramshackle home. Surely no one has ever worn a hat so smartly. When he turns to me, my admiration of his profile is outdone by the straight on view. His full lips, a straight, strong nose, those large blue eyes with low brows. I glance at my front door, and then back at him. I want to tell him to keep on driving, and I groan when the car comes to a complete stop. He laughs.

"Shall we?" He reaches over my lap and pops my door handle. The action leaves a trail of his undeniably male scent in the air around me. His woody shaving soap, his pomade. He meets me on the sidewalk and offers me an arm. I take it and lean in toward his body as we walk. The walkway up to the front door is too short, and we arrive at the stoop all too quickly. We stop and he turns toward me. Somehow each moment replays in my mind hundreds of times before the next comes to pass. It's all in satisfying slow motion.

He rests the back of his thumbnail against his lower lip, a nervous tic I realize that I've been paying attention to all along.

"Pip, I, uh, well... if you would accept it, I would like you to have this." He fumbles in his pocket, then lifts his hand, palm down. Something falls from it and stops short in mid air. The porch light catches a glimmer a few inches below his hand, and for a moment I wonder how he has a lightning bug trained to hover just below his fingers.

My eyes slowly focus in on the delicate chain of a necklace. A charm, a four leaf clover, dances back and forth in the air below his hand, its gentle swing hypnotic in this unreal moment. His large fingers are wrestling with the clasp, battling the tiny pieces of silver.

"May I?"

I turn away and hold up my hair; the air electric on my exposed skin. The chain feels cold against the skin of my neck.

"Let's see," he says and pulls me around to face him. I turn my chin up and to the side so he can see it. The tiny silver piece rests just below the hollow between my clavicles, which are crusty and red with the dried, smeared remnants of my wound.
He rakes his fingers through his hair.

"Nice," he sighs. He's paused, lashes concealing his downcast eyes. The jumble of words that come next melt my heart. "This is to..." he begins uncertainly. "I would like us to, well..." he pauses and swallows. "I'd like you to, to be my gal."

Finally, he looks up, and the dark hedges masking the sapphire blue of his irises lift out of the way. I'm transfixed by the warm, twinkling gold around his pupils. His eyelashes swoop down and mask his gaze again.

"Hmmm," I answer coyly. "Well... I suppose..." He pulls my chin up and holds it there with his hand. He grins. When he moves in to kiss me again, I stop him with my dirty hand on his stained chest.

"Jackson."

"Jack," he corrects.

"Whatever," I continue, waving the correction away like a an irritating fly. "I have been fighting against this... this... um, *feeling* for quite a while now..."

"I'll say," he teases, rolling his eyes.

"Stop that!" I scold and pull my thought together again, fingers grasping the charm. "Well, anyway, I... I just don't understand how you could have, well; I mean, you had this in your pocket, as though..." I stutter.

He grins like a cat. "A fella can hope."

Warmth floods my cheeks. "But we only ran into each other."

"I was coming to ambush you at work. And, well, you know, you may be more transparent than you think, tough gal." He punches me lightly on the arm. I punch him back, not at all lightly.

He laughs and pulls me into his chest. I feel his heart thumping at my ear.

"You scare me, too," he whispers into my hair. As he turns and walks with natural grace back down the walkway, I watch him go, moving his long legs and arms smoothly, his hips moving with each step.

A squeal forms in my throat. I hold it back like a bull kickingat the gate until he lowers into the car, pausing to flash a smile at me as he pulls away.

My façade isn't necessary; the farmhouse is as still as a tomb. May and Mama must already be curled up under the quilt. I exhale the puff of air that I had held to stifle my concealed glee, and let loose a floppy, drunken grin. I tiptoe across the boards slowly, without a creak. I step lightly toward our bed so I won't rouse them. When my head hits the pillow and my hair fans out behind me, a satisfied sigh escapes me. I stare into the darkness for a moment, reveling in the feeling of being Penelope, the Luscious and Desired Being.

"P?"

I roll my eyes.

"Yes, Miss Mayhem?" I whisper. On my arm that hangs over the side of the bed, I feel the tickle of a cold draft from a crack in the corner. With my skin's heightened sensitivity, it feels fantastic.

"Where have you been, Sis?"

I button my lip. The one that is still a little moist

from Jack's kiss.

A squeal chokes in her throat.   She spasms a little, impatient.

"*Where* have you been?   Jack came by here looking for you, and he seemed pretty determined about it.   I told him you were at St. Christopher's. Did he find you? Anything to tell?"

In the dark room, she can't see that I am covered with evidence of things to tell.

Blood.

Wounds.

Jewelry.

Contentedness.

I close my eyes, my lashes resting lightly on the tops of my cheeks, fully enjoying the light pull of the chain on my neck.   I'll have to wash away these stains before I ruin the bed sheet, but I don't want to interrupt this reflective moment.

"Nothing really." I yawn. "G'night." While she exhales in frustration, a flicker show of the encounter plays in my head from all angles, encore after delicious encore.

FIFTEEN

September 8th, 1941

I sit beside Doris's bed, watching her ribs float up and down with her slow, light breaths. Her pallor seems terribly pale, but the pulse on her slim neck beats with vigor.

She's okay.

Nurse Adler shuffles in slowly, avoiding my eyes. I wonder if she is embarrassed that I know such intimate details of her story or if she's uncomfortable with the fear that I'll want to discuss it. Does she think I will require a show of gratitude? Some big "thank you"? I'd really rather just forget all of it, especially the unsettling feel of Stark pressed up against my body.

Well, not all *of it,* Imp giggles. Even if I tried, I will never forget what happened over that steam grate with Jack. And I don't hardly want to. I grin to myself.

"Ah, our pachent is thrivink!" Nurse Adler

bellows. I witness the oddest sight as her tight pucker relaxes into a thin, straight smile. Oh. My. Goodness. Adler is *smiling*.

My heart pounds, pushing me to ask a question. "And... you? How are you faring?"

Her entire face reddens. Her small green eyes finally look up at me from beneath her lowered lids, assessing my sincerity. She shifts the stiff white fabric of her uniform.

"Very vell, tank you," she warbles and her eyes well up with tears.

Aw, nuts. My arms reach out to her without my permission, feet closing in on her stout, trembling form.

"Ja, I em German, bet not a Nazi," she declares tearily.

I pull back, my hands on her shoulders, and assure her, "I know." And I do.

Doris's eyes flutter. Her sleepy gaze shifts between Adler and me in this unusual stance, and her eyes open wide with amazement.

"Hiya, Sleepyhead," I greet her with a smile, perching on the edge of her bed near her hip. She scowls.

"Don't think this makes us girlfriends or anything," echoes in my head. I retract a bit, but insist on doting on her regardless.

"Do you need anything? Are you thirsty? Doc

said you can drink fluids now." I jingle the ice in the cup of juice I've brought her.

She tries to sit up, but groans. I gently guide her back to lying down.

"Here," I say as I offer her a straw, supporting her head. She drinks deeply and drains the cup. The emptiness rattles in her straw until she gives up.

"How do you feel?" I ask softly. She closes her eyes and grimaces in pain. Nurse Adler, newly composed, reaches for the gas mask.

"Here you ah," she croons, placing the mask over Doris's nose and mouth. "A leettle geeft from me to you." Doris's body visibly relaxes into the bed. Her eyes roll.

"Hale, git to verk," Adler says. Old habits die hard.

"I'm not actually on shift today."

"Oh! Two stripahs down today? Geesh!" Stripers are supposed to be volunteers, not paid members of the staff that Adler should rely on. "Vell den. Carry on." She lumbers out the door and I hear it click behind her.

"This was Sweeney, wasn't it?" I ask Doris, who now wears a goofy grin.

"Sweeney. Sweeeeeney llllllikes me," she draws out.

I sigh in frustration. I should've asked her

before she got the giggle gas.

"I told the police it was him. What he did to you is evil. Pure evil," I whisper. "Scumbag."

"Yooooooooou don't like me," she says, her tongue lolling around in her mouth like bubble gum. I wonder where exactly in time her thoughts are.

"I like you fine, Doris."

"I tricked yoooou. I made you clean up puke!" she laughs groggily.

I roll my eyes. I won't be able to ask her about her attacker, or her baby, when she's this loopy, but at least she's breathing. I slip to the door and slide her chart off of the small hook.

"...*estimated gestation of fourteen weeks at time of injuries. Contusion to occipital skull; multiple contusions to anterior trunk. Superficial lacerations to the groin area, severe bleeding. Multiple lacerations to the cervical and surrounding tissue...*" I read, horrified. I shudder as my mind supplies images against my will: the back of her head slamming against the wall, the crushing blows to her newly-swollen belly, her stockings tearing away from her trembling legs, that vile metal object stabbing her tender flesh again and again. I look over at the slap happy gal in the bed, wondering how she could grin after such an occurrence, even high as a kite.

I continue reluctantly reading.

"...fetal remains..." My eyes close instantly. The tiny human, so protected in its mothers cushioned womb, so innocent and fresh; torn from its soft cocoon. Dead.

Sweeney is a monster.

I replace the chart on the hook and rest my fevered forehead on the cool wall. It feels wonderful against the heat of my face. I have lived through a lot. I've seen desperation, greed, hunger, loss. I've seen a span of years during which I was so weak with malnourishment that when I lay in bed at night, I prayed desperately to be alive the next morning. However, this realization of a world where people *kill* is pretty new to me. I can't control my hands from shaking the way that they are. Too many revelations, too much loss of my already thin veil of innocence, rocks me to my core. Stark was ready to slit my throat last night. Doctor Sweeney brutally assaulted Doris and slaughtered his own baby. And someone murdered my father.

I stumble to the chair beside Doris's bed. *Has the world always been this cold?*

Yes. Sense reminds me that a man across the Atlantic is slaughtering hordes of people simply because he doesn't like their family tree. I pull my knees up to my chest and squeeze my eyes shut. I wish I could squeeze them against the images in my head.

How can our nation stand by so quietly while this horrible man carries on? We are just letting this monster slit throats and murder babies and make desperate widows out of dignified women, over and over and over!

No, no; you don't want us to fight, Sense pipes up. *Eddie and Max will be right in the thick of it.*

And Phin, Imp agrees from my other shoulder. I squeeze my eyes tighter. I can't think about Phin! Guilt trickles into the sick, unsettled stew brewing in my belly. What kind of person coils around a sweet, handsome fella one night, and pines for another in the same turn of the clock? I have got to banish the memory of the downward slant of Phin's eyelids, cradled over those burnished green eyes. I must stuff the clear image of the apples of his freckled cheeks gathering prominence with every unleashing of his mischievous grin. His lashes, deceptively long, pale as wheat at the tips. That dark hollow between his cheekbone and the strong point of his jaw...

Stop it, Sense scolds me. Tears spill out of the corners of my eyes. I'm rocking forward and backward toward agony.

"What'ssss yooooooour problem?" Doris slurs groggily. I open my eyes and peer at her sideways. A little more lucid, she watches my silent pity party curiously.

I laugh humorlessly. "Nothing." I push off the chair and perch myself on the edge of her bed.

"I'm. Not. *Dead*." she articulates, mystified by the sound of each word, and laughs.

"Yeah, no thanks to Doctor *Sweeney*." His name tastes bitter.

"Sweeeeeney. Sweeneeeee. Sweeney is a *baaad* man." She wags a finger at me like a teacher; a drunk teacher.

I latch on to her awareness. "Yes. Yes! He is. He did this, didn't he?"

"He's not fatherly material," she slurrs in a low, mocking voice. Her face looks like Shirley Temple's playful scowl. "Not fath-th-ther-leeee."

No kidding.

September 20th, 1941

Bee-dum. Bee-dum. Bee-dum. My cheek, pressed against Jack's chest, absorbs the steady rhythm of his heartbeat. Safely tucked under his arm as we lie under the tendrils of the willow at the Spot, the vibration of his heart echoes in my head while his fingers twirl my hair. Somehow the ground near this thick trunk feels warmer, as though this tree puts off its own heat.

While the river rushes beside us, he tells me stories about his family. How he's always loved to embarrass Bentley, who has been being primed for a political career since he could talk. How his overwhelmed nanny often yelled, *"you little devil!"* and how the ensuing punishment never matched his glee at what he'd done to deserve it. I can perfectly imagine his mischievous grin on a smaller Jack, with the same lock of hair sticking up.

He tells me about his mother, always poised and diplomatic. His father, who taught him to fish and would tousle his sons' hair when they'd earned his pride. Usually Bentley would earn a tousle for his marks at school or learning to tie his own tie, while Jack earned them more privately for his pranks on the nanny and the driver. Again, I draw parallels between Jack and my brothers, and I wonder if Max and Eddie would have the same sort of misdeeds to laugh about if life had gone on as it should have. The misdeeds of a carefree boy, just looking to liven things up a little.

Jack sighs, and his heartbeat lulls me into deep thought. The reply I've been waiting for from Eddie arrived yesterday, only now I feel more confused than satiated.

"Isn't it obvious, Squeak? Who had the most to gain from Dad 'accidentally' dying? Madge! Dad was the guarantor of Grandpa's estate. He had the choice of whether or not to share any of the inheritance with Madge, and it's pretty clear she's

the most greedy, vile serpent of a woman the devil
has ever let out of Hell."

Sure, Madge is cruel and greedy. But the Quinns
have always had plenty of money. Madge brought
her Hale Oil trust fund into the marriage, but Uncle
Harry sweats gold. They had no need for a dime of
Grandpa Hale's money. It doesn't make sense for
her to kill for it. Of course, it didn't make sense for
a family member to kick us out of our home and
claim all of our things, either.

*"They say he was drunk, even though Charles
Kerr (remember him? The guy with the big mole on
his neck?) swears up and down that Dad only
drank lemonade that day. C'mon, had you ever
seen Dad with anything other than juice or a soda?
Anyway, wanna guess who served it to him?
You've got it- Madge. And they say his foot was
'caught' in the stirrup, only when I read the
autopsy report two years ago- they're a matter of
public record, you know- it listed 'bruising around
the ankle appears to be caused by chafing from a
cord or rope' among his injuries. Who's to say she
didn't spike his drink with something, tie his foot to
the stirrup, then hide in the woods and spook his
horse on purpose? The facts are all in line.*

Now you've done it, Squeak. I'm as hopping

mad as I was when I first read that report! I feel like jumping in the ocean and swimming back to the mainland to hunt down the beast who stole our lives from us! Ma won't tell us where Ole Madge lives now; I'm not sure if she even knows anymore. But Max and I are saving up to hire a private investigator when we get back. Ten years is long enough for her to dance on his grave! It's time for her to pay."

After a while the sensation of Jack's fingertips tracing my earlobe brings me back to the present. It's impossible to describe how it feels: the drag of his skin over the tender nerve endings of my ear. I'm still learning to just enjoy the sensation of his touch instead of being stiff with nervousness. A tiny sigh escapes from me.

My head bounces on his chest as he laughs, "Yeah, me too," as though he can read my reaction to his touch.

I reposition my head on him, wondering why I ever denied this fella. I sure wasted a lot of lazy afternoons like this one.

"Pip," Jack starts. I can hear it both in the air and resounding in his throat.

I mumble in response, "Mmm."

"You've gotta meet my mom now, you know," he says. It sounds a little like a warning.

My stomach flips. Hopefully, Jack's mother is more open minded than Mama.

October 2nd, 1941

"Doris, you've met a guy's parents before, right?" I ask her while she lies in the hospital bed, cheeks much pinker than a few days ago.

"Sure. You mean at the dinner table or sneaking past them to his bedroom?" She laughs hysterically. "I'm kidding, the only fella I ever pulled that with was a fella named Georgie." She swoons. "A guy's mother is the gatekeeper, you know, and crabby ol' Missus Quinn didn't like me much."

Quinn? George? My *cousin* George? This town isn't large enough for two Joes with the same name.

"George Quinn?"

"George, Georgie," plays on her jaw. My cousin George is just a year older than my cousin Claire, which makes me three years younger than he is. He's always been sort of mischievous- a family trait- but sneaking a gal into his room?

Well, this gal in front of you is not quite riding on high moral standards, either, Imp pipes up.

I shake the fuzzy vision out of my thoughts.

"At the dinner table," I confirm.

"Well, *my,* how proper," she mocks, bobbling her head atop her neck. "Well, let me enlighten you. You'll want to flirt with the father," she begins with a decisive nod, as though no conquest is truly won without reeling in his father, too.

I feel myself stiffen; it's highly unlikely that I'll bat my eyelashes at Mister Sharpe. I don't think I even know how to flirt to begin with. I bat my eyelashes in clumsy practice.

Doris continues, "Make sure and be kinda subtle, so his wife doesn't notice. Be an angel to the mother, and give just the right amount of adoring glances to her son; you know, show her you prize him as much as she does. Then maybe she'll let you pass through her gate." I imagine a tall iron gate with pointed finials at the top. "But if he's got a sister, she's your real hurdle."

Mentally, I scribble down her notes and commit them to memory. Thankfully, Jack never mentioned a sister, just his big brother, Bentley. Hopefully, he won't be a hurdle. I scrunch my nose.

Am I supposed to flirt with him, too? Crackers. I really am no good at this.

"So, some fella's taking you home to Mommy?" she asks me.

I nod. "Tonight."

"Well congratulations, Miss Prim Pretty Princess. You're way ahead of me." She waves to her fragile body in the hospital bed. My stomach twinges guiltily. I shouldn't have come here to ask her about this. Every eligible male doctor in this hospital will know exactly how she got into this mess, and how Sweeney weaseled his way out of it, by now. She may as well be wearing a sandwich board that reads, 'used goods'. I'm a real crumb. I admire her for her relatively mild mood despite this pickle.

"You've got nothin' to worry about. If I were this fella's mother, I'd like you instantly." Doris just gave me a compliment. Wow. "Of course... as another fish in the sea, I have to hate you. Remember, we're-" she begins.

"Not girlfriends or anything," I finish for her, but she doesn't pull her hand away from mine as I take it. She stares at me.

"Thanks for saving me, Penelope." Her big brown eyes shine sincerely. I wish she hadn't needed saving in the first place.

She narrows her eyes and shakes her bed-head ferociously. "Go get 'em."

SIXTEEN

I am a frantic tornado with my arms flying at gale force speed through the closet. I shove my hangers left to right, then right to left. Whatever I expect to find is not in this closet. I'm beginning to hyperventilate; I'll be picked up in thirty minutes and my hair is still tied up in rag curls. My foot stomps in frustration against the old floorboards, and I bite my lip. With a sinking, searing pain right through my middle, I resign myself to the reality that there will be nothing to wear here, so I just crumple to the floor in utter defeat.

May pads in. I know that all that's visible of me are my splayed legs from the closet.

"You look like the wicked witch dead under Dorothy's house!" she says with a scrunched nose, poking her head in.

"I am dead," I groan dramatically, with all the self-pity I feel. "Well, I'm dying! I have nothing to wear tonight, nothing!" I cry.

What has happened to me? I'm a pathetic heap on the floor. Two days ago, I would be content wearing a paper bag, and all I wanted was for the fella to leave me alone.

You never wanted that. He's had you from day one, Sense whispers reasonably.

Well, it was much easier being a porcupine, Imp shoots back sourly.

While the memory of Jack's lips pressing into mine floats to the forefront of my brain, all three of us become temporarily drunk.

"C'mon, Pip," May croons, pulling on one of my feet. I stand and follow, limp as a frowning rag doll as she leads me to the small cupboard in the entryway. If she thinks something of Mama's will work, she must not be paying much attention to the tattered frocks our mother wears to church.

"Darling, we don't steal; it's a *commandment*," I lecture in my best imitation of Mama, eyebrows nearly at my hairline, as she disappears into the closet.

"*Borrow,* not steal," she corrects from inside of the cupboard with only her hand visible. How I had underestimated my little sister.

She emerges on one foot with an ivory bag on a hanger. She hangs it on the drapery rod and unzips it carefully, top to bottom. A rich, navy blue fabric peeks out from the opening. It seems promising.

"This," she announces as she slips the bag off of the hanger, "is my personal favorite." She holds it up like a trophy. The fabric sways a little on its own, as if this dress contains life in its silken threads. My chin bounces down and up while my mouth tries to form words. I'm speechless.

"Wha? How?" A dim memory of Mama floating down the staircase of the estate wearing this rich blue fabric plays in my head. I suppose Madge didn't take everything from her, after all.

"I like to dress up sometimes, y'know," May admits sheepishly, hands clasped, swaying a bit. A vision of May and her friends trying on dresses and heels far too large for them makes me smile.

"You've been holding out on me!" I exclaim as my limbs regain their life force, and my eager fingers close on the silken fabric. I never knew I'd been living with something so fine in my home all these years.

What use did you have for it until now? Sense reasons. *Milking your cow?*

After all, it's not a paper bag, Imp teases.

"Well, try it on, then," she urges. My shirt flies over my head and on the floor in a quarter of a second. I fumble with the buttons on my skirt and kick off my shoes. I take the dress gently. The satin slides down my skin and bounces at the hem, mid calf, when it falls into place. I look down at it; it seems to fit pretty well. I look up expectantly for May's assessment.

Her eyes glow at me. "It fits you way better than it fits me," she muses, giving a forlorn glance down at her own budding chest. "Good enough to meet the queen."

"Or Jack's mama." My stomach balls up again at the thought of meeting Missus Sharpe for the first time; the gatekeeper.

As I admire the dress in the mirror, I begin removing rag ties from my hair. Tendril after tendril of honey hair tumbles over my shoulders, springing back up in curls. I hug my brilliant sister, whisper a sincere thank you, and make my way back to my room for stockings. I have to crane my neck over my shoulder to make sure the seams are straight. This gives me a rear view of the frock. Pleased, I pull on a worn pair of mustard-colored T-strap heels. They pinch a bit, but I'll probably still have toes by the end of the night.

May enters a moment later with a white coat, also calf length, over her arm. It sharpens my memories of my mother in the bygone days: the fashionable Missus Hale.

The Sharpes' driver is satisfyingly admiring when he picks me up. I hope that Jackson will feel the same. It feels funny to walk over my shabby yard and take his gloved hand to step into the supple leather of the car's interior. We drive back across town to Jackson's family's sprawling vineyard. I feel like a little girl, staring up out of the car window at the brilliantly lit home, like I'm looking up at a Ferris wheel. As we drive past rows of delicately tended, artfully designed flower beds and tall, flowing fountains in the yard, my stomach becomes a cocktail of one part excitement and two parts nervousness, on the rocks with a serious twist. It sloshes around in me as we pull next to a row of gleaming cars.

The driver opens my door with a bow. My heels click up the stone steps, jerking along the path to the warmly lit grand entrance with the grace of a windup toy.

With the backdrop of the dark sky, his home looks regal. Maybe the home I grew up in oozed the same opulence, but when I lived in it, I was either too young to notice or too privileged to appreciate it. The sheer size of the place is impressive alone. The lines of the home, clearly built by a skilled craftsman, flow beautifully over the rooftop. Dormers peek up in threes. A large, sweeping arch of white welcomes me at the doorway, and warm light from within beckons. It's as though the Sharpes have turned on every lamp in the home to greet me with. My heart burns warm; this is going well.

A butler greets me graciously, slipping Mama's coat from my tense shoulders while my heels click over the marble entryway. I feel my lipstick stretch when I smile at him, and smooth the carefully waved lock of hair across my forehead. My eyes go wide, taking in the grandeur of the home. Large paintings hang on nearly every wall, stretching from ceiling to floor. Through stately pillars, I can see that a fire is lit in each room flanking the entryway, warming the intricate rugs that hug the dark wood floors. Fresh floral arrangements adorn every possible surface. I try to imagine silly Jack being raised in this grandeur.

Once my ears register the vibration of muted shouting, which doesn't match the cheery mood of these bright lamps and lush furniture, my smile fades to a curious "O". Muffled words float through the entrance.

"....guests, dear!" a high pitched, feminine voice trills.

"...*told* you... guest!" a lower one growls, barely audible to my perked ears.

The hum of the muffled female voice arcs from scolding to soothing. A door slams, and I jump. A bang and the tinkling of glass shattering follow.

"Jackson!" the woman's clear voice bounces sharply down the marble entry. Then a gal appears, stopping short, but the voice is not hers; the tone of the scolding voice can only belong to a parent.

I recognize the girl. We haven't seen each other in a decade, though I've never met another person so physically well suited to be a forest sprite- tiny, dainty, elfish. One of her small, pointed ears holds back a lock of her caramelly hair. It's undeniably my cousin, Claire; Madge's daughter.

Claire is here? Aunt Madge's daughter, at Jackson's house? She shakes her head in disbelief when she sees me, apparently as surprised to see me as I am her.

Jack appears down the hallway, his mouth set in a tight line as he paces the long rug toward me. His eyes are steely, and I realize that the growling voice belonged to him. When I meet his gaze, I get an unsmiling, terse nod in return.

The owner of the woman's voice rounds the corner. A stunning, raven haired beauty with high cheekbones and a full pout spouts the unmistakable voice of a scolding mother. Her soft tendrils float behind her with her smooth, angry steps as she glides past Claire.

Jack keeps up his determined pace past me and grabs my upper arm as he passes me.

"C'mon," he urges, and I struggle to match his velocity. My head keeps pulling back to take in the beauty of his mother.

Out the door, a sheet of autumn balm nips at my

bare arms. I glance behind me, bemoaning giving the butler Mama's coat. Jack picks up the pace and soon we're running, loping as fast as we can into the trees of the orchard. My shoes are long gone behind me as we run, and the cold, hard earth tears up my delicate hose.

There goes twenty cents! I think to myself.

Thin, gangly trees thick with ground fog act as our cover as we dash deep into the woods. When we finally slow to a stop, a safe distance from the house, we both pant heavily and pull leaves off of our clothing and hair. I lean one hand against a tree trunk to sturdy myself, weak from the exertion.

"What," I pant breathlessly, "are we running from?" I lean into the stitch in my side. He steps close to me. My pulse races from the sprint and the excitement of escape, and now becomes triple-timed by his vicinity. His cheeks are bright pink from the run and the cold. The bite of the frosty air prickles my skin.

He cups his hand on the small of my back, allowing me to collapse a little into him. I give in to the thing inside me that wants to trust him, to be near him and to feel safe in the fingers of this encircling fog.

Except for the barely-audible trickle of a half frozen stream near us, it's absolutely silent out here in the open air. It amplifies the leaves' crunch with each tiny shift of weight from either of us. I wonder what this exact moment is like for him, because I, myself, am exploding inside. My bare feet feel the tiny pricking of dry, dead leaves and the cold of the earth beneath their blanket.

Everything that I know tells me that a gal doesn't make the advances; the man holds the reins and makes the calls. I feel frustrated to have to hold in these feelings and maintain a smooth façade; it's like holding back a team of bulls. They buck and toss about inside of me; restless, fighting the stall that holds them, chafed by these restraints. I fight against them to maintain a ladylike status, even in the thick of these woods.

Jack moves closely in and our foreheads kiss. The ground crackles beneath him as he moves; the only sound my ears register. Every inch of my skin has become covered in goosebumps from the biting chill, and ever the gentleman, he encircles me in his warmth for body heat. He can't know that this move sets off explosions of heat like a scorching inferno in my core. I lean into the embrace, taking in his scent with a deep, belly filling breath. He smells sweet, like maple syrup, and woody like cedar in a fire.

He rubs my bare arms to warm them. He touches my shoulders, my neck, and my cheeks as though he's trying to memorize the feel of them. He holds my face with his pinkies slipped behind my ears and laughs.

"Your nose is pink," he smiles, and touches the tip of his own cold nose to mine.

"So is yours," I reply, unable to stop grinning as my chin bounces along with my chattering teeth.

He moves in and suddenly my cold mouth becomes warm.

Not warm. *On fire.*

We are mouth to mouth, a chemical reaction instantly sending my frozen purple lips ablaze with scorching electric currents. He pulls back, and it actually hurts me when he does. His arms drop, and he steps back from me.

The cold, thick air goes screamingly silent, except for the light sound of our breaths. I steal a glance at him, and watch the smooth steam from his breath rise to the heavens with each exhale. His cheeks are perfectly pink from the bite of the cold, but his expression doesn't seem to match my elated one. Furrowed brows shroud his serious eyes as they drop to the ground.

I'm about to ask, "*what?*" when he provides the answer.

"I had to do that." I don't mind a bit that he did. In fact, I hope he will again. "I shouldn't have, but I had to. Kiss you, I mean."

My brows pull together, and a knot twists my formerly content belly into a tight coil as he looks sadly into my eyes. *What is he saying? What is that look for?*

He continues, "Maybe for the last time, because..."

My heart stops in anticipation.

"Apparently, I'm engaged."

SEVENTEEN

I recoil from him and stumble backward to the ground, punctuated by the startled shuffle of crispy leaves under me. I know he's not engaged to me.

"What?" I gasp. My chest heaves against the silken fabric of my mother's dress. It's suddenly very hard to breathe this cold air.

"According to my *mother*," he spits out like an insult, "I have no say in the matter." His endless lashes sweep upward, his tight eyes focused off into the distance. I appreciate the diversion of his gaze while my face crumples. "Some lousy debutant daughter of her 'dear' friend."

"Oh," I say quietly while my stomach drops down, dangerously close to detaching and flopping all the way to my feet. I connect his words to the people I saw in his entryway. His mother, painfully graceful and elegant. His scowl as he charged toward the door. Claire. My tiny, elfish cousin... is engaged to Jackson.

I feel like an utter fool. The bright red lipstick on my lips feels foreign. My dress, a prop. The magic they'd held earlier this evening fades away with his revelation. How foolish to have allowed myself to climb so high up this hopeful ladder; the fall is long and the crash is so hard and cruel! My shattered bones tremble on this cold forest floor. His mother. His beautiful mother, the gatekeeper, has slammed the gates on me with a resonating metallic rattle. I failed to charm her... I didn't even get the chance.

"Of course," I stammer in a heap on the ground as I try to pull myself together, quickly circling thick bricks and a heaping layer of mortar up around myself. My splattered heart sinks down inside them like dishwater down a drain. "You should be engaged to a debutant."

"I'm not saying I want to marry her!" he exclaims, then straightens. Quietly, he murmurs, "Or that I will." My sagging heart flutters weakly, until his tone turns explanatory; "It's just... my family..." and my heart slaps back against the bricks and sinks to the floor.

"I get it, Jackson," I say, cutting him off. My voice sounds too soft for the heavy artillery I've intended. "Let me make it easy on you," I hiss much more severely, and start to stand.

He catches my arm easily and pulls me up

into him with brute strength. It infuriates me that I'm such a rag doll in his arms. I flail to escape from his hold around my waist, but I'm maddeningly confined. I pull my head as far back as I can from his face, turning my head away, and focus on stamping out the warm embers of my feelings for him. I will them to lose their fire and go cold. That will make this so much easier for both of us.

"No, Pip, you need to understand," he growls through his clenched jaw. He has to catch my chin and hold it, like a toddler's, to get me to face him. I feel my mouth pinched into duck lips between his strong fingers, as ridiculous and stupid looking as I feel inside. I furrow my brows to match his stubbornness. We're two mules in a battle of wills. I can feel the heat from his body against my middle, and it feels good, but I wriggle to get away. This isn't allowed to feel good anymore.

My eyes strain away; it's my only defense. His fingers soften on my face.

"This is bigger than me. Sharpes have been, well, *bethroth-ing* of sorts for ages, climbing the screwy social ladder with gainful marriages. I thought that when Bentley chose his own wife that I'd be free to choose my own, too. I guess since he just happened to fall in love with a debutant that there was no need for my parents to handpick a gal to help the Sharpes 'climb the social ladder'. Well, I have no interest in the *social ladder* if it means I have to spend my life with a wet blanket like the gal in there!" He jabs a finger toward the house while he kicks the dirt. I think of Claire back at the house; his debutant.

I feel sick. My eyes scan the ground for the best place to vomit as bile climbs eagerly up my throat.

"How could you..." I start to shout, then I double over and lose it. Acrid bile forces its way out of my mouth. While I'm humiliated, hot tears burn down the bridge of my nose into the puddle of vomit. I spit out the acidic dregs into the dirt.

"Why did you bring me here?" I squeak pathetically, loose strings of hair hanging in my face and sticking to my clammy skin. My tongue tastes tangy and revolting. This feels like a cruel joke.

He answers, sidestepping while I crawl on all fours toward the stream, "To meet my parents, of course!" It almost sounds believable. "I didn't know that *that* family would be here."

Family? Her entire family is there? George, Uncle Harry, and Aunt Madge? Was one of the fine cars parked along the drive bought with my inheritance? A shiny piece of metal on four wheels whose sticker price could have fed my family all of these years?

My stomach rolls. *Will the Quinns always haunt me?* I feel like I may vomit again.

"You have to know that I didn't have any idea about any of this!" he pleads, following my pathetic shuffle down the bank. "Where are you going?"

I answer him by dipping a cupped palm into the icy water, freezing my teeth as I swish it through my mouth, and spitting it back out into the trickling flow. The mint of my toothpaste was burned away when I threw up, but at least the acrid taste isn't as strong on my tongue now. I sit back on my bare heels and shove the damp hair from my face. I can feel the naked parts of my lips where I've accidentally wiped away my lipstick. Why bother fixing it? I'm a mess, inside and out.

"Who am I to stand in your family's way?" I mumble, and my raw throat protests. It's a weak argument on my part; undeniable electricity arcs between us. He'd made me a 'someone' to him when he gave me the charm. Maybe even when he first visited the farm. I struggle to pull a hand to my neck and break his chain away. I gasp at the stinging pain as it reopens the cut on my neck, but I'm furious enough to use the pain as fuel and toss the charm at him.

"Go ahead and give this to your new gal," I snarl as it hits his chest and falls into the leaves. I don't attempt to hold back the whirling dervish that fights the fight for me so I can crumple into a ball behind it.

I start back toward the house, but I'm caught quickly from behind in one strong swoop that I'm not strong enough to squirm from. I'm a storming, stubborn baby pony against his grip. He shakes me gently.

"P," he breathes into my ear. "Pip, please," he pleads and turns me toward him. He plants his lips deep into mine. I feel a sensation like sincerity and surety in this kiss, dim through my thick wall. For a moment, I'm lost in his affection.

I yank my head away and slap him, fuming. He releases my body on contact and throws up a hand to tend his stinging cheek.

"Ow, oooooh," he groans. I'm pleased by the sound, but my hand stings as well. I take the opportunity and run for the house, swooping down to collect my shoes on the way. I ignore the sharp clods of cold earth beneath my bare feet as I run for the main road and don't look back.

Once I'm home, I brush my teeth with angry resolve to wash away any traces of that adulterous kiss. *How dare he? How dare he tell me he's off the market and then kiss me! Does he think I'll just agree to be his plaything until he ties the knot with someone else? Who does Jack think he is? He's a philandering playboy, that's who he is, and I will not be his toy! Oh, I've brushed too hard.* I spit blood into the sink. I lick across my stinging, protesting gums in an apologetic caress. *All* of me stings. Bitter, jealous stinging, from my bleeding gums to my raw, aching feet.

He said himself that his family has been betrothing for ages, so he must have always known that this was coming. He knew, but he still pursued me! *Me!* A gal his mother never would have selected for him; no riches, no privilege, no social standing. And like a blind fool, I let myself fall for him.

When she happens into the kitchen, May is beyond appalled to find the fruit of her fairy godmothering in this disheveled state. Stringy, leaf-encrusted hair tangled around my dirty, clammy face. Thin streams of blood run around my neck where the chain had reopened the cut from Stark's bottle. The scarlet face of May's Cinderella is marred with a scowl, the mask atop a fresh, tender wound. The panic in her eyes at the sight of my dirt soiled hem dissolves into worry when she takes in the shredded strings around my ankles that once were silk stockings.

"Did you..." she begins, quivering with disbelief, "...meet his mama?"

I awaken with a jolt when my head hits the wooden barn floor. Tilly, who had made a fine pillow for my head during the night, has lumbered to her hooves, standing up. I scramble out of her way to avoid having my head crushed by her hooves. I crawl to the hay bales, dragging Jack's quilt behind me. I hope it gets stained with cow plop and dust. He deserves it.

Because even the crickets have gone silent, I know it's not time to wake yet. I make a nest on the bales and curl up in the quilt. It's freezing out here, but I have my anger burning hot inside of me to keep me warm. I was mad at Jack at first, but now I'm just peeved at myself. I knew better! I broke my own rules, violated my own personal code, and I'm paying for that now. Mama warned me that it would be trouble to get mixed up with a high hat socialite, and I did it anyway.

Just because he was too charming to resist. And breathtakingly attractive. Sensitive, kind, not at all stuck up, Sense lists before I snap the lid on her. As much as it elevated me into the clouds to feel his affection, crashing back down to the ground again hurts.

The juvenile taunt plays in my head, *"sticks and stones may break my bones, but words can never hurt me."* Whoever wrote that verse has never heard words like I have, because I hurt so badly from Jack's news that I feel like all of my bones have broken. I don't think I can ever heal from these wounds. I sigh heavily.

Sleep beckons, and I can hardly resist. I'd rather just go to sleep for a long, long time and wake up when I'm old and unattractive, and there's no danger of romance on the horizon. Life would be simpler with white hair, saddlebags and bare, toothless gums. Sure, there'd be no thrill of a beau's fingers grazing my cheek, or the slow-spreading warmth from a tender kiss; but I think it would be safer to just not feel anything at all.

October 3rd, 1941

I pace over the linoleum tiles in front of the hospital supply closet. The strong odor of ammonia leaks from under the door, and I know that the mess inside has been cleaned away. Still, I cannot bring myself to open the door and retrieve the towels Adler has requested. The last time I'd entered this very closet, I'd found Doris in a spreading pool of crimson blood. Though I know she thrives in a hospital bed just down the hall-- I just saw her living, breathing body with my own eyes when I went to tell her we're in the same broken hearts club-- it feels as though her ghost resides behind this door.

"Psst!" I hear, and I jump a mile. Adrenaline shoots down my limbs, and my heart thunders in my chest. I can't tell where the sound is coming from, and I'm thoroughly unnerved. I whip my head around, trying to find the source of the sound.

"In here," the voice whispers. I turn around and locate a beckoning hand extended from the curtain in the room across the hall. It's small and feminine, like Doris's. I walk tentatively toward the hand, wondering if I may be walking toward Doris's ghost. But the hand is alive and firm, and it pulls me behind the curtain.

"Claire!" I gasp. My cousin stands beside me, short and slender with glistening caramel hair pinned attractively around her face. "What are you-why are you?" My eyes volley from her left eye to right under my furrowed brows as I pull away from her.

"What do *you* want?" I ask flatly, arms folded across my chest. Before last night, I hadn't seen my cousin since I was seven years old, when her family left mine destitute. I thought they'd moved away. Right after I lost Daddy, Claire's mother took away every other comfort I knew. I could've used my soft pillow to cry into, and the comfort of familiar surroundings. But a cold, unfeeling aunt had thrown us out-- in essence, thrown us away, and ten years later, we still suffer from her cruelty. My mouth tightens into a thin line. Now her pampered daughter, Claire, has swept away my first glimmer of real happiness in a decade. How *dare* she show her face to me?

"Jack sent me," she explains. I hate how easy his name sounds on her lips. What kind of creep sends his fiancee to brag to the broken-hearted? I turn on my heel to leave, suddenly not as afraid of the haunted supply closet, but Claire catches my arm.

"Wait, P," she urges, making up for the lack of strength in her tiny hands by digging her claws into my skin.

I look at her stonily. It's like she's cruelly twisting the dagger in my heart.

"He didn't know! He had no idea what his mother had arranged! And he didn't know she was going to be there. He was as surprised as you were! Ruby had just told him about her seconds before you came!" The explanation tumbles from her dainty lips.

"Wha-who? Who's *she?*" I ask, twisting my arm out from under her fingernails.

"Ruby? Bent- well, Jack's mother. I'll tell you, it was pretty awkward at that dinner table with the Barretts and Samantha and, anyway," she rants on in the chirpy, rapid-fire manner I remember her being famous for as a child; "Jack didn't take the news too well!" She snorts a laugh. Her hazel eyes grow wide with a mix of amusement and urgency.

"No, you said, 'He didn't know *she* was going to be there'."

"Yeah, 'she'. The debutant, Samantha Barrett,"

Claire explains as if this was obvious.

"Oh," I mutter. Jack's intended beau is a gal named Samantha Barrett, not Claire. I feel sheepish for being so hostile to my cousin, and try to sweep away the dirt I'd piled against her. "Well, then what were you doing at his house?"

"I'm his sister-in-law, of course!"

"Huh?" All this new information confuses me, especially through the blur of my foggy, sad eyes.

"Yeah, Pip, I married his big brother, Bentley, three years ago," she tells me in a 'reminding' tone, though this is the first I've heard of it. It suddenly dawns on me why Mama was so cold to Jack when she heard he was a Sharpe.

A fresh, angry heat sears my chest; if Mama knew Claire was getting married, she hadn't shared it with us kids. *Why does she insist on keeping me in the dark? This opens a twelfth story window of possibility; what else don't I know?* I can't seem to find any solid ground in all of this secrecy.

I remind myself that Claire was only nine when Daddy died. She couldn't have had anything to do with the management of the family fortune. My current anger at Mama starts to melt the frost on my heart for Claire.

"Oh," is all I can say.

"Jack is a mess over you," she explains.

This fact should make me sad for him, but instead,

my sagging heart leaps with possibility. I'd been feeling left behind in the dust, but maybe Jack's in a dust cloud of his own. Maybe one I created.

"If you hadn't run out on him, he could've explained that he didn't know the Barretts were going to be there, or that he was suddenly supposed to marry their daughter and..."

"He already told me that," I interrupt grimly, shaking my head ever so slightly, and kick up the dust cloud around myself again. "It's just, Jack and me, we're from different stock, you know? If his mama wants a Deb, she's going to be real disappointed with a horse-apple-flingin' milk maid with holes in her shoes and straw in her hair." Regardless of how Jack feels, this is probably for the best. We aren't meant to be a couple.

"What are you talking about? Hales don't work! *You're loaded!*" she exclaims in a whisper, so as not to brag in this public setting.

I narrow my eyes at her. *Does she really think we're still rich?* Her face looks very convincingly confused. Is it actually possible that Claire has no idea what her parents have done to us?

"Claire, why do you think you haven't seen me, or May, or Eddie, or Max, or Mama for ten years?" I ask her evenly, ticking each member of my family off my fingers.

She rolls her shoulders uncomfortably. "I

dunno. My mother said you didn't want to be part of the family once... you know, once you didn't have to be."

"What?" I bubble over with hot red anger. *Her mother told her we didn't want to be in the family, and she believed it, just like that? We used to be spit sisters!* "We didn't leave the family, Claire! Your mother kicked us out of our house and sold everything we owned and cut us out of the family fortune. We've lived in a tiny farmhouse on my uncle's land for the last decade, thank you very much! It doesn't even have an indoor toilet!" I shout.

I watch her delicate features absorb this new information. Her eyes flicker with confusion as she entertains this new possibility. It marrs her pretty face and her chin bobs under her trembling lip. Her large eyes swim.

"That, that can't be true," she whispers thickly. Images of the indulgent lifestyle she was raised in flood my head, soft and shiny against the hard, dark pictures of my much tougher rearing. Maybe it's not her fault, but I'm scarred all the same.

I was just fine before Jack picked me up- even fine with walking over cold clods of dirt to the outhouse in the middle of the night to relieve myself. Perfectly at ease with my station in life; making my own way in the world. I didn't know

Claire was around, or that she was innocent of her mother's evils. I didn't know fellas were still being married off by their mothers for social gain. It's archaic! We're not living in medieval times! All this drama and jockeying for family social position? I don't want any part of it. Maybe it's just better if we all forget any of it happened.

At least Claire knows the truth now. Perhaps she will stick it to her mom for kicking my family to the curb.

"Well, you know, Claire, sometimes the truth hurts," I sneer, and I barge right into the supply closet without fear.

She doesn't follow.

October 4th, 1941

"You are bleeding all over me, Penny," Mama complains while I sulk past her in the kitchen. I barely notice the pungent peach scent in our home anymore.

"Uh huh," I reply dully and begin drying our breakfast dishes. Of course I'm not spilling red blood over the weathered grey floorboards, but there's no doubt that an air of depression seeps from my skin, following me like a cloud of bad scent.

"Well, time to put a bandage on the wound. It'll heal soon enough if you let it," she wisely counsels. Is she speaking about the fresh gash on my heart from Jack, or the festering sore that won't heal closed until I find out what really happened to Daddy? Because the latter won't heal until it's clean, and the deeper I go, the dirtier it's getting.

"Did you know, Mama, that when Daddy died, Madge told Claire and George that we didn't want to be in the family anymore, since we didn't 'have to be'?" My outrage hurls the words out into the air.

"*What?*" Mama's shocked response is so genuine that I know this information is new to her.

"Yeah, Claire didn't even know that we've been living on this farm for a decade."

Mama's mouth sets in a tight line. "Claire? When did you see Claire? Oh, at the Sharpe's." Her large, beautiful eyes look dull. "Sorry." She knows that since he revealed his engagement to me, Jack has become a taboo subject.

I've become a miserable skunk, spraying on everyone and everything in defense. The stench of my misery saturates the entire house, but I can't clear it away. Everything reminds me of Jack, and I have nowhere to run to escape these memories. It makes it so much harder to forget someone when they've been to your home, your barn, your hospital, your orchard, your river. Spray, spray; smelly spray. Tilly can barely keep her hooves planted still for the weak monologue I've been providing her each day. It's a wonder I have a drop of her milk to deliver.

Regardless of my personal tragedy, life rolls on. Even with her softened dictatorship over me, Adler doesn't allow days off to nurse a broken heart; so I am off to the hospital to drown my sorrows in urine samples, paperwork, and bed pans. My feet still ache from the torturous acrobatics the heels I'd worn to the Sharpes had demanded that night, and from running all the way home from their estate in my bare feet. The bruises on my soles echo the bruises on my heart.

Just as I turn off of Radcliffe down the road to the trolley stop and my sore feet twinge in pain, a long, creamy white Rolls Royce slows along next to me; its presence wildly out of place on these dusty farm roads. A crease appears between my brows, but I keep walking. The Rolls crawls alongside me, keeping pace, even when I quicken my steps. My neck tingles with the feeling that I'm being watched, so I slow to the crawl of a tortoise. Its whitewall tires roll along in time with my steps.

The rear window slides down smoothly. "Penelope Hale?"

I halt; so does the car. "Yeah?"

"Get in."

I peer into the dark interior of the car, but the figure inside is protected by darkly shaded windows. I jump back a little when the back door pops open. My heart, which has felt tired and sagging these last few days, begins a lively death march.

Don't just hop into a dark car with a stranger! Sense chastens, pushing back against my curiosity.

"May I ask what for?" What is a Rolls Royce doing on this side of the tracks?

"I'm sure you'd like a ride to Saint Christopher's, wouldn't you?" the silky female voice coaxes.

Hasn't your mother taught you anything?

"I was just walking to the trolley stop."

Curiosity killed the cat! Sense screams in my head.

My feet protest and the door swings wider. I surrender to my curiosity. *Clink, clink;* two more pennies for May's indoor toilet fund.

Inside, perched on the cool leather seat, my eyes slowly adjust to the dim light. This person knows I volunteer at the hospital.

What else do they know about me?

EIGHTEEN

"Miss Hale," floats off the tongue of my companion. "I was hoping we could come to some sort of agreement." Still hazy, my eyes strain to place her shadowed features.

"May I ask with whom this agreement would be?" I ask in my best imitation of Emily Post. Nervous and guarded, I cross and re-cross my legs several times. I can't seem to remember how to sit properly.

The mystery woman's laugh tinkles lightly in the air.

"My dear," she draws out the endearment with a warmth that feels ice cold to me. "Surely you must recognize the mother of your beau." She leans in a bit with her dry laugh, and suddenly I know exactly whose car I'm in. Jack's mother. The gatekeeper who slammed the gate on me.

My stomach spasms and I sit up ramrod straight to reply, "You're mistaken, Ma'am. I don't have a beau."

Her warm laughter drips with condescension.

"Please, Darling, don't call me 'Ma'am'! You'll make me feel *old*." She flicks her thin wrist. While there's no mistaking this woman is devastatingly beautiful, her features have indeed wilted with age. She definitely qualifies as a 'Ma'am'. "And there's no need for falsehoods with me; Jack's told me *all* about you." I blink rapidly, trying to match the serene, sleepy eyes, tiny nose and sultry lips across from me with her anger-distorted face that night at Jack's house.

"Pardon me, er, *Miss*;" I try, though I know she's married and should be at least a 'Madam'. However, I don't want to be scolded again for acknowledging her age. "But, if he's told you everything, then you must have heard how I slugged him and ran away as soon as I heard about his engagement," I tell her, fighting the bitter warble in my voice. I want nothing more than to get out of this car, sore feet and indoor toilet fund or not. My bottom scoots across the leather seat toward the door.

Her pause tells me that this is new information for her.

"Hard to get, hmm?" She looks down her nose at her long, dainty fingers that drum on her thigh. It's a wonder she can lift them, what with the heavy baubles that weigh each thin one down. "I've played that game in my day, Darling. *Hardly* one to keep a man away. In fact, any girl worth her salt should know that that game is a very attractive invitation for a fellow." The long, sweeping lengths of her lashes fly upward, and her eyes dissect me.

I feel like I'm on trial, and I shift uncomfortably on the leather seat. Missus Sharpe's quietly dominating presence causes a chill to run up my spine.

"What is it that you want from me, Missus Sharpe?" I ask, my hand on the door. We can't be moving much faster than a galloping horse, and I've fallen from Nell's back plenty of times, back when she could still move faster than a turtle. If I can open the door and jump out...

"You may call me Ruby, for now. Naturally, dear, my son's preoccupation with you is a problem. I want you to end it, immediately. Now, do I make myself clear?" She says this to me as though she's giving an order to her servant. I get the feeling that she doesn't meet with any resistance very often. Like a petulant princess, she expects me to follow her command.

Didn't she hear me? "I *did* end it."

"No, no, my dear; whatever you did, you left him pining after you."

I sigh. Girl's games are not my area of expertise.

I don't have room in my head for *'Twenty Six Ways to Make Him Notice You'* and the other cheesecake articles in the Vogue magazines in the hospital lobby. Doris flips through them all of the time, but I actually work when I'm at work.

"I don't know how to play those games, Ruby," I tell her honestly, shrugging.

She scans me up and down and smirks. "Dear, you don't have to; those legs and lips play all the games for you."

Should I take that as a compliment? I wonder. It certainly doesn't make me feel too swell, in this context.

"End it with *finality*," she insists. "And it wouldn't hurt if you 'forgot' to wear lipstick when you did it, hmm?" She stares at my legs longingly, sighing. I try to tuck them away, but there is nowhere else to put them. I wish I were wearing pants.

"Why should I do that? I don't want to hurt him." Even though I'm still spitting mad at Jack, I really don't wish for him to feel as awful as I have felt these last few days.

"If you ever cared for my boy, then you will allow him the kind of marriage that will keep him elevated. Marrying *down* would just damage his social standing, close doors and waste opportunities for him..."

My cheeks flush hot and pink as I choke out, "I never- I wasn't trying to *marry* him!" I reconsider jumping from the car, half because I'm uncomfortable and half because I suddenly feel like I'm going to lose my breakfast all over this fancy upholstery.

"Silly girl! What do you think that seeing someone socially is for? *Fun?*" she guffaws, rolling her large brown eyes.

My eyes stare at her blankly, focusing hard on calming the inferno of my cheeks. Breathe in, breathe out. Deep breath in...

"It's like trying on dresses, dear. When you find one you like, you buy it."

I have no memory of dress shopping in a boutique, choosing whichever I like. My scanty wardrobe consists of mended hand me downs and skirts sewn from scraps.

"Well I really wouldn't know," I retort, holding my throat with one hand, the other set of fingers gripping the door handle.

Her eyes light up. "That's precisely my point! You're from completely different stock, Dear."

That's what I'd told Claire. Ruby needn't press this point on me. As the car rolls to a stop at a four way, I throw the door open, legs fumbling their way free of the cage. I don't bother retorting that the stock I'm from is far wealthier than she could ever hope to be. It doesn't matter, because even with my pedigree, I milk a cow and shovel poop on a daily basis.

"End it!" she calls out after me in a sing song voice. The fine car jerks forward, and my door closes on its own. Though unsaid, I heard the pressure of the words, "or else" in her tone.

Even though I made it out with my handbag and both of my shoes, I still feel she's somehow taken something away from me.

I try to make it through my chores, but I just can't shake the bothersome memory of the way Ruby looked down at me. It's as if her opinion is a horde of tiny fleas crawling all over my skin, and I can't brush them all away. They're irritating and uncomfortable.

The thought pops into my head that if I had grown up on the Hale estate, she'd be simpering at my feet, sending me fruit baskets and inviting me to tea. She'd use those sultry lips to coax me into friendship. She'd be begging me to court and marry her handsome son, not to break his heart. I'm beyond disgusted. I can't help but wonder, *Did my worth really disappear when my trust fund did?*

No, you're still the same girl, Sense insists.

Am I?

The lips and legs that she insists have drawn

Jack in have grown just the same as they would've in the estate. My hands, though calloused, were destined to be just this size and shape regardless of my upbringing. The features of my face were decided long before I moved to the old farm. I try to envision myself, where I would be this very moment, if my daddy had never died.

With Ruby's prejudice against me, just because I'm poor, I realize that I've been given a gift by growing up on the farm. I've learned how to work. I've had to fight for everything I own, so I appreciate every one of my meager belongings. Instead of spending my years perfecting my posture, I was forced to forge a path for myself; and because of that, I discovered an aptitude for nursing. I developed strength. Sure, my muscles are strong, but I'd also gained real inner strength through all of this. My personal worth isn't measured in riches!

Ruby doesn't want me, but neither do I want anything to do with her.

October 20th, 1941

Fall is the season for lovers, snuggling close together against the cold as they walk, the buzzing warmth in their hearts setting their faces aglow. To someone trying to stifle hope and warmth in herself, these couples are supremely irritating. They're all out this evening, as though just to torture me on my eighteenth birthday.

As I walk from Saint Christopher's to catch the trolley, the Friday afternoon witching hour has just begun; couples, couples everywhere. Holding hands, laughing, blushing. It gouges my belly so that I'm truly near retching when I reach the trolley bench, where I can finally avert my eyes from oncoming walkers. I plop my bag down and stretch out my legs. I click my heels together idly, imagining they are clad in red sparkles and I can be home already, out of the depths of this sea of gaiety.

"Excuse me, Miss," a particularly wrinkled old man in a bow tie and vest rouses me from my reverie. I look up at him, standing next to the bench. "You've dropped this," he says and smiles kindly, handing me a slip of paper, which is folded in half. Clearly the effort of standing back up is a strenuous move for him. I don't recognize ever having picked up this paper, let alone dropping it. *A mysterious birthday gift?*

"Thank you, sir," I say with skepticism as I take the paper and sit up straight, studying the deep wrinkles in the man's face as his lips curl into a grin. Clearly this isn't his first smile. Complex webs surround his eyes, folding easily into his ancient laugh lines. Deep ravines run from his nose to his chin, with graduating wrinkles rippling out onto his cheeks as though a pebble has been thrown in water.

His drooping cheeks hang from his jawbone, giving him the look of a ventriloquist's puppet. I contemplate what the man sees in my own young face. The despair I'm wallowing in won't produce wrinkles in happy shapes like his. Surely, I'll be a hag by the age of twenty.

I manage a small smile for him. He looks satisfied, and continues a crooked hobble down the street. I open the paper, revealing masculine penmanship. The letters look practiced, near perfect, as though a tutor has spent many lessons urging the writer to hone the skill. *Jack's writing.* It reads *Ruth 1:16-17.*

He's brought the Bible into our argument. Stubborn mule. *How can someone argue with the word of God?* In my mind, I scan through Bible stories. *Ruth, Ruth...*

I'm suddenly desperate for a pair of Dorothy's red sparkling shoes so I can be home, at our mantle with our old family Bible, where I can read this passage. *Why can't I remember it?*

I tear down the street, ignoring the disapproval of my sore feet as I run. I'm eager to get to that Bible. If only Reverend Bell could see me now! The trolley that stops at nearly every corner won't be quick enough for my burning curiosity.

When I get home and pull the Bible off the mantle, I feel a pang of guilt that I have to blow dust from its cover. *Ruth, Old Testament or New?* My fingers fan the delicate red-edged pages, giving me a flicker show of the words in the top right corner: *Genesis, Exodus, Leviticus.... Ah hah! Ruth!*

"16: And Ruth said, entreat me not to leave thee, or to return from following after thee: for whither thou goest, I will go; and where thou lodgest, I will lodge: thy people shall be my people, and thy God my God:

17: Where thou diest, will I die, and there will I be buried: the Lord do so to me, and more also, if ought but death part thee and me."

Twin tears slide down my cheeks, dripping onto my collar as Mama walks by.

"Aw, Penny, it does my heart some good to see you feasting upon the word," she swoons, nodding in approval and going on her way.

If Jack truly claims that death alone can keep us apart, than I hope he knows what his mother is clearly capable of. She terrifies me. There isn't a chance I will fit in among 'his people'; is he really willing to sink down and dwell among 'my people'? *What can I possibly offer him that's worth abandoning a life of comfort?* Perhaps he doesn't truly realize that his family will shun him in half a minute for marrying so far beneath him. Does he know how hard he'll have to work to support a family without a endless flow of family funds? His perfect hands will become calloused and rough from hard work. In fact, we'll barely have time to spend together. He'll work long hours, and I'll be engaged in cooking, cleaning and caring for our children from sunup till long after the sun goes down. And what if he dies? I'll be left to scramble for bread just as my mother does now. And our children will have to work instead of learning and imagining and playing. Childhood is a short season for the offspring of the poor.

Even with this threat on my mind, the flattened happiness I've shoved into deep, dark corners shakes off the dust. Apparently, we have something together that Jack finds worth his downgrading to a gal with ragged fingernails. I feel confused, but excited. Hope-filled, but at the same time, hopeless. Happy, angry, lovesick, and afraid. There is only one thing I can do with all this unbridled emotion.

The screen door bangs behind me. I know just where I need to go.

I'm not sure what I expect to happen, but my eager legs move in long strides. A trail of dust dances behind me as I make my way toward the familiar tree line ahead.

When I brush aside the sweeping tendrils of the willow, which have faded from green to golden, I sigh at the sight of the empty riverbank in front of me. There were no tire tracks in the road; no shiny black Merc parked on the trail. I shouldn't have expected to see him here, but my heart falls even so. The tiny glimmer of hope inside of me that survived the train-wreck attempt at meeting his parents had indeed expected him to be waiting here.

Without even thinking about it, my feet slip out of my shoes and I start over the cool grey rocks, seeking comfort in the river as they have done hundreds of times. With the crisper air, the water doesn't bring the same relief to my soles as it does in deep, sweltering summer. I teeter across the log to the base of the jumping rocks, and hoist myself up. At the tip-top of the ledge, I lean back on my palms and listen to the autumn wind rustle the dying leaves.

Think he has brought Samantha here? Imp asks. My stomach turns. This place, so far out of town that its guaranteed solitude, but whimsical and green, has its own special magic. It's a wonderful spot to inspire romance.

Naw, Sense replies. *This is our place.* Jack wouldn't betray me like that.

Oh, but he has, Imp insists. My heart squeezes.
Will it always hurt to be here?

Out of the corner of my eye, I catch movements. I automatically swivel my head down toward it, expecting to see a family of thirsty deer. The willow's swaying wisps bend unnaturally, and Jack appears. He stops, rests a palm on his stomach, his thumbnail on his lower lip. The leaves rustle with a strong gust of wind, and he walks forward to the bank. He settles himself onto the rocks, heaving a sigh, and his shoulders slump.

He doesn't see me up here, I realize. It feels sort of wrong and impish to spy on him; but after all, I submit to Imp's advice quite often. It's who I am. Rooted in place behind the rock, staying absolutely still, I observe him quietly while his brows pull together, forming two lines between them. He stares solemnly at the river. Stones plop into the water, some skimming the surface, some just plunking on in.

I watch his head fall between his knees. I've never seen his strong, confident body look so broken and sad. His back begins to shake. When he finally looks up, he cups his hand over his mouth and I can see lines of moisture running off of his chin and down his throat. He drags his thumb under each eye.

He's crying.

After awhile, he puffs out a breath that I can't hear over the wind, but I can see the movement in his chest and cheeks. He starts to stand.

You can't just let him leave! screams Sense.

"Leaving already?" I call out. His head snaps up

and he looks around. When his eyes find mine, they are large and full of wonder. The rogue lock of hair on his crown sways in the wind. He looks like a young boy until a determined look washes over his features and he steps over to the jumping rocks.

In the minute it takes him to climb, I wipe my clammy palms on my skirt and smooth my hair. I bite and lick my lips to make them pink and soft. I breathe as deeply as I can to steady my pulse, wiping my palms again. And again.

When I see the top of his head rise over the last rock, I tuck my legs hastily under me in a ladylike fashion, giving my palms one last swipe over the fabric of my skirt.

"Pip," he breathes, his mouth spreading into a smile. "You got my note."

"Yes, I did," I say, shifting my legs around. Swipe. "And you called *me* stubborn." We smile together, though it does little to soothe me. Questions swirl around in my head: *did Jack ask the old man to give me the note? Or, did he somehow slip it to me earlier, and I really had dropped it? How could Jack be sure I'd meet him here when I'd read it? What exactly does he want? Should I even be here?* Relentless buckets of sweat pour from my palms.

"I wasn't sure you'd know to come here," he says, looking from my right eye to my left and right again.

"But you did." A tiny smile plays on his lips. The creases appear beside them, and I am undone.

"This is *my* thinking place," I argue possessively. Before his smile can completely suck me in, I come right out with it.

"What do you want, Jack?" I question, finding it difficult to keep my guard up with the stark blue of his eyes directly in my view. "Why would you want me?"

He frowns thoughtfully. "Want. You."

My fingers idly run over the mended tears of my hem. My eyes register the dusty cake on my feet and legs, the bruises on my shins, the scabs on my knees. I examine my fingernails, bitten short but still with enough length to hold crescents of brown grime underneath them. I am no match for his debutant. My mouth puckers sourly.

"Yeah, when this other gal can offer you so much more."

"Penelope," he begins, sounding a lot like Mama opening up a lecture. "So much more of what?"

"Please don't call me that. It makes me feel like I'm in trouble," I say.

"You are in trouble," Jack argues. "If you don't realize why I want you, then we're both in trouble. I don't understand what you think will make my life so much better with an arranged marriage. So I can be sure my wife knows just how to hold out her pinkie while she's drinking tea?" In my lap, my pinkie twitches. I haven't even begun to perfect that art. "So I can be sure that she's only marrying me for my family's money? So I can never make a choice on my own? So I can be certain to make the guest list of every high-hat's party? I don't care about that fuddy-duddy Fifth Avenue scene, Doll." His voice is so sure, so even, that I know he means it. Perhaps I need to be the one to shake some sense into him.

"I mean, doesn't this Deb realize that her fiancee is chasing some other gal?" I contend. "Doesn't this mess things up for you? What if your mother disowns you? You barely know me, and you're throwing away your future on the chance that you might still like me once you do." I feel a sinking surge of self doubt in my belly. There's so much more to living with privilege than the short list he has provided. I was robbed of the opportunity to be a child when my days filled up with hard labor and farm chores.

He's quiet for a moment; pensive, with his thumbnail resting against his lower lip. It aches, how handsome he looks this way.

"When a fella dates a gal, she puts her best foot forward. Rouge, stockings, earrings, the whole bit. She smiles and agrees with him, laughs whether she thinks his jokes are funny or not, barely eats a bite from her plate so he won't think she's a pig." He shakes his head. "But you, Penelope, you've been fighting me from the beginning!"

I think of the day I met him, dripping with grimy water, snatching my hand away when he'd tried to hold it. Ruby was right; I guess he does like 'hard to get'. My lips twist into a bitter scowl.

"Thrill of the hunt, huh?"

"Pffha! I don't know many 'hunters' who'll shovel horse crap to catch a kill," he looks at me pointedly with those big blue eyes.

I smile shyly, slightly softened. What he's saying *is* true. There's got to be much easier prey in this town.

He continues. "Naw, it's that I know you're not just putting me on; showing me what you think I want to see. I know you don't mind getting dirty when you need to. I know that you know how to work hard and take pride in it. I know you're not a pampered princess who thinks only of her next whim. I know you're strong and you can handle just about anything," he ticks off on his fingers. "And I know you're not afraid to eat."

Blood rushes to my cheeks. Feeding me must be like watching a pig at its trough.

"I know you're brave enough to defend a friend," he continues, and I think of Nurse Adler, and Doris. "And tough enough to knock a slimeball where it hurts."

I shudder as Stark's wet breath comes to mind. My earlobe crawls at the thought of his creepy tongue touching it.

"I know you have the softest, sweetest lips I've ever kissed," he declares, resting his fingertips lightly on my lower lip. The spot ignites with heat where they touch.

My eyes close involuntarily with pleasure.

"And the way you are with your little sister... Well, let's just say, I can tell you're going to be one heck of a mother."

I choke. He is pretty forward thinking if he's considering my parenting skills.

"Wha- a mother?"

"You were right, I *have* been thinking about my future. Only, I just can't see one with a drag like Samantha. I want my kids to have fun, and run and play, and jump off rocks, and know their mama is someone to look up to. Someone like you." He looks directly into my eyes.

"You want me to..." I cough. "...have your *babies?*"

He scoots over, kneeling right in front of me. He takes both of my hands, running his thumbs over my rough, cracked knuckles.

He whispers, "I realized something when I didn't get to see you every day: I missed you. Before I met you I was just fine on my own. But now... I need you, P. I-"

I hold up a firm hand to stop him. I feel what is coming, and I scan through the visions I'd created as a little girl, making sure this moment will live up to her starry-eyed expectations. I nod, satisfied, and drop my hand, allowing him to continue.

"I'm in love with you, Miss Penelope Hale."

An explosion bursts from my heart, sending sparks shooting down my spine and out my limbs. My fingers and toes have gone numb, and my head is pleasantly dizzy. Young Me could have never foreseen a feeling quite like this. Ruby may think I'm lower than dirt, but she hasn't effectively passed on her blinders to her son. He loves me, for me. My fingers run over the ragged edges of my nails, for once not feeling humbled by them.

I stare into his eyes, trying to see past the vivid colors into the depths of emotion behind them. He's true and kind. He isn't fooling himself; what we have is real. I open the hatch that I've stuffed my feelings for him into, allowing them to float freely to the surface while I examine them closely. It's my turn to realize something.

I pull his neck to mine and take in deep breaths of his skin. The tip of my nose runs up his neck, over his jaw and across his cheek until it finds his nose. My weight shifts to my knees and I cradle his head in my fingers as I stare into the hypnotic bursts of yellow in his eyes.

"Well, that's the best birthday gift a gal could've asked for," I grin. He rolls his eyes at me. "I love you, too, Jack." A feeling explodes from my chest, and I know it's true.

He settles his lips over my upper lip, and rests them ever so lightly there. My lower lip drops open, welcoming the fullness of his pout between them. His palms rest on my cheeks and cool the fire that's blazing there. He wraps his forearms around my back, holding us as close as two sheets of paper.

"I want you to marry me, Pip," he breathes into my ear. The little girl dreaming of her proposal could not fathom the trembling warmth that runs through me, the shiver of my spine, or the feeling of nestling into the very spot you are meant to be in life.

Does he want to get kicked out of his family? Sense pipes up. I deflate a little. I wonder if he's really thought this through.

"Jack, you know your mother..." I begin, and he rolls his eyes. "She, um, gave me a ride and we had a little chat. She was quite... convincing."

His face slackens and he blows out a puff of air. I can tell he knows the exact purpose and pretense of the "ride".

"Sheesh! She is relentless!"

And smart. Admit it: she's wise enough to know that this wasn't over, adds Sense.

"She 'asked' me to end things with you," I continue.

Imp laughs, *Ha! Ask? More like 'command'.*

"And I don't think I'm doing a very good job," I admit.

A terrible job! Sense corrects.

"My mother likes to meddle," he explains with a grimace.

Meddle? Imp asks sarcastically. *Like a general 'meddles' with his troops! She ran you over like a tank!*

I try to shut out the loud voices in my head. I don't want to be distracted from the nice view in front of me.

He sighs, and it deflates his countenance.

"You're going to let my mother keep us from being together?"

"Can you just talk to her, Jack? To see how she'd feel about it? Maybe if she really knew your heart wasn't in it with Samantha," I start, but deep down, I think Ruby isn't the type to change her mind over something as trivial as his feelings.

"Please? I mean, I... I want me to marry you, too." We laugh together. I feel like a shaken, bubbly bottle of soda waiting to burst. "I just won't do it if it will ruin your life."

He bites his lip.

"Sure, I'll talk to her." In his tone of voice, I hear his skepticism. His mother is very set in her ways, I'm learning.

We rise together, and walk to the sheer drop-off before us. Here we stand as a couple. We're fully clothed on the ledge, ready to take a plunge into the icy swirls below, when a nagging thought pokes at me.

Naw, don't ruin the moment, Sense halts me from speaking it aloud. Something he'd said is nagging me-- something he'd said about kissing my sweet lips.

No, go ahead, let's find out, Imp urges.

"So, precisely how many lips *have* you kissed?"

NINETEEN

October 24th, 1941

"Mama?" I begin tentatively, wringing my hands.

She hums as she rinses clods of dirt from dark green leaves of kale, but she gives me a sideways glance to indicate that her attention is mine. Her eyes assess my new, perked-up countenance.

I clear my throat. "I have something to tell you."

"Oh?"

"It's about Jack," I continue shakily. "And me."

She smiles, and the years fall away from her face. "So, you're finally admitting you're sweet on him, huh? Oh, Penny, I knew you wouldn't be able to stay away from that darling fellow for long." She shakes water from the bunch of kale in her fist and turns to me, leaning her hip against the sink.

"Between you and me, I think he's rather handsome." Mama's brow arches over a sparkling look in her eyes.

"Oh. You like him, then?"

"Well, besides his unfortunate family tree, who couldn't adore a sweetheart like Jack? Makes me feel like the boys are home again." With her indulgent girl talk, and the softness in her smile, a ribbon of warm hope dances in my veins along with nervous adrenaline. This is going well.

"Good, because..., he, uh..." my cheeks ignite, "he asked me to marry him."

The kale hits the floor with a leafy thunk. Mama's lashes flutter faster than a moth's wings while she musters a forced grin.

"You're pulling my leg, aren't you?" Her eyes search mine for a hint of a joke. "My *barely eighteen-year-old* daughter can't possibly be telling me that a fellow she's known for a couple of months proposed marriage to her," her tone and stature grow with each word; "and that she is actually considering abandoning her dreams, *not to mention her family,* to accept that proposal!"

The Stare flares hot in her eyes, and my tiny thread of hope is washed away with a fresh wave of anxiety.

"You didn't accept, did you?"

"No," I answer in a tiny voice, and hope brightens her face. Before it glows too brightly there, I continue, "I'm waiting to hear how his family will take the idea." The glow burns out. I wipe my palms over my shirt, heart pounding.

"This is my new new dream, Mama." I assure her, my voice weak and wobbly.

"Penny!" she gasps in irritation and pinches the bridge of her nose, as though she can barely handle me. She leans her thin frame heavily on the sink.

"This dream still includes my career, Mama," I assure her.

"You are smarter than this," she jeers. She whispers a word under her breath that sounds like "lust".

My face flushes as red as a beet, humiliated by her assumption. "Lust" belittles the feelings Jack and I share to an animal instinct.

"This is not *lust*, Mama!" Oh, crackers. The claws-bared, reckless tiger in me has reappeared for a fight. Mama has a special way of drawing her out. In this way, I do give in to an animal instinct.

"Doris is lying in a hospital bed because the man she lusted after got her pregnant and then ripped the baby right out of her body! Then a bunch of creeps came after Nurse Adler to attack her, and one of them cut my neck with a broken bottle!"

As I shudder, recalling the feeling of Stark's thin, odorous body pressed up against mine, breathing his rancid breath onto my skin, Mama's large blue eyes go still and wide. They fall to the diagonal pink scar on my neck with sudden awareness of its presence there, and so I stretch my shirt collar wider for her view.

"Yes, Mama, I am aware that some fellas out there would be an unwise bet. I get it! But do you know who stopped that hooligan from completely slitting my throat? *Jack!*" I release my collar, and it snaps back into place.

Mama's own feral animal joins in the scuffle.

"Do you think that reminding me of the evils out in this world really make me want to turn you loose into it?"

"Gahhh!" I growl, exasperated. I cannot win with this woman. "Jack is a good man!" She rolls her eyes.

"*Man?* Penny, please, he's still just a boy! And I am not half as concerned about him as I am about his parents. You have no idea... oh, my. You don't even have their blessing to run off and get married!" Her head bobbles on her neck, daring me to contend with that fact.

I think of Ruby's warm, silky voice, urging me to end my relationship with Jack. *Can she can be convinced to forget the social power a union with the Barrett family will gain for her?* I can't begin to compete with Samantha's fortune. *What can I offer to Ruby? An old horse? A stubborn milk cow? An orchard of peach trees?*

"Not *yet*," I point out quietly. "But maybe." I sincerely hope Jack's talk with his own mother is going better than this one. Mama's doing an excellent job of trampling all over my happy flame, stamping out the coals.

"Hmmph!" she scoffs. Her face darkens. "I knew it, Penny, I knew it! When you brought him home, I knew he'd be a load of trouble for you." While she tosses the kale into the sink, she wears a wry smile that looks ugly on her pretty lips. Her nostrils flare over and over with yet unexpressed emotion.

She murmurs, "He even had me drawn in." It's true; Jack had somehow flipped Mama's opinion of him. Unfortunately, with both hands grasping the sides of the sink and her back hunched like she's about to vomit into the basin, I think it's flipped right back. All of her original bitterness toward the wealthy is resurrected, stronger than before, and concentrated on Jack. A tsunami of resentment and anguish floods over her; and Jack is caught right in that killer tide.

Suddenly, her face awakens with surprise and she whispers harshly, "You... are you *with child*, Penelope?" as her eyes narrow into The Stare.

I sputter as I reply, "N-*no!*" I recoil as though her accusation were a venomous snake. "Mama, I would never!" Truthfully, virtuous thoughts are difficult to cling to when I'm with Jack, but I decided long ago not to let things get quite *that* hot before a honeymoon. I just bottle it up, waiting to pop the cork on my wedding night.

"I'm not *loose!* We haven't even come close to... y'know..." My cheeks deepen to a record-setting shade of red, finishing the sentence that I cannot.

My reaction must be enough for her, because The Stare melts from her features. Through a tight grimace on her lips, I sense a hint of her satisfaction that she has at least raised me to be virtuous.

However, she's still shaking her head when she says, "I can't believe you didn't tell me someone threatened your life. And now you're threatening to run off and get..." she pants breathlessly, "...*married!*" With her tone, she may have well said, *"run off and join the circus!"*

"Sorry to disappoint you, Mother! Maybe I knew I'd be nagged to death if I did!" My chest rises and falls heavily, drawing steaming hot breaths that fail to relieve the tightness around my heart.

Mama looks stung.

"If you leave, I'll have to sell the cow. I cannot possibly take on another chore, and May is loaded enough with duties for a little girl." She places her hands on her hips, right at her apron string, to show her seriousness.

I narrow my eyes at her. May hardly pulls half the weight I did at her age, and milking and deliveries barely use up an hour of the day. Mama is just playing dirty.

"You wouldn't sell Tilly,"   I growl, and immediately wish I hadn't said it with so much emotion. If I'd played it coy, I would've taken away the advantage of her threat. I scramble to gain back the dominant position in this argument.

"Speaking of sharing the truth, thank you, Mama, for lying to me for ten years about how Daddy died." My eyes go steeled and hard while my heart slams into my chest wall again and again. Allowing myself to get this angry feels like teetering on a thin tightrope high up in the air, terrifying and thrilling.

Mama's eyes glisten with anger and sadness, enhanced by a sheen of fresh wetness.

"There have been angry theories, Penelope, but I have never told you a lie." Her voice trembles as her eyes fill with tears.

I hate that I'm so sensitive to crying. It's hard to be as mad when there are tears involved. Guilt cuts across my swollen heart with its burning blade.

"Withholding the truth is exactly the same as lying, Mama."

She walks for the door, tears spilling over her lower lids. "Your behavior is hardly proving you're adult enough to get *married*, Penelope!" Penelope. She is angry.

Apparently, I'm only allowed to have her love if

I do exactly as she says. I scan my thoughts to find another time that I've strayed from her word. No, this will be the first.

Acid eats away at the walls of my stomach, dripping in clumps down into my legs. How foolish I had been to trust her affection. What an idiot to feel safe in the net of her "love"! I can see in her belittling look that she will never respect my opinion unless it's perfectly in line with hers.

While I take her in, this new woman who I'm not sure I know at all, she sees my look and blows a pale lock of hair from her eyes with an exasperated *"puff"* and throws up her hands. Then she walks out the door. It hits the frame with a resounding bang.

As Mama abandons our argument, I ache to feel anything but this naked, vulnerable feeling. It's cold and far too much like losing my dad: solid ground turning into tissue; truth being turned upside down; feeling like I can't trust anything I know, or any*one*. Mercifully, hatred slips in, hotter than scorching, even, and wraps around my pain, choking it out. Fierce throbs of hot blood course through me.

I embrace the heat as it fills my emptiness.

I *hate* her right now.

November 1st, 1941
"May," I whisper, shaking her shoulder. "Mayhem, wake up."

She moans, and nestles deeper into her pillow.

"May!" I lick my pointer finger and give her ear a wet willie.

Her eyelids flutter, revealing a sleepy, annoyed look in her eyes.

"Shhh," I mouth softly with my damp finger to my lips.

She follows me on tiptoe out to the barn.

"What are we doing?" she complains, rubbing her eyes; but she sounds curious. I lead her inside and we shuffle through the straw toward Tilly. She needs to learn Tilly's secrets for after I'm gone. Jack has a gift prepared for Mama: enough wages to cover two farm hands for a decade; but I can't leave the handling of my best friend to some stranger. Tilly needs someone special to look after her. So does May.

"Why are we..." she complains, grinding at the sleep in her eyes with her fists. "I'm going back to bed."

"No! May." My tone halts her parting steps. "I may not be around forever. You need to learn this stuff," I explain while trying to impress the gravity of the situation upon her with the intensity of my expression. "And I've got to show you how to do your hair each day..."

Her eyes search mine in the low light. "What, are you dying, Sis?" She scrunches her nose skeptically before her face alights with understanding.

"You're going to run away?   With him?" Suddenly, she doesn't seem so sleepy. "No! No," she whines. "Don't leave! You can't marry him!"

My brows pull together. I feel a repeat lecture coming on, and I brace myself.

"This isn't nineteen-twelve, P! You can wait a little longer these days!"

As if I'm marrying him to save myself from becoming a spinster.

"And, you know..." she trails off, piquing my curiosity despite my defiance. She's not bringing *him* up, I hope.

"...Phin will be back in town for Christmas, when they're all on leave."

"Pffsha!" I sputter. "What, you want me to *wait* for him before I decide on another guy? What for? So Phin can look right through me, like I'm made of glass?" My arms slap pitifully at my sides.

"He's paid more attention to you than you think," she argues, and I hate that my heart flips hopefully at her words. I hate myself even more for entertaining her argument.

"What do you mean?" I ask guardedly, inching a toe toward the idea.

"Ha! I knew it!" she caws, a mischievous look on her face. "You like him!"

You love him, Sense corrects.

"Are you just pulling my leg?" What a mean thing to do. *Mayhem.*

"Aw, c'mon P, you never noticed how he always helped you with your chores before you all left for the woods?" she challenges with a hand on her hip. Every summer, Phin, who didn't have a list of daily labor at home, would show up each day on his bicycle to help hurry along our farm chores so we could get to The Spot more quickly. I had noticed his help, but I thought it was chivalrous pity.

"And when Eddie and Max would take off, he'd hang back a little and wait for you?" My mind searches my memories. At the time they happened, I was far too busy denying the possibility of feelings between us to notice anything like that; but I suppose he did usually pause at the edge of the orchard until he saw me coming. It makes my toes tingle to think that I may have been something special to him once. But now? Now someone thinks I'm more than special, and I plan to marry him. It would be so much easier to do with some support from my family.

"Didn't you read Max's letter, May? Phin's keeping pretty busy with the naval nurses and local gals lining up for him," I say with a sneer. "'sides, *Jack* loves me for real. Not some 'maybe' in a memory." I feel my heart glow for Jack.

"I just think you're rushing this." In the low light, her eyes are pleading. "What's the hurry?"

Samantha Barrett, Imp answers.

I drop to my knees next to Tilly and stroke her belly. *Are we moving too fast? How quickly could Jack and Samantha's grand wedding come together, anyhow?* Engraved invitations, a cake taller than May, fresh flowers, a custom-made lace gown for the bride. Surely a gal prestigious enough to gain Ruby's approval wouldn't settle for a thrown-together affair. This would be the biggest day of Samantha's life! That is, if her groom were planning to show up.

"C'mon May," I plead. "I get enough flak from Mama. Can you just be my sister for a minute and let me show you how this is done?" I run my hand down Tilly's back and find her sweet spot. She stands up on her hooves and presses her hip toward me, leaning into my circular scratching. May takes a step back in the hay.

"I'm sorry, P. I think you're making a huge mistake, and I can't help you make it," she says quietly. "And I can do my own hair. I just like spending time with you when you do it."

It would be a much bigger mistake to allow Jack to be pushed into a loveless marriage, on the sliver of hope that Phin ever cared about me.

"Fine! Well, good luck figuring out how to milk

her on your own," I warn, pulling the stool under me.

"Pfha!" She mimics squeezing imaginary teets with her fists and flippantly challenges, "How hard can it be to *mmn mnn?*"

Oh, she's in for it. There's so much more to milking this gal than squeezing her milk into the tin bucket. The only thing that ended my wrestling match with Tilly on the first day we met was her finally deciding that she wanted some relief from her bulging udders, and stopping in the middle of the tall grass so I could catch up to her with my bucket. We may have been equally-matched in stubbornness, but Tilly outweighed my seven-year-old self sixfold! Ah, well. With May's current attitude, I'd say she deserves to learn this the hard way.

That doesn't stop angry tears from coming when she stalks out of the barn.

November 8th, 1941

I'm walking down the cold, sterile hall of Saint Christopher's Hospital, ten paces from the supply closet. I feel the muscles in my back tense, followed by the prickle of the hairs on my neck rising to attention. I hate that closet. I actively push away the memory of the vivid red of Doris's blood from my thoughts.

A cold hand grazes the back of my arm.

"Aaaagh!" I shriek, jumping out of my skin.

"Hey, hey; it's just me," the hand's owner soothes in his low, honeyed voice.

Jack.

"You sure are wound up. Nervous about...?" he asks, turning his fingers around my bare left ring finger suggestively.

I shake my head. "No, it's just... that closet. I hate that closet," I accuse and point to the haunted door.

"Well, I have something that should soothe you," he suggests, swinging a bag around his shoulder. It hangs from a hook looped over his finger, sweeping down to where it brushes against his calves.

I reach out for the garment bag and he pulls it back, just out of my reach. I laugh and stretch farther. He flicks it a few more inches away. I stamp my foot, and his eyes crinkle happily while he lifts me by the waist with one arm and carries me, kicking, into the room across from the supply closet. We sweep under the curtain.

His nose buries in my hair, breathing hot breaths on my ear. I shiver. His mouth presses against my lips. I hear a rustling sound, and with my lips still on his, I look for the source in my peripheral vision. He holds the bag out just within my reach. I dive at it and pull the zipper down. I push the plastic off of the hanger. The glossy, sleek fabric can only mean one thing.

"You got it?"

He smiles. His eyes sparkle. "I got it," he says as his free hand wrestles a crinkling paper from his pocket. I rock to my toes and grin. We have a marriage license! And thanks to my fiancee, the dress I'll be married in hangs right in front of me. It's like a plastic sheath over my impending reality, and it forces an unpleasant question to my lips. I can't go through with this without knowing.

"Jack."

"Pip," he says as he mimics my serious expression.

"Jack, am I just your escape plan?" The thought has been brewing in my mind since my argument with Mama, when I'd retreated into the solitude of the barn, hiding among the hay bales. It's clear that that Jack doesn't want to marry Samantha. I've never met her, but to me, she represents the path Jack's parents have created for him. Marrying her would be giving in to that parental control. Marrying *me* is rebellion.

"Escape plan? From what?" his eyes appear truly confused. The solid picture in my head of his motivations goes fuzzy with his brow furrowed like that.

"You know: Samantha, your parents' wishes..."

He rolls his eyes upward and sighs.

"As for my parents, oh, Doll; this is *anything* but the easy road."

That's true. Ruby hadn't even entertained the idea of Jack marrying beneath him for a moment. I was disappointed, as was Jack, but when his mother fought back by arranging a full-page announcement in the society papers of his engagement to Samantha, we both felt the squeeze of time running out. "There'll be the devil to pay for running off with you. I just happen to think it's a very, very good idea anyway."

I'm skeptical. "A good idea to do it now, before the engraved invitations for your other wedding go out?"

The corner of his mouth slides up. I love that look; it intrigues me.

"I thought it would be cruel to allow that gal to plan a future with me when I have no intention of following through."

That is true; the poor gal. Jack *is* quite a catch. His sensitivity toward her endears him to me; he really is a good guy.

"The longer we wait; the heavier the damage. More people involved, more plans made, more money spent. I mean, the entire town thinks I intend to marry Samantha. So, I went to talk to her."

My mouth drops open involuntarily. I think of how it must have felt for her to be given bad news by her intended future husband.

"How did she take it? I mean, is she okay?" I wonder. I feel guilty for taking this dream from her.

Jack's expression is amused. "She was thrilled."

I blink twice. I have no words.

Who wouldn't want to marry a darb fella like Jack?

"It seems she doesn't like having her choices made for her, either."

My guilt for hurting her slips off of my shoulders like a blanket; I hadn't realized just how heavy it had felt there. Without that weight on me, I can take a deeper breath, but I'm still shrouded in a thick sadness because of my family.

He whispers behind his hand, "and just between you and me, she was wearing pants. That girl is a rebel!"

I don't know her at all, but I think I may just like Samantha Barrett.

"Thank you, Jack." My eyes well up a little. He puts his palms on my cheeks and searches my eyes. I realize that I've never before let someone look into my soul deeply.

"Are you all right? Do you need more time?" I know that he'd give it to me if that's what I wanted, especially since my early request didn't work out.

I shake my head. There's damage no matter what, or when. Once May lies in bed tonight, shoving her arm under her pillow as she always does to get comfortable, she'll find the letter I left for her there. She'll know that Jack has paid for two farm hands for the next ten years, but that I don't trust anyone else besides her to milk Tilly until Mama inevitably follows through with her threat and sells my cow. There's no doubt May will immediately tell Mama, who will be a boiling pot of fury and disappointment. I don't need more time, because more time means more pretending for Jack and me. Jack and Samantha, pretending to carry on their engagement to please their parents, keeping the wrath of Ruby off of me. May and Mama know me far too well not to see my real intentions in my face.

"Did you make the appointment at City Hall?"

"You doubt me," he accuses with one handsome eyebrow comically arched.

"When?"

"Well, all they could squeeze in on short notice is one-thirty."

I look up on the wall. "Forty five minutes? I'll still be on shift!"

"C'mon. Run away with me," he purrs into my hair. "Tell the boss you're sick or something."

It isn't a lie when I tell Nurse Adler that my stomach is upset. Each time I think of Mama's utter refusal to participate in my wedding day and her forbidding May to attend, my belly wrenches. Her threat to sell Tilly if I leave the farm boils the acid within, and I get a good hefty twist when I remember Jackson's sad look about his parents' reaction. Ruby's firm "end it" echoes in the mix of my anxieties.

Perhaps the worst ache of all is the empty hollow where Daddy should be. I never allowed myself to form a new thought about my wedding ceremony since I was a little girl imagining herself swathed in lace and satin, arm-in-arm with her daddy, marching proudly down the aisle toward her would-be husband. No picture has replaced it. It hurts to mourn him freshly.

Still, as we run through the relentless downpour outside toward the car, I'm sure. When we climb in the Merc and our winded, quick breaths fog up the glass, Jack draws a heart with his finger on the window, that surety solidifies to a concrete hardness. I know I'm making the right choice as we drive through torrential rain toward the courthouse under heavy, dark grey clouds. I just wish this trip felt less like two convicts on their way to rob a bank, and more like my wedding day. Perhaps a beam of encouraging sunlight through these ominous dark clouds would soothe me? A small break in the heavy, pounding rain?

"Hey, slow down," I tell Jack. Within the hour I'll be his wife, I justify, so I may as well get a jump start on the nagging. He's going at least ten miles an hour over the speed limit in this slush.

"Hey, and you're not even the missus yet," he jokes and winks at me. He has read my mind. It calms me to remember that we are so in sync, and I sigh contentedly as I feel the freight train of my pounding heart slow to a normal pace.

I sigh and lean into the door.

Jack is going to be my husband.

The nasally whine of a siren starts behind us. Jack's eyes jump to the rearview mirror.

"Aw, nuts." When a navy blue uniform approaches Jack's window, he rolls it down. An officer crouches to peek into the car.

"Well, I'll be," he says and relaxes onto the sill. "Sharpie."

"Hey, Dalton," Jack greets lazily, punching the officer lightly on the arm. They smile at each other while the rain drizzles on Dalton's head and into the car. His gaze finds me and runs from my head to feet and back up.

"Don't I know you, Dollface?"

"Yes, you took my report when I turned in that scumbag doc for attacking my friend."

"And then you kicked Stark right in the clams," he grins appreciatively.

"I hope Stark and the doc are sharing a cell," I retort. Dalton pushes an amused breath out of his nose, barely audible over the chorus of raindrops behind him.

"Well, aren't you a piece of work?" He cracks his neck and his eyes jump to Jack. "You look real gussied up there, Tiger. Where you headed?"

Because I feel as guilty as a convict, my heart revs in my chest at his question.

"City Hall," Jack answers smoothly.

"Oh," Dalton nods, then stiffens.

I stiffen along with him, bracing myself for his reaction. He's the first of our friends, family and acquaintances to know what we're up to, so whatever he says will represent all of them. "*Oh.*"

My heart falls at the note of disapproval in his voice.

"City Hall, huh? Your mother know about this, Sharpie?"

I can't see his eyes, but I know Jack glares at the policeman.

"Heard about your engagement, but I thought it was to a certain Miss Barrett. And you're off to sign papers with this... this..." Dalton lets the question die away as he looks at me mockingly.

My eyes close to escape this prickly moment. I can feel blood collecting in the skin of my face.

"My maid has this real doll of a daughter,"

Dalton begins, licking his lips hungrily. "And you know I've gone there," he laughs and shakes his head. "Mmm-mm. I mean, we've all gone slummin' a time or two, Sharpie, but you're really gonna take on this pretty little pile of trash over a *Barrett?*"

The car jostles, and I hear a sickening crunch. My eyes fly open. Jack leans halfway out the window with his feet in my lap, and Dalton is invisible from my view. Jack slips out and onto his feet. I crawl across the bench seat and peer out the window, where the officer lies curled up on the ground, the rain thinning the rivulets of blood that pour from his nose. The rain intensifies, and he bats his eyes to keep a clear view of his opponent. Jack stands over him, chest heaving.

"Jack! You're really sinking this low?" Dalton shouts over the rain and sissy kicks Jack in the shin. Jack stomps on his fingers and Dalton recoils his hand to his chest, his howling drowned in the downpour.

"No lower than you. Get up," Jack challenges, standing slack while brown street water ricochets around his ankles.

Dalton wobbles to his feet, his elbows and knees bent like a prize fighter. He jabs at Jack's cheek. His fist makes contact, but slides over the rainwater. Jack stands still.

"I'm being a friend, Sharpie. You're better than

this! This...this is a mistake. Marrying a Barrett will take you places! C'mon, what are you doing? Marrying her," he points at me with his nose, "will just drain all of your resources!" Pink-tinged water sprays off his lips as he speaks, his chest heaving.

Why is it always about money with the people in Jack's circle?

Dalton bobs defensively in the downpour, anticipating payback, then uppercuts Jack's chin. I wince when I hear Jack's teeth knock together, but he doesn't swing back. Through the soaked cotton of his dress shirt, which clings to the rolling muscles of his back, I see intensity waiting to strike.

"C'mon, hit me," Dalton taunts, jutting out his dripping chin. "Defend Little Miss Scrub."

Jack swings his arm around, and I see droplets fly sideways across the downpour along with Dalton's jaw.

"Don't you make any trouble for me, Dalton, or I'll go straight to the papers with the *real* reason your father kept his fortune," Jack growls.

Dalton's angry look melts into one of defeat. He spits a bloody tooth onto the pavement and it disappears into a milky brown puddle.

"Is she worth it, Sharpie?" Dalton sneers as he wipes blood from his mouth. "Is she really worth throwing your entire life away?"

Am I worth it? I wonder along with Dalton.

"Absolutely," Jack replies with certainty as he opens the driver's side door. "She *is* my entire life."

TWENTY

My racing heart leaps at Jack's declaration. He swoops down into the car, sopping wet, and his left arm works the window shut. The Mercury roars to life under us, and Dalton's hunched, pathetic form gets sprayed with muddy water as we pull away.

Jack's mouth sets in a line. His soggy chest heaves, and I'm entranced by the wet cotton of his shirt clinging to his skin. On either side of the thin tie running down his soggy shirt, faint hints of peachy skin show through the transparent fabric.

"You punched him," I say, still stunned.

"That guy is the backside of a donkey." Residual rainwater sprays off his lips onto the dash and windshield. "No; he's the crap that comes out of the backside of a donkey! No; he's a fly that feeds on the crap that comes out of the backside of a donkey."

"You punched a cop!" I shriek. Now I really feel like a convict.

"He had it comin', Pip," he grits through his teeth.

Though the veins in my limbs course with nervous adrenaline, my heart leaps a little. He's just showed me that I mean more to him than public opinion, which is good, since he's going to catch trouble from people who are higher up than Dalton.

We run under the shelter of Jack's suit coat into the courthouse, even though the rain has lightened to a mere sprinkling, and the sun has broken through the dreary gray cloud cover.

"Are you sure about this?" I ask him again, looking up from under the small veil that shrouds my eyes. Even though I've asked nearly twenty times, I want to allow him one last chance to pump the brakes.

Jack nods, smiling as he buttons his slightly-damp grey suit coat over his sopping wet shirt and pants. Droplets of rain water escape from his hairline and run down his forehead.

"Because I will absolutely understand--" I begin, but he cuts me off.

"Pip, I've never been more sure about anything in my life," he answers, looking me squarely in the eye, standing tall. His eyes are steeled with certainty.

While I take in the tiny details of his face: the lone freckle on his cheek, the length of his eyelashes, the tiny spot of stubble below his lip, I can't doubt that he is as sure as I am. So when he straightens his damp tie and takes my arm, our chins and chests simultaneously rise. We push through the doors and march to the podium.

Light streams in through the tall windows of the chambers, illuminating flecks of dust that drift downward. They seem magical, moving slower than my breath. They'll be the only decoration for our ceremony. Rows and rows of empty wooden benches threaten to remind us that we are completely alone and totally unsupported in our decision.

It is far too quiet in these chambers to match how I've envisioned this happening. No one has burst through the doors wielding torches and pitchforks, angrily protesting and spitting at us. We can surely expect it all once this news gets out, but for now, the only sounds that echo through the room are the sound of our footsteps and the whisper-light shuffling of the judge's robes.

The balding, graying judge is bent and knobbed under his robes, but when he turns to face us, the twinkle in his kind eyes tells me instantly that his decades of adulthood haven't spoiled his appreciation of young love. His calm gaze strengthens me as we walk arm-in-arm toward him.

"And what brings the two of you here today?" He

asks with a knowing grin. His strong, mellifluous voice gives him a fatherly quality, which endears him to me. Since we are doing this alone, I welcome a fatherly figure.

Jack holds up the marriage license with his free arm.

"Oh, I see," the aging man says, still grinning, and takes the paper.

"Just the two of you here?" I nod shamefully.

"No shame in eloping, Dear. I entered matrimony with my dear Rose in just the same manner."

My cheeks flush. I hope when we're as old and knobbed as he, Jack will have a similar twinkle in his eye for me.

He clears his throat, rousing a slumped form on the front bench. The sleeping man shoots upright, instantly alert. I hadn't noticed him there before.

"Evans," the judge prods. The man skitters over and signs the license. My brow rises in question.

"Our witness, you see," explains the judge, who winks at me. I blush.

"Well, then. Shall we get started?" He begins at a pace that suggests these words are well practiced. Without flowery pretense, he asks me to be Jackson's lawfully wedded wife, and pauses.

I clear my throat, and look through the yellow centers of Jack's eyes. They are illuminated from within, glowing with promise.

"Oh, yes."

He turns to Jack and asks him the same.

"I-"

The doors burst open; our heads turn and our hands drop. A figure hurries across the room. Her heels click with her frantic pace, distracting all four of us. Her scream bounces through the hollow room.

"I object! I *object!*"

My heart pounds against my ribs, trying to beat its way out. I knew something like this was going to happen!

The judge replies, "This is not a trial, Madam. This is a wedding." He has the calming tone of a father soothing a tantruming child.

Ruby's cheeks have flushed to a blotchy pink, hair going wild, and her eyes glint with fury. The judge's serenity seems to fan the inferno within her, as though she can burn her opinion into him with her added intensity. I wait for her to explode right in front of us as her feet slam down the aisle. Her fast gasping and hunched posture have me thinking she will pounce on me when she reaches us, claws bared.

"That depends on who you ask! I forbid the union of my son to this *gold digger!*" she hisses with a shiny, accusing fingernail pointed at me.

The judge steps between us, blocking my body from the raging woman, a sigh pulling his shoulders low. I admire him for either his courage or his disinterest. I'm not sure which makes him feel safe near a woman who's shooting fireballs from her eyes and who looks as though she will burst into flames at any moment.

The lethargic witness catches my attention by hissing, "pssst!" and nods his head to the side door, his eyes wide. "You can escape that way!" he seems to say. The scent of liquor wafts with the sound of his warning, and I glance back at Ruby to see if she's also noticed him. All I can see of her around the judge's robes are her arms, flinging about wildly as her tongue lashes the gentle old man.

Jack pulls me by the arm and punches the side door open with a huge palm. The thunderous spatter of rain on concrete roars through the opening. It looks like the rain is back with a vengeance, and we're instantly drenched. My eyes are fixed on Ruby, but her eyes are trained on the judge as she tears into him with an utter lack of gentility. Emily Post would be scandalized.

Once out the door, we fly down the damp alleyway that leads to the street. We're a full ten paces along when the door slams behind us with a very noticeable bang. Ruby will have heard that for sure.

My heeled feet struggle to keep up with Jack's long strides. Dirty puddle water licks up my shins while torrential buckets pour upon our ducked heads. My bare ankles feel as though Ruby's fingers will close around them at any second, so my heart jumps hopefully when the parked Mercury comes into view up ahead. Adrenaline courses through my veins, so I have to stamp the heels of my feet to slow down near the car. Jack pants as he pauses to open my door for me, water dripping off of his nose.

"Missus Sharpe?" he dramatically gestures with his arm for me to enter the vehicle. My heart barely has a moment to spin in a cartwheel at his grin as I throw myself into the car like a bank robber fleeing the scene. He tears away from the curb and yanks the wheel across three lanes of traffic.

"Dalton," he growls. Through the back glass I can see Ruby's desperate figure, arms thrashing to flag her driver. Jack flies through the downtown traffic, dangerously maneuvering through the city streets with the erratic path of a swerving bee. Three blocks up, he pulls a sharp turn to the left. My body is thrown into the door.

"Till death do us part, remember?" I nervously point out with slick hands steadying me on the seat and ceiling. "Let's not kill ourselves within two minutes of that promise!" I look out the fogged back window again for the other possible source of certain death, my neck straining. "You think Dalton called her?" If he'd gone back to the station with his broken, bloodied nose beginning to swell to make that call, there's an excellent chance that Jack is now a fugitive.

He blows a breath out his nose in affirmation, swinging recklessly around the next corner. "Without a doubt."

As I'm thrown against the door through the turn, I don't press him to explain what he'd said to Dalton about his father's dirty fortune, but I'm burning with curiosity to know more. I'm also thoroughly perplexed as to why the wealthy in Saratoga seem to have a secret society that they want to keep everyone else out of. *Really, why should Dalton care who Jack takes as a wife? And why would a middle aged woman and a young bachelor share secrets with each other? Come to think of it, why does Dalton work a nine-to-fiver when his family is supposedly as well off as the Sharpes?* I can't keep these questions from bursting through my lips another minute.

"Why is he working, anyway?" I ask Jack. When he furrows his brows, I clarify, "Dalton, I mean. Isn't he up on a pedestal with all the rest of the east-siders?" I reposition my hands to keep me from flying into the backseat. One palm is pressed into the roof lining, and the other firmly on the dash.

Clearly, thinking about Dalton cripples Jack's ability to drive safely.

Jack lets out a long breath. "That, my dear, is a long story," he says with a meaningful look. "I don't want to think about that rat right now, anyhow." The set of his lips tells me I'll have to satisfy my curiosity another time.

"I think we've lost her," I hint lightly, hoping he'll ease his lead foot off of the gas pedal. Still, he guns it onto the northbound highway, wipers frantically clearing the windshield.

He turns to me and smiles that devilishly lopsided grin I'm beginning to know so well, wagging his brows. Rows of straight white teeth flash through his lips and droplets of water dance off his earlobes.

"Sorry, Pip, I've got some unfinished business to attend to."

It's exactly that sort of business that's twisted my tender stomach back into a knot. I haven't spoken to anyone truly knowledgeable about the details of a honeymoon; only the whispered giggles of schoolgirl speculation. I have no idea how enlightened Jack is. I feel like a nervous actress being pushed on stage, a full audience waiting for a winning performance, and I haven't even read the script!

The only thing that assures my thumping heart is the instinct that takes over every time his fingers graze my skin. He has my pulse racing, heart fluttering, cheeks flushed with heat, knees weakened, stomach up in my chest. I know that when he wraps his arm around my back, a fire alarm goes off inside me. My body longs to re-live this feeling, but my head throbs with nerves.

I push his grinning jaw forward so he can watch the traffic. I can only handle so much excitement in my stomach before I'm bound to throw up. We're routed upstate, but I am blind to the finer details; he has me in the dark. He flies along the soggy state highway at the pace of an eager young man. Thankfully, the sky gets clearer and the roads get drier the further north we press.

When we pull up to the entrance of a quaint little hotel in the woods, the sky is bright with afternoon light. I want to jump out and cling to the firm, unmoving ground. The curves and turns of the rural roads didn't seem to slow him down, and I had worked to hold the contents of my stomach in. But as he escorts me to the door of a small, quaint inn, I am reminded that the queasiness I felt as we drove wasn't entirely carsickness. I can't be sure if the faint glow on the rosebushes is real or if my vision is fuzzy.

We check in quickly, which suits me just fine. I don't want the gal at reception looking at me with that knowing grin any longer than is necessary.

We're led to our suite by a gangly teenage bellhop with a goofy smile. I want to smack it right off his face, but instead I restrain my hands by pressing them into tight balls at my sides. I should have removed the soggy little veil from my hair before we got out. It marks me as a bride as much as the white dress marks me as virtuous. The pock-faced bellhop opens the door to our suite with a swoop of his long, thin arm. Jack takes that as his cue to sweep me up in his arms and carries me through the door frame, holding me close.

The bellhop misses his cue to shut our door and leave. He remains standing there with that stupid grin, watching us as we cross the threshold. Jack gives him a brutal look and he quickly shuts the door like a dog with its tail between its legs.

I'm jostled in Jack's arms as one of the hands supporting me works the lock.

"Hmmm. Alone," he purrs into my hair, his voice low with intent.

I feel myself trembling and I hope he can't feel it as he carries me all the way over to the large bed and tosses me lightly onto it. I sink into the fluff of the down comforter, which is so soft that it's difficult to sit up on. It is pure white and has the same halo around it as the rose bushes outside did.

Jack jumps into the fluff beside me.

"Whoa, whoa, Jack..." I start to say. "I need a

minute. My case?" I scan the room for the little blue suitcase. Nothing.

"Hmmm," he murmurs with a sigh as he reluctantly pushes himself up off of the bed and opens the door of the suite.

The teenage bellhop stands there sheepishly with our bags dangling from his spindly arms. His timid smile tells us he's been too effectively intimidated by Jack's scowl to knock on the door and disturb us, but too responsible to just leave our bags outside our door. He holds out his arms awkwardly, surrendering our bags. Jack fishes in his pocket for a tip, presses a coin into the boy's hand, then grabs the bags and stows them near the door. He shuts it, turning the lock with finality.

He turns to face me, biting down on a grin as he sheds his jacket. It pools on the floor, abandoned, as he strides toward the bed with thumbs latched under his suspenders. The stiff, dead-cat rigidity returns to my limbs. He crawls onto the foot of the bed, then makes his way toward me so that he's on all fours over me, holding himself up by his hands on either side of my face. I feel as though he's a lion, and I'm his helpless prey awaiting the inevitable kill. His eyes shine with intention, the gold in them flickering eagerly. He lowers his face, eyes smoldering into mine.

I find that I am no longer nervous.

Twenty-One

I wake feeling light and new. Parts of me are sore, and parts of me are newly-healed. Light filters gently in, casting a skewed rectangle on the floor. I examine this phenomenon as my mind catches up with my surroundings. My toes caress the soft sheets; my head enjoys the cushy depth of the pillow beneath it; my arm dangles lazily off the side of the bed.

Still halfway asleep, I feel the bed jiggle as Jack tries to quietly slip back into it. He feathers his palm down my exposed shoulder, my ribs, then my side, finally wrapping a strong arm around my waist when I stir. Having never been touched this way before, the sensation dances between pleasure and ticklishness. He pulls me to him.

"Good morning, Missus Sharpe," he whispers into my hair. The title is too new to feel right.

"Buyer's remorse?" I tease him.

"Not one bit," he whispers into my ear, biting the

lobe softly. When he moves, I smell a fresh wave of his familiar soapy scent. I could get drunk off the stuff. It's a pleasant sensation, but deep down I feel the flutterings of guilt. I don't want to ruin this pleasant morning by asking Jack if he shares my concern. When Hurricane Ruby stormed in with her torch and pitchfork, Jack never got to say that last famous word to seal our union. He said, "I", but not "do". No one gave Jack permission to "kiss the bride". So I can't help but wonder, *Are we really married? Did I just give all the milk away without him actually buying the cow? Am I a two-bit floozy?*

The judge signs the paper to make it official; the I do's are just fluff, Sense insists.

I try to take comfort from her, but two days later, the guilt still tickles my insides as we reluctantly return to Saratoga. I'm like a jittering windup toy as we step into Mama's kitchen with my hand entwined in Jack's calm, steady grip. Hopefully, she's had time to hear the news from May, bounce off the walls with anger, and calm down about it.

"Oh, Penny, what have you done?" Mama sighs into her hands, dramatically leaning into the small kitchen table. Despite my best efforts to hold my neck straight with the poise of an independent adult, I shrink under The Stare like a single cube of ice under the summer sun.

"Penelope," she sighs like I am an impossible three-year-old. "Didn't I explain to you that after marriage comes *children?*"

The memory of our awkward discussion on the birds and the bees replays in my head. I had tried to appear composed while not directly meeting her gaze, nodding as she stumbled over the uncomfortable words. Inside, I'd been traumatized; *could it really be true that my parents had done that three times? Once to conceive my brothers, once for me, once for May?*

I've realized since that I had largely underestimated the frequency of the act. At the time, I couldn't quite grasp what motivation besides creating a child would drive people to do something so barbaric together.

I'm slightly more enlightened now.

"Are you ready for that? How will you complete your training with a baby on your hip?" Mama scolds.

I blush deeply, as though her penetrating eyes have witnessed all of the moments I've shared with Jack since Tuesday.

"Mama!" I groan, cheeks flooded with crimson heat. I 'm trying to shut her out of my head and the memories of the last few days with Jack. For once in my life, I'd like a little privacy.

"Ma'am," Jack interjects, clearing his throat, "I

want Penny to reach her goals as much as you do. I'll personally see to it that she does," he promises. He's never called me Penny before; that's what Mama calls me. I can see that he's trying to find some common ground with her, but her eyes have rolled up to the ceiling. Her arms are crossed tightly over her chest until she explodes with a fresh lecture.

"You can't know what will happen! You are just children!" Jack coughs, and my eyebrows rise. He doesn't seem like a child to me at all.

"The world hasn't eaten you alive yet! You don't just make a plan," she says in bitter-flecked mockery, throwing her hands up into the air, "and then expect it will go perfectly. It's not all *peaches* and *roses!*"

I think of the roses outside the honeymoon inn, and recall the peach of his skin peeking out above the sheets.

It's a darn good thing she doesn't know that you're not sure if you're actually married or not, Imp chimes in. *It would only add to her arsenal.*

I am angry. Mama is so stubborn! Why can't she see that Jack is a good man, probably the best that I could ever ask for?

You could ask for Phi- Imp interjects before I cut her off.

I am *married!* Well, I think I am.

I know that Jack won Mama over before. Why can't she let go of her hard-set ideals? My angry tiger charges out of hiding, claws bared.

"What would Daddy think of the way you are now, Mama? So shot down and so... so bitter all the time? He'd be ashamed! You're just an old, angry hag!" I spit.

As soon as the words leave my tongue, I want them back. They are bullets from a pistol and they sear her flesh as they burn through her. But they don't pass through; this wasn't a clean shot. They are embedded deep inside her flesh. I don't think I'll ever be able to dig them out.

"Sorry, Mama, I didn't mean..." I begin, sobered. I send the tiger in me back into her cage.

"No; you did mean it," she stops me with her voice hard and cool. "I think you should just go, Penelope," she says, eerily soft.

She's used my full name, which is a very bad sign from Mama. She won't meet my eyes, so I search May's for a glimmer of atonement. Hers are also cast down.

No one speaks.

Jack and I shuffle out through the peeling screen door, and it's slammed behind us as hard as a half inch of rickety pine can slam. The sound resonates through the new hollow inside of me.

November, 1941

There's nothing quite like opening your eyes in the morning and instantly being excited by the person lying next to you. Or brushing your teeth with your best friend, and even with white foam dripping down your chin, he still looks at you like you're the most beautiful creature on the earth.   Nestling yourself between his cello and chest and absorbing the warm vibration of his cello playing.   Realizing that ironically, snorers fall asleep faster than non-snorers, making it nearly impossible for the victim of bear-like snoring to doze off. Then kicking him at midnight for snoring loudly enough to wake you from a dead sleep. Or, being tickled until you wet your underpants a little, and learning that he did it on purpose to get you to strip down.

We are living in marital bliss; the happiest newlyweds in the entire state of New York.

Liar, Imp and Sense chorus together.

Well, we would be the happiest couple, if not for the general disapproval of our union by our loved ones.   There is an ugly, gaping hole in my heart where Mama was. Since I know I am unwelcome at the farmhouse, May comes by the hospital every few days to say hello, and to give me updates on Mama's attitude toward my marriage.

It never changes.

"She's still hoppin' mad, P. She even grumbles

about it in her sleep." May doesn't seem upset at me anymore, but there seems to be an inexplicable barrier between us anyway. Maybe that's just what happens when you don't live together anymore, or when you let another person become as important to you as a sister was. She reports that Mama held good on her threat to sell Tilly; just to spite me, I guess.

Sigh. I miss that stubborn old cow.

Tilly, I mean; not Mama.

And, of course, Jack's mother is beyond hysterical about our marriage, which somewhat dampens his joy. Needless to say, the marriage of Penelope Hale to Jackson Sharpe did not make the society pages of the newspaper. As for me, I'm secretly thrilled and relieved at Ruby's anger. A dog on the hunt, she has explored every avenue possible to dissolve our union. If someone with that much power and influence can't sniff out a legal issue with our shortened ceremony, then it is undoubtedly rock solid. I'm not a tramp after all! Maybe I can start writing to Emily Post again.

Ruby has cut Jackson off from his weekly allowance until he moves home-- alone. She has also banned him from Sunday dinners, unless he comes without me; but he's known her long enough to be sure that the main course will be annulment papers wrapped in a tongue lashing and drizzled in guilt.

Perhaps we're not the most content couple in the state, but we do love each other.

At least a few folks share our joy. Lyla was thrilled when we shared our news with her. She'd clapped her bony hands together and her eyes had gleamed.

"Wonderful!" she kept repeating, grinning as though it were the best news she'd ever gotten. She now wears a permanent expression of glee, which on Lyla, looks very odd. Her nose is wrinkled, her eyes scrunched and twinkling; with her mouth in a tight "o" for a smile. Her shoulders are up at her ears, and her fingers continuously flutter together like an evil scientist.

From what I know of her, the woman doesn't gleam over someone else's happiness. Surely it fills her with great satisfaction to know that Ruby is irreparably scandalized, and that is what makes Lyla's cheeks glow. She has become our greatest ally, providing Jack with enough of an allowance for us to rent a small apartment, buy groceries, and fill the Merc with gasoline. She's even filled our tiny space with her hand-picked furniture. It's a generous gift that makes me feel like I am living in a seventy year old woman's home. I am drowning in doilies!

Really, the only visitor who gets to enjoy the

granny decor is Claire, who is kind enough to forgive my bitterness toward her. As a granddaughter-in-law of Lyla, Claire was also presented with a vast collection of hand-tatted doilies as a warm welcome into the Sharpe family when she wed Bentley. She throws one of ours away every time she visits us.

"Phase them out slowly," she has instructed me. My heart has softened enough to realize that my sweet cousin was an innocent party in our eviction from our home, and that she had no part in her mother's cruelty so many years ago. Clearly, she had no idea of what her mother had done. Truthfully, she is a walking contradiction of everything the bitter version of Mama had taught me about wealthy folks. Claire was raised in the lap of luxury, the way I would have been, but it didn't seem to spoil her. She is unfailingly kind, gentle, and generous. I haven't sniffed a whiff of snobbery or exclusivity on her.

See, Mama doesn't know it all, Imp declares with satisfaction.

Things have been smooth between us, with the exception of my bumbling mention of the topic of babies. After all, Bentley and Claire have been married for years, and their home is yet to be warmed by the presence of a little Sharpe. To my surprise and chagrin, Claire had instantly bubbled over with tears. I worked out through her mucous-y sobs that after three unsuccessful years of trying for a baby, she and Bentley are considering drastic measures for fertility with their doctor. It's clear that Claire's heart is broken, and that she feels like she has failed as a woman.

I haven't mentioned a baby since.

Instead, we busy ourselves with working on Doris's romantic life. We don't even have to use Doris's last name for George to remember his old girlfriend with a thoughtful smile. Though he has the token protruding ears of a Hale, George has grown into a somewhat handsome fella: blonde and green eyed with a square jaw. It feels strange to talk and laugh with both of my cousins after ten years. The impish voice in my head is right; Mama fed us a lot of false truths. George and Claire are all right.

Lyla is sharp enough to give us some newlywed space, though today, she's dragging me to bingo with her, still wearing her impishly triumphant expression. On the way, she fills my ears to the brim with the hottest gossip on the geriatric circuit while her fingers dance with satisfaction; the Sharpe family is still in scandal! To change the tired, guilt-inducing subject, I ask how she had become a widow at such an early age.

"Did they teach you about the Titanic at that public school?" she asks in her usual warbling croak.

I smile. I'm used to her condescending,

mischievous nature by now.

"Of course. I wasn't raised in a cave, you know."

"Well, Mister Sharpe was on that big old boat.. 'A business trip', he'd called it. Pshaw! I'm told he and his companion made it into one of the rescue boats, but it was overturned by a crowd of desperate souls trying to climb in to safety..."

Companion? I wonder. Her tone of voice tells me she doesn't mean a business partner. She must be referring to a mistress, and she sounds quite bitter about it.

"...and I thank every one of them for their service to me," she concludes.

I wonder if there was ever a time when Lyla was soft and sweet, instead of peppery and hard.

"Oh," I reply reverently. "Drowning sounds like a horrible way to die." Before I have a second to linger on the horrible thought, her hands are in the air, brushing away my concern for her late husband.

"Ack!" she crows. "His mistress drowned right along with him. Got just what was comin' to them, if you ask this old prune." I never knew Mister Sharpe, but looking at Lyla's scowl and feeling the sting of her wrath, I just can't blame the fella for taking a mistress. And I thought *Mama* was bitter!

At bingo, I sit between Lyla, wearing her glow of evil satisfaction, and the oldest man my eyes have ever beheld. He has an impressive amount of salt-

and-pepper hair reaching out to me from his ears, nose, and brows, though his freckled head is bald and scaly. He coughs like the last remaining victim of the plague, the jowls on his walnut-like, wrinkled face swinging with the force of his hacking, but he never excuses himself from the game. Even on his deathbed, the sweaty fellow apparently can't pass up this excitement.

It's probably the last day of his mortal life, so I let him slide.

Curse that old man! Thanks to his germs, after just a week, I'm now wrapped up in an old-lady afghan on our old-lady couch, alternating between being hot and nauseated and having bone-shaking chills. My sinuses feel like balloons under my skin. My lids are thick and heavy. My throat burns from repeated vomiting.

I'm going to die, I lament. And I haven't spoken to Mama in weeks. My gravestone will read, *"Penelope Hale Sharpe, beloved wife; horrible daughter"*. I moan just as the front door swings open and my vigorous, healthy husband strides in.

"No more bingo for you," Jack scolds. He brings me a cup of cool water, mopping the sweat from my forehead with the closest available doily.

"Oh, c'mon," I croak, trying to sit up. "The least I can do for our sugar mama is to escort her to the biggest social event of her week." I hope Jack remembers my sense of humor when I'm gone.

"Pshh! She owes us big-time for burning her daughter-in-law," he says, coaxing me to take a sip.

I rinse my mouth and spit into the trashcan I keep close for emergencies. I think I've tossed my cookies three times already today and I'm starting to see stars. I snag the damp doily from his fingers and blow my swollen nose with it. The last time I looked in the mirror, I had bright red dots around my eyes from the force of the heaving. How had that old man survived this? The elderly don't often pull through influenza. I wonder if he's still kicking.

"I didn't marry you to burn your mother," I tell him. "I married you for the swell furniture." I crack a weak smile and throw a doily at his wide grin.

He catches it before it reaches his face. "Yeah, well, I think Granny still sees it as a personal favor from us to her."

I'm sure he's right. Anytime I speak to Lyla, I wonder who on earth raised such a cold snob of a daughter. He balls up the doily and throws it over his shoulder.

"Anyhow, I've got something to talk to you about. I ran into my old coach from Rigby, and he's got an idea that might help us stand on our own two feet," he says with an arched brow. I've come to know that this means something interesting is coming.

"Oh?" I ask.

He sucks in a breath. "Well, he was wondering why I wasn't at Columbia with the rest of the fellas for fall term. I gave him the gloss of it. He gets it. He's blue collar; college is expensive. Well, his boy enlisted with the Navy, and they're going to totally pay for his education!" He lets the word ring through the air and waits for my reaction.

"Oh," I reply, somewhat anti-climactic against the excited expression on his face. "Isn't that... dangerous?"

"Dangerous! Ha! We're in practically the safest nation there is. We're not even at war!" he justifies confidently. "Uncle Sam's just throwing money at these soldiers. Why not have a piece of the pie?"

It's a sensible thought. We really can't continue this Lyla-sponsored honeymoon forever. She'll be bored of the scandal soon enough and take her purse with her to a new interest.

"Okaaaay, let's think about it," I concede.

"Aaaaw, you're a doll!" he crows, leaning toward me.

"Don't kiss me! You'll catch it!" I warn, so he diverts his aim to my neck.

"That's not the only surprise I have for you," he says. I roll my eyes. His first "surprise" was certainly surprising. I don't know if I can stomach anything more.

"Well, what is it?" I ask.

"I'll have to show you," he says and pulls me to standing. As he leads me down the hallway, pulling out the car keys, I protest.

"If we're driving somewhere, you've gotta let me drive or I'll-"

He presses the keys into my palm instantly. We're both tired of vomit. He directs me through the city streets, onto the back roads, toward the Ferring plantation.

"Oh, no you don't, Mister," I protest, taking my foot off the gas pedal, when I see he's directed me to drive to his old house. The car slows to a coasting crawl. "I'm not going in to beg your mama to let me into the family..." But I smooth my pitiful hair and pinch my cheeks just in case. A picture in my head of Ruby's flared nostrils and fiery eyes makes my tender stomach roll.

"Oh," I moan, feeling an overwhelming wave of nausea. My limbs go limp and weak with the feeling, and my foot can't find the brake pedal. "Oh no!"

The car is still slowly rolling when I swing open the door and throw up on the middle of the road. Jack throws himself over my lap and presses down on the brake with his palm, but I barely notice him there. My eyes water from the force of vomiting up my nerves over Ruby. I wipe my mouth and sit back up, sighing. My mouth tastes rotten, but at least my stomach doesn't feel sour anymore.

"Aw, Doll," Jack groans sympathetically, petting my head. I turn to him, remembering Mama's words about how real love can survive through vomit. If only she could see us now.

"Actually, I feel the best right after I yak." And I do, so my eyes are abnormally bright when I ask, "Where's my surprise?"

He directs me forward down the road.

"No, not the big house. Around back," he coaches, and I coax the Merc around the trees with a sigh of relief. The frame of a smaller version of the Sharpe home comes into view.

"Granny's," he explains.

When I'm old, if I live in a house half this large by myself, I'll turn it into an orphanage. There is no way an old woman can really need what appears to be at least eight bedrooms! I can't even begin to imagine how many doilies there are inside Lyla's sprawling home. I start to pull toward her driveway and Jack stops me again.

"No, around back."

When I park, he comes around the car and helps me up to my feet. He ties a silk scarf around my eyes. Blinded, my other senses go on high alert.

"Follow me," he breathes into my ear. I shiver at

the feel of his breath on my earlobe, spreading through my hair, submitting my arm to him so that he can guide me. The cold ground crunches under my awkward, blind steps. What could possibly be behind Lyla's house that would surprise me? I am surprised enough at the size of the "guest cottage" she lives in.

I smell dirty snow, rotting leaves and-

No! Could he have...? I smell the sweet tang of digested grass.

Cow plop! I rip off the scarf and start to run toward the source of the scent. Inside a well-built, ornate building is a row of hay-filled stalls. In the corner, I see the lazy flick of a very familiar tail.

"A late wedding gift," Jack explains, taking the balled up scarf from me.

"Tilly!" I cry and run with my fingers outstretched to her. When they make contact with the reddish hair on her enormous head, I wrap my arms around her neck and kiss her ear. She flicks it and moos a hello. "I missed you, too, Tilly."

When Jack strides over, tears stream down my face, dripping onto her hair.

"Tilly," I whisper thickly.

He looks amused.

"Milking Tilly was the first chore I ever did in my whole life," I explain with much more emotion than I ever knew I had for this stubborn old cow. I feel my cheeks burn red.

"When my world fell apart, it felt like I was falling into nothing; just a big, empty abyss of blackness. Nothing was certain; I had no security; I felt completely helpless. And then I was put in charge of this cow. And with my own little hands, I could milk her, and bottle her milk, and deliver it. I made money. I was doing something useful, and I felt able. I became important to my family."

I stroke the ridge of her back, realizing that Tilly is my trophy of triumph. She made me the protective, strong gal that I am today. I laugh when her familiar long tongue appears, licking the air while I scratch her hip.

Jack's head cocks to the side as he listens to me, wearing a slight frown. I can see the wheels of comprehension straining behind his eyes. I realize that Jack has never worked a day in his life. Maybe he has felt the pride of winning an award or the known the satisfaction of earning high marks in school, but he has surely never brought a scrap of bread to his family's table by the sweat of his handsome brow. But he knows enough to love me so well. Enough to buy back my cow.

Holding Tilly's bristly hairs against my tear-stained cheek wakes me up to a realization: I am not whole without all the pieces of my past.

I've got to go see Mama.

Twenty-Two

When I cut the Merc's engine, its headlights go dark. Under the moonless sky, the landscape of the old farm is as black as if an ink bottle had spilled over everything. Faint stars shimmer above, begging to be admired on a night so dark, but they are dim against the other light I see. *Where is that shadowy light coming from?* Curiosity quickens my pace.

Something lands lightly on my nose, as light as a snowflake, as I hurry toward my old house. I touch it, and it crumbles away under my fingertip. Ash.

Ash?

Ash!

My eyes adjust to the darkness quickly, as any girl's would when she has lived so long on the outskirts of town. I feel the raw tang of smoke burning my throat and nose, stronger now. At that moment, I note the heavy wall of rising, swirling smoke over the barn. The chalky cloud is illuminated only by the flickering licks of the hungry flames below it. While my mind races to catch up with what my racing pulse has already realized, my feet lunge in long strides. The barn is on fire.

Dry, grey wood and hay feed the flames. I shriek, horrified, as the fire explodes into an inferno. The west roof cracks, pops and tumbles in on itself. The gaping hole it leaves brightens the scene as tall, hungry flames fight for height out through the newly-created escape route. It almost looks like a litter of puppies trying to jump out of a box, wrestling one another for position, feeding on the now-plentiful air.

"May? May!" My cry comes out weakly. My throat is dry, and constricted with smoke and panic. "Mama!" My eyes jump around wildly, only able to take in the scene in flashes while the flames lick out of the barn.

"Tilly!" I shriek, and realize my throat is cotton-dry in the smoky air. I cough and sputter. My tender stomach is ready to add substance to the force of air coming from me.

Tilly's on the plantation now, Sense reminds me.

Safe, Imp reaffirms.

Still, I'm flat-out running over the dusty yard toward the barn. I see Mac's lumbering form heaving a tin bucket of water against the barnside. The two-foot-wide splashed area sizzles and goes dark and steaming. I grab the chicken's water bowl, containing at best three quarters of a cup of water thick with the chickens' saliva, and splash it futilely at the blaze.

I dash to the water pump and pump as quickly as I can, my fever-weakened arm fueled by adrenaline. I haven't felt this sort of vigor in my muscles in over a month. The coppery ends of May's curls catch my eye as she appears at my side, taking the bucket from me. Tears burst forth and my chest is flooded with relief, but I continue pumping water into a watering can. A gravelly cry erupts as I push my muscles to their limit, heave up, press down. Up, down. Up, down.

In seconds, May is back with the empty bucket and takes the watering can. I switch arms on the pump; my left arm is just as superhumanly strong as my right.

Mama appears with a pot and catches the sloshing overspill from my wild pumping. Reverend Bell comes at her heels with a bucket of his own. The four of us work as a team, a motley fire brigade until all that is visible in the night is the steady rise of white, steamy vapor. Soot-caked, soaked, and filthy, we all stare dumbly at the hissing remains of the old barn.

We did it.

May comes to me, shoulders hanging limply, and

throws heavy, exhausted arms around me. We crumple to the dirt and breathe heavily, bewildered. The balloon of strength that had held up my frame in the frenzy of action deflates with a sputtering leak, and achy weakness arrests my joints and muscles again. Mama joins our huddle, and I welcome her.

My family is safe.

Mama starts shuddering, and I breathe in as deeply as my scorched lungs will allow to prepare myself to comfort her. *Will she accept comfort from me?* I know the heat of the fire has melted my anger toward her. *Has it softened hers toward me?* My arms start to open toward her. Until...

I realize she's not shuddering; she's chuckling. Soft giggles graduate to peals of laughter until her maniacal cackling has May and me chuckling with her. It's not funny. Nothing about narrowly escaping a horrid death by fire is funny.

But we are alive.

We are safe!

Oh, it feels good to grin. It feels good to laugh with Mama again, regardless of the twisted cause of it; despite the blanket of ash and grime we're covered in; notwithstanding the icy climate between Mama and me, though our relieved glee is doing wonders to melt it.

November 26th, 1941

Even though I've shampooed every flake of ash from my hair, I'm feeling rotten. It seems that yesterday's activity has knocked me right back into the thick of this flu. I slept so late that I woke up to solitude, and I've been watching shadows move across the living room floor for hours. I feel so incredibly lazy lying around all day, but any time that I jostle my stomach, a spurt of bile shoots up my throat. I don't think that little four-letter word, bile, quite captures the horrible acrid smell and taste of the stuff.

When Jack returns home, he wears a funny smile.

"Hiya, Pip! I brought you lunch!" he sings, and kisses my forehead. "Mmm, much better than smoke. Strawberries."

I press a lock of my hair to my nose. I breathe in, searching for a hint of the delicious scent he seems to be smelling. My senses catch on a completely different aroma beyond the strands at my nose. I haven't smelled anything like it since I was a little girl.

"Is that... Chinese food?" I ask, and my mouth suddenly waters. I drop my hair, sniffing the air in search of the source of such an intoxicating smell. I haven't wanted to look at food for days, for fear I'll see it come back up, but for some reason, the scent wafting from the brown bag is heavenly.

"Broccoli beef, ginger chicken, and a couple of spring rolls from a oriental joint in the big city," he replies. "It's still kind of warm."

The thought of the beef pieces in that sauce makes my stomach roll and I gag at the thought of the fried rolls, but the ginger smell makes me ravenous.

He watches my face while his own falls.

"Do I have to eat outside again?"

"No, no; I'll be fine. Maybe just sit over there," I compromise.

He offers me the ginger chicken and chopsticks, and backs to the farthest seat from mine.

Once the sauce hits my tongue, any thought of eating politely, slowly, is gone. I wolf it down, picking up in my fingers the pieces of rice that my fumbling with the chopsticks couldn't claim. I sigh in contentment. This is a nice way to celebrate the first chip in the iceberg between Mama and me.

Jack has trouble chewing around the huge smile on his face. "It's nice to see something going down your throat, instead of the other way around," he jokes.

"Don't remind me, or you're going to see it the other way around!" My stomach is happily full, but still tender from the spasms it has endured for the past two weeks.

Suddenly, Jack's grinning face grows serious.

"Pip, I think I have to tell you something," he begins, his happy expression slightly darkened.

"Mmm?" I mumble while I work on annihilating a single grain of rice between my front teeth. I feel the exact instant the blood sugar hits my veins. I shudder with the newfound strength surging in. My aching body feels almost... normal.

"Is Tilly moving in with us next?"

"I think, well, I'm pretty sure that the barn fire wasn't an accident."

"What? What do you mean? The fire chief said that barn was a bonfire waiting to happen. Old dry wood, hay; Mac even kept the tractor fuel in there," I explain. It's a wonder that giant torch hadn't gone up in flames years ago, now that I think about it.

"Which makes it just plausible enough to look like an accident, but timely enough to send a message," he says in a low voice, his brows furrowed.

"A message from whom?"

"Well, I haven't, um, told you this, but, well, I've been trying to keep you out of all the commotion since you're so under the weather and all," Jack bumbles.

"What?" I really dislike being kept in the dark.

"There have been, well, *threats*. And these." He

tosses me a large manila envelope.

I pull out the papers inside, blinking against the harsh word in bold, official print: *annulment.*

"My mother," he begins.

"You think your mother burned down my barn?" My mind races. "You should've told me, Jack! I, I could have..."

"You could have what? There wasn't anything to be done, except to actually sign these." His tone tells me that he has not once entertained the idea of annulling our marriage. "I figured she was just spinning her wheels, trying to spoil things for us. I never thought she'd really go and..."

I interrupt him. "Go and what? Burn down my barn? Threaten my family? What if May had been inside? Or Mama?" I'm panting with belated fear, cold with sweat.

"Well, I have a plan for us to get away from all this. So far away that my mother won't bother with your family anymore. I went to the recruitment office today in the big city..."

I sit upright, suddenly aware of where he'd acquired our exotic lunch.

"... just to check it out, you know..."

So much for my contented stomach.

"...and, well; Doll, you're looking at the newest candidate for pilot training!" he announces while pulling an overly-excited face, like an advertisement. "I'll still have to pass the qualifying exams and all, but the fella looked at my grades, and he thinks I'm a shoo-in for officer training. I'm gonna be a pilot, Pip! I mean, eventually, we can live anywhere. All the way in California if you like."

"What?" I am confused. *Big decisions take time to come around, don't they?* I don't know that being far away from my family will do anything to soothe my concern for them. *Would it really keep Ruby away from them?*

"I passed my vision test right then and there, so as long as the doc says my ticker's in good shape, I'm gonna take the exam to be a fighter pilot," he grins, thumbs under his suspenders. He looks so proud of himself that I attempt to suppress my concern. I'm sure it can be hard on a man to rely on his aged granny to support him; rather emasculating. But the idea of *fighter* pilot, as in, *combat*, doesn't sit well with my tender stomach.

"Fighter? Fight*ing?*" I ask.

Remember the first day you met him? How is eyes sparkled when he spoke about flying? Sense reminds me.

"C'mon Pip; you know there's no danger. Uncle Sam's kept our hands out of this war. I'll just get to play around with planes for a few months, then they'll pay for my college education. It's pennies from heaven!"

"How do you know ol' Sammy won't join the war tomorrow? What if they're dangling the college education to rope in a bunch of strapping young fellas and then storming on in once they've got a full arsenal of fighters?" I wonder aloud.

"Aw, your Uncle Mac's filled your head with a bunch of baloney," he dismisses and waves the thought away. "It'll be fine." He seems very sure.

"Did you sign a contract?" My voice warbles while my stomach simmers threateningly.

"Yeah." His brow flickers. It is clear that my lukewarm reaction disappoints him. My stomach sinks. "And they gave me a signing bonus. So this lunch is on me," he says proudly. Even though I'm wracked with anxiety, he has just earned his first dollar. I feel like it would be wrong to burst his bubble.

"When do you start training?" I ask nervously, trying to keep the warble out of my voice.

"Erm, next Monday," he says hesitantly, "in the city." Suddenly, I am standing more upright than I've been in more than a week, including fighting the fire. Jack's pride be hanged!

"*Monday?* You're leaving?" My face flushes; I can feel my skin burning white hot. "I thought marriage was about making decisions *together!*" I bellow.

"Shhh, the neighbors will hear you!" he soothes.

"I don't care! Lottie!" I call obnoxiously and knock on the wall to the old woman in the next apartment. "My husband is ditching me for Uncle Sam after just three weeks of wedded bliss!"

His ears are red and his mouth is set. "You. Are. *Overreacting.*"

"No. I. Am. *Not!* If you want to commit suicide, I think you should consult your *wife* first! Or have you forgotten that you have a wife?" My hands gesture wildly in the tense air; I've been learning from Lyla. "Don't you care what I think?"

Crackers. I've really become a bona fide nag.

"I *do* care what you think! Why do you think I signed up in the first place?" he hollers back.

My standing, fuming form bears no resemblance to the roadkill I've been; lying around the house feeling like death would be a welcome relief from my misery. I am buoyed by my anger.

"Don't pretend you did this for me. You did this for *you!* The rest is just the cherry on top!" I argue.

His strong, square chest heaves under his shirt, and his nostrils flare angrily. "Why do you insist on pushing away everyone you love?"

"Well, don't you fight dirty! Must've learned that from your *mother!*" I shout. He throws his hands up and marches to the door.

Though I watch the door swing shut, the loud *crack* it makes still makes me jump. My eye catches the brown bag by the chair he had been sitting in. I snatch it up in my fist. I open the door and heave it at the back of his head.

"Don't forget your lunch, Dear!" I sing in a falsely merry voice and then slam the door harder than he had, locking it. I know he has his keys in his pocket, but it gives me a satisfying sense of finality to throw the bolt.

With each heaving puff of air I gulp in the lingering silence, I begin to deflate. I fall onto the couch and close my eyes. My ring catches on the pillow. I grab it and wrestle it off of my finger, shoving in deep between the cushions. With the last air left in my balloon of indignation, I sit hard on the cushions to bury the symbol of our promise to each other. I lay stone-still, except for my rolling stomach.

I'm fairly certain that the ginger chicken is about to come back up.

A contract is a contract, like a marriage is a marriage. After a heated, apologetic reunion, Jack left for training on the base near the big city. He qualified for pilot training, of course, because a dream that big just won't be denied. All I have now to curl up with at night is his cold pillow and ration his lingering scent on it, so as not to sniff it all up. That, and his letters.

I had to smile when I read his narration about how he paced and stewed, waiting for his test results to be posted. When he ran his finger down the list and saw, "Sharpe, Jackson", he nearly burst the buttons of his uniform. I wrote back, instilling as much enthusiasm into my reply as I possibly could. I am proud of him, but I'm afraid, too. His letters, full of enthusiasm and his obvious fulfillment, are nourishment to my hungry soul.

Today, I jump when I hear the mail slot clink shut and letters fluttering to the floor. When I see his boxy penmanship, neat and clean, I hold it against my heart. Eagerly, I rip open the envelope, unfold the paper, and lean back against the door to savor it:

"Dearest Pip,

I hope Granny is leaving you in peace while you recover from the bingo-itis. The boys here are giving me a hard time about writing to my old lady back home every day, but I just can't resist! A Joe from Georgia read your name from the envelope and pronounced it "Pen-el-owp" instead of "Pen-el-oh-pee". I got a good laugh out of that, but he still seems pretty confused as to what all the fuss is about.

They call me Jack-o, which is short for jack-o-lantern, after I punched out a fella's tooth. Now he looks like a jack-o-lantern. Don't get all in a lather, now. We just box for fun and none of them are any bigger than Dalton. It gets boring at night, and we do what we can to entertain ourselves. Some guys just smoke all night, and I know you don't want me to get going with that. I'll try to keep all my teeth where they belong.

Besides missing you, I'm getting along fine. I'm like a kid with a new toy airplane, only this plane is real! Some fellas have painted theirs with pictures of their old lady as "nose art", they call it. You can bet your knickers I'll be painting you on my nose, Doll! What color do you want me to paint your ribbon?

I went to see Mother before I left. She flatly denies being involved with the barn (of course), but I think I have her convinced that no fire on earth will get me to sign those annulment papers. I told her that if she ever even thinks of pulling another stunt like that, she'll never see me again. So, you can rest easy, since I'm her favorite son. I'm certain that will do the trick.
Give ol' Gran a kiss from me, but don't let her drag you to bingo!

Your loving husband,
Jack-o"

I exhale. His letter should perk me up, and it

does; but his voice in my head, narrating each word, fills me with loneliness, too. I imagine the faces he'd pull while he said this, or the way his eyes would crinkle over that. It's rather painful, but I'm certain it would be more painful not to hear anything at all. If anything, I realize that the feeling I get from a letter from Jack bears no resemblance to the way I feel reading letters from my brothers. Jack's leave can't come fast enough!

TWENTY-THREE

December 7th, 1941

My insides feel as cold as the drifts of snow my blank eyes stare over. At the window of Saint Christopher's Hospital, my fingers are vises on the sill while the slightly-nasally but authoritative voice booms from the radio that someone has turned up so loud that it crackles. Hospital staff stand packed like sardines around it, and the entire room is blanketed in a general feeling of shock. The entire nation must be in shock with the crushing news that the Army and Naval bases on Oahu have been heavily attacked by Japanese forces. Pearl Harbor, the *"lucky spot so far away from the fighting that we're as safe as kittens"*, was ambushed early this morning, before most of the inhabitants were even awake.

I feel sick with dread, because Max, Eddie, and Phin are on that base.

Innumerable casualties are still being tallied.

Many injured, many survivors, sure; but with the Hale family lucky streak, I just know Eddie or Max is injured. Or... worse. The announcer calmly advises us to stay calm, and that the families of the deceased will be notified as soon as possible. *"Please do not inundate the Naval and Army offices with calls, as they have much more important matters to attend to at this difficult time."* Spoken like a man who does not have a family member stationed at Pearl Harbor!

The drifts of snow start to spin.

"Go home, Hale," Nurse Adler's gravelly voice commands. "You look terrible." She has been much easier on me since the incident in the alley, though that tense encounter feels like years ago.

The shocked crowd of white uniforms around the radio stares at me with sick pride that they know me, the sister of not one, but two Pearl Harbor uniforms. I can barely take a step through them before I falter, almost crumpling from terror. Their eager hands are all around to catch me. I snatch my arm away from the searing grip of Doctor Sweeney and I shoot icicles at him through my eyes.

He puts his palms up defensively and says, "Okay, okay; the lady is independent."

I'd spit in his face if I thought I could get away with it. I hate that he is still employed here. I hate that he's not rotting in prison. After his repulsive touch, I am remarkably strengthened enough to walk on my own.

Go home, Adler had said. *Home.*

I stumble down the hall toward the exit, toward home, with one hand grazing the wall, in case I need to lean on it for support. My spinning head makes plans to get home to my empty apartment and crawl under the blankets of my lonely bed. I'll pull the covers over my head and scream out this feeling before it can burrow into my flesh, causing my soul to collapse and decay.

But the very instant the frigid air outside bites at my skin, a new plan is set in my mind. I can't just stand here and wait for a yellow cab. I know I couldn't hold still for a second at the trolley stop. And I can't go to an empty apartment.

I need to go *home.*

I skip the last step of the hospital's front steps, teetering on the snowy sidewalk before I hit the asphalt running. The road salt has melted the snow to an icy slurry that soaks through my shoes, but I don't care. I ignore the protests of my chilled nose and earlobes and run with all of my might.

When I leap over a snow drift, it claims one of my shoes. I leave it behind, soggy and useless, so my feet have a musical quality as they move. *Pad, thump, pad, thump, pad, thump.*

When I'm so far outside of town that the silence

screams, I rip off my other shoe and throw it with all of my might. I barely hear over my ragged breathing the soft "plop" it makes as it lands in the distance.

The cold air makes my lungs burn from within.

I can smell the smoky ghost of the barn fire when I turn onto Radcliffe; a hint of smoldering ashes preserved in the cold air. Both of my sides have stitches, so it's at a pathetic pace that I jog toward my old house. My home.

The faces of Mama and May appear at the window. A rush of relief arrests me and I halt in the yard, swaying breathlessly and holding my sides. They come out onto the porch.

"Welcome home, Penny," Mama greets me with glassy eyes. Her voice is steady and her posture is straight, but her hands tremble at her sides like I've never seen them. She has heard the news.

"Did you hear?" May sobs, not one to bridle her emotions. She throws her body forward to run down the steps toward me.

Oh, yes, I heard every word. The voice from the radio's words are playing on an endless loop in my head.

Within the safety of the gate of my childhood home, the sheer horror of what has happened bubbles up into my throat. Like a marionette with no control over her body, I double over and heave it out all onto the snow. May's outstretched hand snaps back when I retch, and with the foul stench, up comes my fear for Eddie. Another stomach spasm, and the terror that Max has been killed runs out in a stream. My forehead beads over with sweat, and the panicked dread that a Japanese bomb has claimed Phin rushes out of my mouth. My throat burns as I retch and gag, and my eyes gush with the salty streams that vomiting forces from my tear ducts.

Somehow my body hasn't realized yet that my stomach can produce no more. Dry, fruitless heaves threaten to turn my esophagus inside out. Deep, guttural sounds accompany each spasm. I look up. May's eyes are huge and terrified. Combined with the awful news, I think my violent lurching may be traumatizing her.

Mama rushes to me and presses a handful of snow onto my forehead. Like a magic potion, it calms the storm within me, and I can breathe. I crumple into the snow. I'm a shuddering, barefoot, sickly grey mess with purple fingers, lips and toes.

"It's alright, Penny," Mama soothes in the voice I remember falling asleep to as a little girl. "Everything's alright," she fairly sings. "You're home now."

I am home now.

I'm home.

Home.

Mama's fingers carefully pour hot water from the tea kettle into a basin. She tenderly lifts up my feet and places them in the water, one by one. At first, it feels oddly as though my feet are being frozen again, but then the heat seeps in. As they begin to thaw, it feels like my feet are being stabbed with a mixture of searing red-hot pins and ice-cold needles. I grimace, sucking a sharp breath in through my teeth.

"There, now," she coos. I drink in the soothing sound of her voice. I may be a married woman now, but I still need my mama. And we all need some soothing today.

"Do you think, I mean, when will we know that they're alive?" I ask her. I'm still shivering; I'm unsure if I'm still cold or still terrified for my brothers. Or both.

I recognize the shift in stature my mother adopts when she decides to be the strong one. She breathes in deeply and her shoulders lift, straight and strong.

"We'll just have to wait to hear, from the boys or from the army. For now, we can only believe they're alive."

If we hear news from the army, it will be bad news: "We regret to inform you" news. I pray that we'll get personal letters from Max and Eddie instead, but it could take at least five or six days for any mail to make it over the Pacific and across the country.

"We'll just have to find some way to distract ourselves until then," Mama says. "So cheer up, girls. Worrying is like a rocking chair, remember?"

I smile because she's just used one of Daddy's favorite sayings.

May wraps a quilt around my shuddering shoulders and I snuggle into it, pulling it up to my nose. I breathe in the familiar smell of it.

"Hey," I say, pulling my head back to examine the quilt. I know this smell. This is not the blanket embedded with the scent of every living Hale from years of sleeping under it. It's sweet and woody, with notes of straw and cow plop.

"Jack's," Mama supplies knowingly.

I watch her carefully. I never told Mama whose quilt this was. I never even pulled it out in the daylight! *How could she know it belongs to Jack?*

A shudder runs up my spine. Maybe mothers do have eyes everywhere. I wish she had eyes at Pearl Harbor, so we could have some clue how Max and Eddie are faring in the fray.

And Phin, Imp adds.

Mama presses a warm mug into my hands, and I shudder in pleasure at the comforting feel. I take a tentative sip to see if it's too hot to drink.

"Chicken broth?" I gasp in surprise. The savory taste is delicious. I had expected bitter tea, and now my throat and belly bask in the warmth of a rich broth. We've never had something so precious at this table before; chicken is expensive! My tender stomach accepts it eagerly, begging for more. I pull in another mouthful and gulp it down greedily.

"Well, Jack's gift was very generous," Mama says in a guarded manner. I know she is a proud woman, and rightfully so after toiling herself half-dead in an effort to feed four hungry bellies by the sweat of her brow, but it's clear she doesn't want to be called out for accepting money from a Sharpe. Curiosity begs to know how she's used the bills intended to hire help in my place, but I know better than to make her turn into a porcupine. I just quietly bask in the satisfaction that May and Mama have been cared for. Warm. Fed. May pounces on the mention of money.

"Wait 'till you see *this!*" May sings, eyes dancing with excitement. She pulls me up out of the chair, and the steaming water splashes onto the floorboards. It runs through the cracks and disappears.

My curiosity is piqued, but I take another quick gulp of the delicious broth before setting it on the table and pulling Jack's quilt tighter around my shoulders. She shakes my arm impatiently, so I shuffle behind her toward the back door.

Only, it's not a back door anymore. The smell of new wood fills the little room that has been built onto the back of our house. A beautiful porcelain toilet gleams in the center, next to a wash basin and a hanging hand towel. A round mirror hangs behind the little sink.

"You got your indoor toilet," I smile at May with real delight. I turn to Mama, who leans onto the doorframe. "Did you do this?" I ask in wonder. It seems out of character for Mama to throw dollars at a luxury like this.

"A crew just showed up one day," she says with her hands up.

This smells of Jack.

How had he managed this? And he didn't even tell me!

I purse my lips, but my eyes communicate to Mama that I know she knows that my husband did this for them.

She looks down, and I burn to know what she is thinking.

"I wrote to thank him," she sighs. I grin happily; it seems Jack has finally weaseled his way back into her good graces. Her quiet concession is enough of an apology for me. I won't rub her nose in it.

May swoops onto the toilet seat and beams. "Isn't it the most incredible thing you've ever seen?"

She hugs the tank.

In my mind's eye, I watch myself stumbling over frozen clods of dirt in the cold moonlight toward the outhouse. The memory of holding my breath in the heat of August before dashing into that rancid hot box to relieve my bladder is seared into my brain. This really is an amazing gift.

"It's beautiful," I agree, but my stomach feels twisted into a knot as the dark, looming possibility of tragedy creeps back into my head. I really hope Max and Eddie are still alive to see this.

* * *

"
December 10th, 1941

Hello Little Lady,

Thanks for the note you sent. It always brightens my day to hear from my best gal! I wouldn't complain if you wrote me every day, even if it's only about how wiry the hairs on the head nurse's chin are, because I love to see your penmanship. The curlicues on your 'y's' and 'g's' never fail to bring a smile to my face. Bring 'em on.

As much as I'd love to take the credit for the new addition to your mother's house, I cannot. It wasn't my doing, though I really should have thought of it first! I'm kicking myself for missing that opportunity. My mother and father wouldn't have noticed that missing chunk of change before they cut me off. I'm a fool. I'm writing your mother back, too, but hopefully the truth won't undo this peace treaty between us.

If I had to guess who the mysterious benefactor is, I'd guess 1) Gran or 2) Claire. Gran is still basking in the glow of how well we burned her daughter-in-law, and maybe she did it for them as another grand thank you. She may just be eternally grateful, and she does love to spend Grandpa's money wherever she can, so my mother will inherit that much less when she dies. Perhaps electric lighting or a bathtub will show up next? A crystal chandelier over the dining table? However, I've never known Gran to keep quiet about anything, so maybe count her out. She'd want the credit. Mac wouldn't happen to be a very generous landlord, would he?

If not, then I suspect Claire. She was pretty upset after she went to talk to you for me. Now that I think about it, she did mention at least three times that your family had been forced to work on a farm and use an outhouse because of her mother. P, I really don't think she had any idea about the events surrounding your father's untimely death. Claire's a spitting awful liar, and she would have had to really dig deep to put on a performance like she gave me that day. And just between you and me, Bentley and Claire Sharpe may well be the wealthiest folks in all of upstate New York, even wealthier than my parents. (Please don't breathe a word, because my mother would faint if she knew). Bentley is a wise investor. It wouldn't be any skin off of their noses to build your family a bathroom. If she is in fact your family's benefactor, then it sounds like she is a wise investor as well. There is nothing more precious than family.

When I return, we're going to make things right with my parents. Not for the wealth of money, but for the wealth of love. I think my mother will be sufficiently humbled by our nation being pulled into this war, and the dust over this situation will settle. We're going to be very happy, P. We'll buy a little house and fill it with children. I promise we'll plant a vegetable garden and you can get as dirty as you want, anytime you please! I love you. Wait for me.

Your devoted husband, Jack "

December 13th, 1941

My ears buzz, pulling me back from far away. It seems like it has only been a few minutes since Roosevelt's voice came through the radio, lamenting that "many American lives have been lost," though

I've really been drowning in those words for six days.

I hear the lightest knock at the door. I stiffly walk to it and open it, wondering if I'd imagined such a soft noise. The familiar form in the doorway takes my breath away.

"Jack!" I throw my arms around his neck. Joy bubbles up from my toes to the crown of my head, and I try to squeeze the sensation out of my body and into his. "But I thought you weren't due for leave for another..." my voice trails off when I register the look in his eyes. "What? What? What do you know?"

Without a word, Jack tugs on my hands and leads me to the car. He doesn't meet my eyes again.

He doesn't speak as he drives me home to the farm.

My stomach sinks lower and lower with every block. I know what the news will be; I can feel it. I just want to know which brother I've lost. I try to prepare myself by comparing Eddie and Max; *which one can I live without?* A terrible feeling grips my stomach, squeezing it and wringing it in its clutches.

Not both. Or all three. No! Please, God. Not all of them!

Jack supports my weight as we shuffle toward the house.

No, no, no! I can't move on my own. I don't

want to go inside! I don't want to hear this out loud! His hand is steady on my back, and we make it through the door.

May shakes where she stands. Her streaming eyes and trembling chin tell me all that I feared before she can stutter, "They- they s-sent an of-of-official notice." Her little frame gives up and crumples in the entryway.

I catch her and pull her to me, trying to soothe her sobs so I can find out more. An official notice is not the letter we've been hoping for.

"Eddie? Max? Who?" I beg. Her chin dimples with a restricted sob. "Which one? Tell me!" She can't seem to speak.

Mama shuffles in, hunched with sorrow, and supplies the answer I'm desperate for: "Ed."

My gut hits the floor with a sickening splat. *Eddie? My big brother? The ringleader of the very wildest of the Hale family shenanigans? The fella who could shake the outhouse with his loud singing in midday, not at all ashamed to be taking his time in there?* Yes, Eddie; the boy who had become half of a set of stand-in father figures for May and me.

Eddie's gone.

"How? I mean, what exactly-" I start, wanting to know just what form of cruelty stopped Eddie's heart from beating, and how he had taken his last breath. May's wrist twitches, and I take the folded, crumpled paper from it. The official notice is short, diplomatic, and uninformative; there is no specific information about the cause of his death.

"And what about Max?"

Were they together? I wonder. *Were they sleeping?* The attack was very early in the morning. If so, I hope they didn't have to feel any fear or any pain. My throat clenches. *Were they with Phin?* Even though I'm married, even though I can't begin to imagine life without Jack, and what I'm about to ask feels like utter betrayal, I just can't stop myself from asking it anyway.

"D-did you hear about anyone else, uh, local? About... Phin?"

May looks at me, each eyebrow taking a turn lifting and falling. It's her look that communicates that I am pathetic.

I am. I'm pathetic.

I sob without restraint. I have no father, and now, no Eddie. Jack has traveled hours to be with me for this news, and here I am, worried about some other guy.

He's been a family friend for over a decade, Sense soothes.

Mama hands over a rumpled newspaper. Front page: *Saratoga's Own Pearl Harbor Heroes.* A large black-and-white print photo of a sullen-looking fella fills half of the front page. His head is turned, looking over the wreckage from the attack. His face is streaked with soot. His mouth is turned down. His eyes are sad; and familiar. Phineas O'Shea has made the front page of our local paper as one of Saratoga's Pearl Harbor survivors.

I want to embrace him and soothe that tortured expression on his face. I want him to embrace me, and soothe the torture inside of me. But even though this is just a stack of inked papers, my chest swells with relief. Phin is alive. I run a finger over the cheek in the photo.

Family friends don't caress one another's pictures, Imp teases.

I retract my traitorous finger before Jack can notice. Below the headline and gigantic photo are three smaller photos. One of Robbie Bryce and Lawrence Thomas in their Naval uniforms, also Saratoga locals who were killed in the attack; one of Harold Hansen, the fella who used to work at the garage downtown, with a lei and a surfboard; and the third is the photo of Phin, Eddie and Max that had made me so jealous when Max sent it home. It feels like an invasion of privacy for this personal photo to be emblazoned in print, being sold on every city corner. This is not hot news; these are my people.

I don't even know how to feel. I'm devastated. Heartbroken. Relieved. Ashamed. I had no idea that a person could feel so many emotions at once. It's a hurricane inside of me, so uncomfortable that I may just pass out. Despite Jack's old sales pitches about how the United States Army is as at peace as a roomful of nuns, there's no way we can lie down and let the Japanese do this again.

My hands tremble as the full impact hits me hard. No more safety. No more assurance. No guarantee. Surely, all of Jack's idle training is about to be put to use.

December 28th, 1941

The low warmth of Jack's cello bounces through the deep hollow of the cavernous chapel, echoing through the hollow inside of me. My chest feels like a deep, endless pool of blackness. I can see the inky outlines of fellow mourners offering me their condolences, but I can't hear them at all. To keep from becoming lost in the sorrow, I'm clinging with two tight fists to the hauntingly beautiful notes he creates; to this moment. However, I can't seem to do much about my sagging jaw or drooping head. I don't have the fight in me to sit properly in this pew.

My eyes have been wet for so many hours that I can't remember a time that they haven't felt soggy, so when they need to see, it takes a round of furious blinking to clear them of tears. I can't trust the foggy image in front of me, but my ears clearly register the sound of a violin joining in the strains of "Nearer My God To Thee" along with the deep hum of Jack's cello. A solemn-faced fella with slick blond hair stands at Jack's side, playing the hauntingly beautiful notes with him in perfect harmony.

Dalton.

My heart is too busy, too heavy with sorrow to allow in any shred of anger. I watch Jack look up to learn the source of the new sound. I watch him as he recognizes Dalton at his right shoulder. None of the fierce anger from my wedding day shows in his expression as Dalton nods to Jack in his chin rest. They seem to have a mutual, silent understanding that today's funeral should overshadow all petty arguments, and for that, I am grateful. Another young player joins in at Jack's left side with a viola, falling perfectly in time with Jack's and Dalton's notes. It's truly beautiful to see them play without concern for their quarrel.

With newly clear, curious eyes, I glance over my shoulder into the rows of pews behind me. I'm surprised by how full they are with people. Yes, I had expected our neighbors to come. I knew I'd see familiar faces from Sundays at church, and surely the gangly crate boys would show up to pay their respects to their boss, Mac's, family member. But the church is filled to bursting with Saratogans from all walks of life. Some are dressed in their Sunday best, some clearly came straight from work; the grocer is still wearing his apron. I see Nurse Adler in a straw church bonnet, and several doctors from Saint Christopher's sitting together near the back. Even Doctor Getz, the busy chief of surgery, has torn himself away from the hospital to pay his respects. The streetcar's morning driver tips his hat to me when I meet his eyes.

Lyla looks regal in a felt tilt hat with feathers reaching heavenward from it. A row of firemen in uniform sit shoulder to shoulder, and the police chief stands near the back with his hat in his hands. Claire's carmelly hair covers her ducked face, but her shoulders are shaking so hard that I know she is in tears. A fella who has to be Bentley has his arm wrapped around her, speaking softly into her ear. Doris and George are next to them, wearing matching frowns. My eyes rest on the profile of a plump woman with dark, rich, caramel skin, and I am almost certain that she is Honey, the housemaid who helped raise us at the Hale Estate. Her vacant expression can only belong to someone who once soothed the deceased as a babe in her arms. Bankers, farm hands, attorneys, chimney sweeps, even the mayor and the judge who married Jack and me have come. It seems that the tragedy of losing a local fella to an unprovoked attack has brought us all to the same level.

How terribly sad that it took something like losing an innocent life to do so.

During the service, Edward James Hale is revered as a hero. He's always been one of my heroes, and I'm so pleased that the rest of the world can see him that way, too. Reverend Bell briefly mentions the short list of brave boys from Saratoga that are either still recovering from the attack in Pearl Harbor hospitals, or helping sift through the rubble for missing men. Max is listed, and it lifts my heart to hear about him living and breathing, even though I know that forty percent of his body is covered in burns from an explosion in his bunk caused by a Japanese bomb. Still, he was luckier than Ed in the blast. I learn that he was sleeping in the same bunk as Max when the barracks were hit, only Max was awake and walking toward the door. The force of the explosion had thrown Max into the wall, cracking the front of his skull, so he is counted among the brave soldiers currently recovering in the infirmary.

It comforts me to know that Eddie slept through his death, and that he didn't feel any fear or pain in his last moments, even though his body was much too damaged to be viewed with an open casket. Blessed unconsciousness! I feel sick to know that I'll never hear Eddie's deep, throaty laugh again, or ever be the victim of his pranks.

I don't think I'll ever stop missing him.

The following morning, I have to say a different sort of goodbye to Jack.

"I don't care if I get sick," he insists when I turn away from his parting kiss at the train station.

I don't want him to catch this nasty flu. I can't be entirely sure if my muscles are weak and aching with this lingering illness, or grief, but he can't go back on duty with these germs. Though he's gotten special leave to attend Eddie's funeral, he is now due back on base, so we're tangled in this miserable goodbye on the train platform.

"Come on, P. If this is the last time I see you, I'm not going to let a few germs spoil it for me." His words are visible in the cold air; a puff of white.

My stomach sinks. The *last* time he'll see me?

"I'm sure that line works on all the other gals," I tease him, but my heavy heart doesn't feel its usual glee at doing so. I poke him in the ribs. "Really, I mean it, don't you dare talk like that. Just go find Hitler, shoot him up, and come back in time for dinner, would'ja?" I manage a weak grin with the teasing that barely masks my nerves. There's no chance he can follow my instructions, but there is a very good chance I will indeed never see this face again. He's headed into the belly of the beast.

Grinning like a mischievous child, he ignores my

warning about the germs, and plants his lips firmly onto mine, pulling me closer with an arm at my waist and kissing me thoroughly. I shiver as my limbs go completely weak. Thankfully, his arms are wrapped tightly around me, supporting me from crumpling to the ground.

I no longer care about infecting him. I'd almost forgotten how sweet the feel of his soft tongue is as it sweeps across the tops of my teeth. I feel as hungry for his kiss as I'd once been for his fried chicken. Warm blood rushes through my limbs, invigorating them, and I curl my fingers around the rigid fabric of his uniform and hold on tight.

The train whistle shrills, pulling us back into the realm of reality. I feel our separation closing in, and my heart won't slow down. Frantic, I rip the chain from my neck.

Guiding the charm into his gloved palm, I say, "For luck, Jack. So you'll come home to me."

He closes his fingers over the cold silver.

"Yes, I'll be coming home, Pip, and we're going to live every second together to the fullest. Wait for me; we're going to make Ed proud!" He kisses my pink nose and pulls himself away from me with obvious regret, stepping up onto the train. He leans out from the railing, just the way I do from the trolley pole.

Yes, we'll live enough to make up for the fact

that Eddie won't, I inwardly agree as the train's rhythmic chugging pulls Jack away from me. Oh, how Eddie loved life! He drank it all in, gulping down experiences both good and bad, and sighing in satisfaction as he wiped his mouth. He'd want me to keep my chin up and push forward, and that's just what I intend to do. Or at least, try my very best to do.

I scan every detail of Jack's face as he moves further into the distance, committing each of his features to memory. As the train gains momentum, the rogue lock of hair at his crown blows straight upward in the frigid wind. He salutes with his free hand, then lets it drag in the wind, fingers absently pointed at me. The shape of his mouth in that handsome sideways grin sears into my brain.

"Come home to me, Jack!" I call desperately into the updraft from the train, but the whistle shrills over my words. He can't have heard me. With my dress and hair being blasted by the furious swirling air from the train's gaining momentum, I run along the snowy platform toward him. By the time the platform ends and my heeled feet have no more solid ground to run on, I've realized that this locomotive moves far faster than I can. A cloud of coal smoke envelopes me as I crumple to the wooden planks beneath my feet.

Why did I let him go?

Chin up, Sense firmly reminds me, like a smack on the bottom. For Eddie, I lift my chin and stand, holding my skirt down in the furious updraft of the train. As my hair swirls around my head and sticks to my tears, I shake the dread from my thoughts. When the last car of the train passes me, and the furious whirlwind dies away, I'm left swaying on the very last knobbed wooden board.

Alone.

Jack had better stay safe out there. With any luck, I'll never stand over a flag-draped coffin ever again.

THE END

Learn more at **alissabright.blogspot.com**
and be sure to 'like' the **Hale's Storm Fan Page**
on **Facebook** for the latest information on the
Hale's Storm series!

ACKNOWLEDGEMENTS

They say it takes a village to raise a child, and it is also true that it takes a crew of friends and family to create a novel. Jen, Carson, Leah, Ashley, and Cindy- your proofing is in the pudding! There's no way I could have looked at the story outside of my head without you guys! Ashley and Leah- Max would be dead without you. You saved his fictional life! Nancy, Karisa, and Ashley- thanks for wrangling my monkeys for me so I could get "in the zone". Grandpa Jim and Mom- how could I have learned proper English without the two of you correcting mine all the time? Carson, thanks for the technical help and innumerable computer fixes! You are the best big brother a gal could ever ask for. (I hope you recognize yourself in Pip's big brothers. If the Hale's shack had had a staircase, I would've written in her brothers sending her down it wrapped in a blanket inside of a box, just to honor your incessant torture!) Cindy, your photographic talent blows my mind. And Cover Girl, I hope you know your soul is even more gorgeous than your face! I must also thank every odd person my subconscious has ever absorbed for teaching me that people are odd and individual. Ben, I count myself lucky to have stumbled upon a guy as loving and supportive as you. Thanks for the writing time, the cheering section, and the love. (I hope you recognize yourself in Jack and Phin!) Lastly, I must thank my Creator, who instilled in me this drive to create (on a smaller scale than Him). Thanks for the inspiration and guidance all along the way!

ABOUT THE AUTHOR

Alissa Bright lives on the Central Coast of California, 126 steps from the sand, with her husband, two children, and their dog, Brutus (who escapes to the beach whenever a window has been left open). She loves being a mom (her dream job), and seeks a creative outlet wherever she can find one. One side of her family tree is full of artists, and the other full of teachers- a great recipe to produce a writer.

She began writing the Hale's Storm series when her son was just a newborn, and completed the first novel in the series just after his sixth birthday. Alissa is not an English major, nor a college graduate, but she does believe creativity and drive can leap traditional hurdles. Her favorite quote is, "Whether you think you can, or you think you can't, you're right," by Henry Ford.

She can't wait to share the rest of this story with the world!

www.ingramcontent.com/pod-product-compliance
Lightning Source LLC
Chambersburg PA
CBHW070735180626
46818CB00007B/2849